First Published November 2021
25 Wiley Road, Wanaka, New Zealand
mgbooks@xtra.co.nz
michaelguest@xtra.co.nz
Phone – 03 4437843

Catalogue record available from
The National Library of New Zealand.

Printed by Colour Print Ltd
1 Turakina Road,
Dunedin

ISBN: 978-0-473-65583-9

DEDICATION
To my wonderful wife, Barbie.

SOUTHERN LAKES LAW

FOREWORD

Queenstown is a beautiful rural town, surrounded by mountains on the shores of Lake Wakatipu in the south of New Zealand. It is one of the country's largest lakes which curls around the front edges of the township and then the town itself spreads up to the magnificent slopes of the Southern Alps.

This delightful setting lies within the most Southern legal district in the world. The only more Southern Courthouse is at the bottom tip of South America in a God-forsaken place named Tierra del Fuego. Queenstown is far more 21st Century.

The storyline follows the daily life and adventures of a very busy and exciting legal practice led by Richard Locksley and his lawyer wife, Mary and two young and talented lawyers, Wiremu and Melinda.

This practice is known as Southern Lakes Law. The story and plots are highly paced, laced with humour and set against a background of true legal situations on all pages. Guilty clients. Innocent clients. Low life crime. White collar crime. Murders to speeding tickets. Family breakup scenarios. Civil cases and defamation. Nothing is too large or too small for Richard and his team.

A wide range of characters permeate the plots and themes – cantankerous Judges, lying cops, snivelling clients, good cops, interesting Judges and a host of fascinating human stories and legal principles.

CHAPTER ONE

Richard Locksley was starting to burn out as a bustling barrister in Auckland. His calling frequently led to 14 hours a day of hard legal slog. There were astonishing characters in every field of the law. Cranky Judges. Wrong Judges. Exceptional Judges. Good and bad cops. Unscrupulous clients. Violent men. Evil women. Corrupt lawyers. High quality lawyers. Perverts. Flashers. Down and outers. Confidence men (and ladies). Liars. Cheats. Pious people. Utter pricks. Tricky witnesses. Abortionists. And we're not finished yet!

All had a tale to tell. And all were innocent – until the Court said otherwise!

Richard's friends were determined to say he was named after Robin Hood, the somewhat fictional Earl of Locksley. They argued that Richard acted for the poor and the dispossessed with passion, even when they could not pay and that his zeal to see that 'justice is done' echoed the tales of Robin of Locksley of the 12th Century. Therein lay the similarity between the two characters. But the modern-day Richard proclaimed that an ancestor from the 16th Century was a humble locksmith in County Durham and took his surname from his trade. His Auckland friends would retort that Richard today should therefore be called Richard Nightcart, but almost everyone who had been touched by Richard's zeal for justice disagreed.

He is a fine man and legal professional and a formidable advocate to his very core. Where there is Whizzbangery to be displayed in Court, Richard was the best one to provide it. Frowns, ringing of hands, verbal fireworks, jokes, faux tears and a bit of clowning around were all tricks in his Courtroom bag. He was a skilled orator.

࿆

Today was a typical rainbow day in Auckland. It had started as a fine and still morning. By 11.00 o'clock there was torrential rain. Lunchtime saw some brief outbreaks of sun and by the middle of the afternoon it was bright and sunny again.

The No 1 Auckland High Court sits in the middle of a magnificent Edwardian red brick building surrounded by wood-lined corridors and internal walls so it is cocooned from the outside elements. This is where bad men come to stay while good men walk free and snivelling businessmen fight over money like dogs fight over bones.

Richard was a very experienced barrister. His 42nd birthday took place last month. Today, he was explosively addressing his jury at the end of a jury trial. This vigorous advocate was a good-looking lawyer with brown hair perhaps a little long for his age. He was a born and bred New Zealander and took his law degree from Otago University in the City of Dunedin on the East coast of the South Island.

Today, he held the Court in the palm of his hand. As he orated, he liked to twist his right palm ever so lightly to make a point. Occasionally, he was known to thump a large textbook on the table in front of him to make another point if he perceived one juror was not paying attention. And fiddling with his pencil case to distract the jury from what a Crown Prosecutor was saying was a well-used and faithful trick by him.

His co-lawyer, Wiremu Pihama, often known as Willie, sat beside him. Willie was just 25 young lawyer, still with much to learn but already a rising star in the younger brigade of dashing young things in the New Zealand legal profession. Willie was of full Ngai Tahu descent and was a calm figure in a courtroom setting. He was tall and looked every inch the reliable young advocate. But he needed a bit more experience.

The public gallery was packed, and the press bench was full. Richard's client was facing two counts of manslaughter and one of GBH. South Auckland dairy owner Ravi Singh looked a clean cut but nervous man about 50 years old. Not to put too fine a point on it, Mr Singh exterminated two robbers with his cricket bat and almost sent the third to the promised land! He hit them each for a six with one massive swipe to each head! Two dead, one seriously injured!

Ravi had been the victim of a violent robbery but his significant response in defence had put this good man in the dock today. The court of public opinion had probably already found him innocent but the law grinds exceedingly slow and he finally came before his own Judge and jury.

The High Court Judge, Justice Malcolm Casey, was grand and full of authority high up on his Bench. The Judge's hair was white, and his complexion ranged between pink and purple, depending on his view of the facts. Today, he was light pink.

Police officers looked grim. The press bench strained forward. It's corny to say it but you could have heard a pin drop.

The Crown Solicitor's name was Lincoln Green. Yes, that was his real name, but it was a worthy link to the name Locksley. Mr Green shook his head from time to time as Richard captivated the jury with his final peroration. He clearly had the jury under his spell. The court room was quite still, except for this skilful advocate persuasively arguing the case that his client was acting in self-defence. He was building up to his final burst. Richard was in full swing.

A very loud burst of thunder shook the building. The jurors looked startled.

"What a perfect time for God to intervene," mocked Richard to Wiremu in sotto voce tones. But in a voice that everyone could hear.

The jurors all smiled.

Richard leaned forward and started to complete his defence address.

"You good citizens! You ask yourself what you would have done! Go on! Just ask yourself."

He pointed to Ravi and twisted his hand ever so slightly.

"Ravi Singh is a corner dairy owner. His shop was invaded by three young thugs holding knives!"

The Crown Solicitor rolled his eyes and shook his head. Richard faced the Judge and then turned on this rather elderly advocate for the Crown.

"Don't you dare roll your eyes and shake your head while I'm addressing this jury."

"Your Honour, please . . ." stammered Green.

"Mr Green! Control yourself!" snapped back the Judge.

"I'm sorry, Your Honour. They were only 15 years old. I was just . . ."

"Not one more word! Mr Locksley has the floor! Continue please, Counsel."

Richard turned back to the jury.

"Yes! Only 15. But armed with knives and full of murderous intent. And there were three of them! There was no back entrance to my client's dairy. Ringing the police was not an option. All three were threatening him with knives. Threatening him! With knives!

Not just his property!

His body!

His face!

His eyes!

His very life!"

Ten of the jurors appeared to be with Richard. The other two did not seem so sure. Richard continued, eyeballing the two potential dissenters.

"The first one actually said - "I'll kill you!" The second one yelled - "How would you like your throat cut, you Indian bastard!?" He raised his voice.

"And what did Mr Singh do? He grabbed his cricket bat from under the till and swung it at head height. Very hard! Once! Twice! Thrice! No more. Three hits were enough! Three thugs lay on the ground, two dead, one injured. He did not intend death. Make no mistake about that. The Crown does not allege that. He did not intend to exact revenge! He did not go too far! The Crown Solicitor has pointed to the "buckets of blood" as he so colourfully complains. But so what?! Richard took one step, possibly too far.

"I dare say this to you – "Who cares? Who cares?"

Justice Casey raised his eyebrows, and the Crown Solicitor almost had a fit. But they did not make a sound. They were not allowed to say it openly, but everyone thought that these young punks got what they deserved!

Richard had got away with his "who cares" comment.

"The law is quite simple as his Honour will explain to you shortly. The law permits you, you and you, as well as the accused, simply to use reasonable force to protect themselves. If you use excessive force, then that is a different matter. But this force was reasonable! When three young men are storming at you with knives then you have available to you the defence of self-defence."

Richard then delivered the killer line.

"... and he grabbed his cricket bat and hit them all for a six!"

Six members of the victims' families made a theatrical show of standing up and walking out in protest.

Richard looked at them with contempt and the jury noted his demeanour.

"You could SHOOT them! – if that's what you need to protect yourself from a fatal knife attack!"

This magnificent advocate directed the last statement at the rabble low-life family leaving the courtroom. They wore hoodies and had dirty mullet hair styles. The parents were large and fat and they all reeked of alcohol. Richard was defiant in his condemnation of the retreating familial detritus.

"Scumbags!" he thought to himself. But he continued to hold the jury in his hands.

"A wise Judge once laid the law down this way – he said that the law does not require a citizen to weigh to a nicety the precise degree of force necessary ... provided it is only reasonable force. What a nice turn of phrase that is! In this case, Mr Singh hit each assailant once! He stopped each assailant from plunging a murderous dagger into his head . . . or throat . . . or eye."

Richard drew himself to his full height and raised both hands and extended his fingers. It was the body language of a final exclamation mark. He called it "personified punctuation."

"This was self-defence, pure and simple. I didn't even want to mention reasonable doubt. But I do go further! I am confident His Honour will instruct you that my client does not have to prove self-defence. He only needs to point to credible evidence capable of amounting to self-defence and the Crown then must disprove that evidence! The Crown simply cannot do that in this case. You must find this man not guilty!"

He sat down with a theatrical flourish.

There was a feeling of dramatic relief. But the jury was clearly convinced of the innocence of the accused, not just whether there was a reasonable doubt.

The Judge commenced his summing up in a monotone, almost droning voice. He took at least 30 minutes to cover the points raised by the prosecution and the defence. Richard surreptitiously kept looking at his watch. He was required in another Court across the city. He whispered to his junior counsel, Wiremu.

"Christ! He's taking his time. I'm due across town in the District Court for several cases. Jeez! I won't get through this week. My heart is thumping already."

Justice Casey finished summing up, rose and left the Court. Richard made a dash for the door giving instructions to Wiremu.

"Willie. You'll have to take the verdict if I'm not back. If it's not guilty, text me and make an appointment for him in a couple of days. If it's guilty, try for bail but it's unlikely. He knows that. Tell him I will see him tomorrow. Shit! Shit! Shit! I'm not going to make it."

Richard dashed out of the building and jumped into the first taxi. He was known by almost every Auckland cab driver.

"District Court, Mr Locksley?"

"Yeah, Harry! What do I say on behalf of a bum tickler? And a druggie?"

"Well, I'd say sayonara to the druggie and cyanide for the other! Good riddance! I'd pull the trigger myself. No. Boiling in oil if you please."

"Yeah! Right! Step on it! I think I'll blame it on their mothers."

They pulled up at the District Court. Richard was on the run. Out of the taxi. Dashed into the foyer and up the escalator and up to Court Room No 4. He passed many colleagues, court staff, former clients and police officers.

"Hi."

"Hi."

"Good to see you!"

"Flat out!"

"Must have a beer."

"Tomorrow after work."

"Yeah."

He crashed open the courtroom door just as Judge Albert Christie appeared on to the Bench. He was a bad-tempered Judge in his mid 60's and Richard delighted in calling him Judge Crusty.

The first case called was his cannabis client, Terry Jenkins. Richard was still out of breath. He opened his soft leather satchel and placed two files on the lectern in front of him. His first case was called within a minute. He just made it with seconds to spare. The clerk of the Court intoned -

"Call - Terry Richard Jenkins."

Mr Jenkins climbed into the dock and acknowledged the Judge with a small nod. He was a 38-year-old plumber. Richard stood up with his customary flourish.

The prosecutor read out the facts and Richard presented his plea in mitigation.

"May it please the Court, this man had only two ounces of cannabis when he was apprehended. The police charged him with possession for supply. It took a plea of not guilty and four months of hard negotiations to get them to reduce it to a charge of simple possession. That was a classic case of overcharging to try and extract a plea of guilty to a lesser charge. That is wrong. It was bordering on prosecutorial abuse. But the police now seek to persuade you to sentence him to imprisonment on the basis that he has a little bit of previous."

"And what is wrong with that, Mr Locksley?"

"Well, the "little bit of previous" are two convictions in 1996 and 1995. He was a teenager then."

"So what? What's your point?"

"My first point is that they were so long ago! It's now only a charge of simple possession."

"But it's his third!"

"But no convictions for 23 years!"

"I think I've have heard enough. Anything more?"

"Well obviously not in this Court, Your Honour!"

"What do you mean by that impertinent remark?"

"As usual, you've made up your mind. This sentencing exercise will have to be determined in the High Court!"

"That's a preposterous remark! Sit down! You're finished!"

The Judge glared at Richard and dismissively waved him to sit down. He started his sentencing remarks.

"Jenkins. Some people think possession of cannabis is a minor offence. I do not. This is your third offence. It does not matter to me that it is 22 years ago that you committed your second offence. You will go to prison. The maximum available to me is only three months. I wish it could be more. You are sentenced to 10 weeks in prison. Stand down. Call the next case."

A very dejected-looking Mr Jenkins stepped down and moved toward the door to the holding cells. He beckoned to Richard and Richard mouthed a "See you soon" signal.

"Call Brian James Grimbsy."

Mr Grimsby was appearing for sentence on a charge of indecent assault. He has patted a 15-year old's bottom as she boarded a bus in front of him.

"Yes, Mr Locksley. Keep it short," snapped the Judge, most improperly.

"I shall take as long as I see fit. My client faces the possibility of imprisonment for one charge of indecently assaulting a young girl aged 13. I cannot hope to mitigate his offending out of existence. More importantly, Mr Grimsby himself acknowledges that he should not have acted the way he did. But surely prison is not inevitable for someone who is 69?"

"Quite the contrary. A definite proposition."

"I trust you do want to hear from defence counsel?"

"Not really. But don't be so objectionable. More impertinence."

"Well please hear from defence counsel before pre-empting the final decision."

"Just get on with it, Mr Locksley."

"Let me summarise the positive points." Richard counted on his fingers.

"Firstly, aged 69, he has no previous convictions of any kind.

Secondly, he has been employed as an electrician at the same firm for just over 40 years.

Thirdly, his employers speak very highly of him. His wife and family stand by him.

Fourthly, he has started an intensive sexual offenders' course of therapy.

Fifthly, and I am obliged to highlight this point, the charge is one of indecent assault, not sexual violation. There is a maximum penalty differentiation between 20 years for the former and 7 years, for the charge he faces.

Sixthly, there was no penetration either digitally or by any other means. No skin was touched."

The Judge butted in.

"That's just disgusting! I don't want to know the detail! It's offensive. Kindly keep your submissions to the facts relating to the offender."

"No, I will not."

"I beg your pardon, Counsel!"

"You know very well is my duty to raise every matter relevant to both the offender and the offence. I respectfully say, NO, I insist that you do not continually interrupt each of my submissions."

"I'm still no wiser, Mr Locksley."

"To be sure, Your Honour, but better informed."

"Now you are meaning to be offensive."

Richard raised his head and stuck his jaw out in defiance of the Court. But the Judge realised he had met his match and glared at this Counsel but said nothing. Richard continued.

"I don't make light of the offence. The victim was only 15. He patted her on her bottom as she stepped on to a bus before him. Bad enough. I accept that. But this is not the stuff of a lengthy prison sentence. He is entitled to come before this Court and point to his previous good character and lack of convictions."

"Indecent assault is indecent assault is indecent assault," replied the Judge.

"There you go again. What does that comment mean?"

"It means what it says."

"But it means nothing."

"I think it's better for you to sit down again, Mr Locksley."

Richard raised his voice, "This case will also end in the High Court. You clearly don't wish to hear submissions for the defence."

"I suppose I better let you finish."

"Too little, too late! I am sorry, Your Honour. It's off to the High Court. You have already obviously pre-determined your decision."

Richard sat down with a shake of his head. The Judge flashed a look of contempt at Richard and then addressed the defendant.

"Mr Grimsby. Your lawyer is an offensive Counsel. Nothing of any value can be said on your behalf. He has said nothing of value. That is why I asked Mr Locksley to sit down. What you did was disgusting. There can be no response from the Bench other than to sentence you to two years' imprisonment. Stand down."

Richard spoke up, "Your Honour, I should be lodging an appeal against sentence within the hour, so I ask that bail be granted pending the appeal."

"Complain to the High Court, Mr Locksley. Mr Grimsby begins his sentence this second."

Richard did not reply but gave a contemptuous bow. As he was leaving the Court Room, he noticed a senior Law Society Council member in the back row of the public gallery. Magnus Denholm was a nasty piece of work, spending much of his time constructing disciplinary actions against fellow lawyers. In his early 50's, he was short and round and looked piously at everyone in sight. A grumpy Mr Plod the Policeman springs to mind.

"Good morning. Not checking up on me are you?" snapped Richard.

"All will be revealed. You can't help abusing judges, can you? I've been sitting up the back. I've taken notes."

"Aw! Go to hell! Take a note to remind yourself to take a happy pill twice daily."

Richard hurried to the front door.

ॐ

Rushing outside the Court building Richard grabbed a taxi.

"Busy day, Richard?"

"Bloody Judge Christie! Prick! Bastard! Ignorant sod! High Court, please."

In the five-minute drive to the High Court, Richard uttered the words "Prick! Bastard!" at least 6 times. He reached the High Court front door, foyer and bounded up to the High Court counter.

"Two Appeal forms, please."

"There you are. Two today, Mr Locksley? Judge Crusty must be on the Bench?" says the court clerk.

"Bloody Hell!! You should have heard him today. He's a mad dog."

Richard knew the drill with appeals against decisions of Judge Christie. He filled in the forms in handwriting and handed them back to the clerk. He read out the third paragraph which he had written in capitals -"I ask you to refer this Appeal Notice to the duty High Court Judge. It is an urgent application for bail. My client is 69. He has no previous convictions. Even the police summary of facts accept that the indecent assault went no further than a touch on the bottom as a schoolgirl who climbed on to a bus before him. Can you please refer this to the Duty Judge as soon as possible?"

The clerk took the forms.

"I'm going up to the Duty Judge's Chambers now and I'll give both appeals to him. I have your cell phone number. We may have a slot for both at 3.00 pm tomorrow. I'll give you a ring. You serve the Crown and tell them that tomorrow afternoon may be available."

"Thanks a lot. I'm grateful. Judge Christie's Court is literally one where justice is dispensed with!"

❧

Richard left the court office and was met by Wiremu, his junior counsel.

"The jury's coming back."

"Bloody hell! I need a pee."

"No time."

"You know what, Willie? One day you will learn that District Court Judges are quick, courteous and wrong. High Court Judges are slow, rude and right. The only exception to the former is Judge Bloody Christie! He is slow, rude and wrong all the time."

They both hurried back to the courtroom just as the jury shuffled in. The crowd was silent. The jury sat down. A very slow 20 seconds ticked by. The High Court Judge appeared through velvet curtains and on to the Bench placing him at least two metres higher than everyone else. Mr Singh stood in the dock flanked by two large prison officers. He looked very worried.

"Mr Foreman, have you reached a verdict?" The court clerk faced them.

"We have." The foreman stood up.

"How say you? Do you find the accused guilty or not guilty?"

"Not guilty! On all three charges."

"And is that the verdict of you all?"

"Yes."

His Honour leant forward.

"Mr Singh, in accordance with the verdict of the jury, you are discharged. You are free to go."

The Judge left the Bench. There was general milling around. Everyone wanted to say something to Richard. The family of Mr Singh gathered around him. The family of the violent robbers glared at Mr Singh and made threatening gestures by sliding their fingers across their own throats. The police rounded them up and pushed them outside.

&

Richard and Willie walked very quickly back to the office.

"The bloody waiting room will be full," panted Richard.

"I've telephoned. Janet says there are six to eight clients. Melinda has started interviewing." replied Wiremu.

"Right, we're on our way. Christ, I met that dick Magnus Denholm at the District Court. I call him "Maximum Venom." Did so in a Law Society dinner one evening. Everyone agreed with me. There is certainly no love lost between us. We almost came to blows. He doesn't have many clients, so the Law Society pays him to persecute practitioners who do have clients."

Willie grinned -

"Bad things come back to haunt people like that."

"You may well be right. A private investigator once gave me some juicy stuff on Denholm. I must look it out, particularly if he's coming after me."

"I look forward to that fight!" replied Willie.

"I must also show you my War Box someday. Full of goodies! Ready to be pulled out and displayed at a moment's notice! Great fun to be used against sods who dish out the dirt themselves."

CHAPTER TWO

Richard's offices were situated in one of the taller buildings in Lower Queen Street with a pretty view of the harbour and the famous bridge.

His secretary, Janet, was doing her best to keep clients happy, serving coffee and biscuits. She was a very pleasant 50-year-old and had been with Richard for over 15 years. She had forgotten most law that young lawyers had not even learned and was able to provide research work for Richard at the push of a Google button. She sat and passed Family Law at Law School in her early days with Richard. Came top with an A+. She was a capable and invaluable member of the office and quite often reviewed relationship property cases of some complexity for the other lawyers in the office. There was not a man in her life at the moment.

"I don't Dabble. I play Scrabble," was her usual answer to inquisitive questions about her sex life. But there obviously had been the odd dalliance or three.

Janet was as cool as a cucumber under pressure and never got rattled or stressed or upset.

"Disgruntled?" she would respond when asked how she was feeling. "I'm not even gruntled."

Melinda, 25, was a quirky young lawyer approximately three years out of law school. She had studied alongside Wiremu at Otago University, although, as she not so delicately put it, she remembered her university years as "mostly vomit and love bites." That's our Melinda. Always full of jokes but quickly learning to become a skilled advocate.

She cracked a joke at every opportunity and was loved by clients. Her hair was short and modern and seemed to change colour almost every other week – usually auburn but sometimes green and sometimes purple. Even orange! Her wardrobe was somewhere between weekend casual and Op Shop colourful things - usually purple, orange, silver and anything that made her look like a rooster. She was introduced to the firm by Wiremu with the winning formula – "But we will have fun. She's a character. One glass of wine and she's a gibbering goblin. She'll dance on the table and burst into song, and you want to take her out because you never know what's going to happen next."

Richard loved the description. Janet was a little more circumspect.

"Not what I would have call an incisive reference," she commented when Richard signed up this legal goblin.

Melinda also occasionally suffered from a mild form of Tourette's syndrome. How much was an act? No one knew. She was full of bonhomie all the time and very, very quirky. Luckily, she only came out infrequently with hilarious one-liners which were entirely inappropriate, but very funny. One famous utterance was to a rather large, unpopular female Family Court Judge when one day Melinda blurted out "Big bum! Stupid girl!" She apologised in the cutest way and was forgiven. But every lawyer present at the time inwardly guffawed because they thought Melinda's comment was entirely accurate.

She was always joking. Sometimes she hung a sign on her door exclaiming –

"OUT OF MY MIND. BACK IN TEN MINUTES."

"At Uni, I had to stop her getting "Out to Lunch" tattooed on her forehead," added Wiremu.

But Melinda turned out to be a very skilled young lawyer and advocate and she was a truckload of fun. Wiremu admired her from afar. He was smitten. She did not know it yet.

Wiremu was also 25 but a little more serious, although he had a container load of one-liners and expressions which brightened up any conversation. The whole office enjoyed the funny side of law with its stuffiness and frequently weird clients. But Willie was inclined to answer a simple question about how he enjoyed his weekend with a retort such as –

"The sex was so good even the neighbours had a cigarette."

He referred a tad irreverently to one warring couple of clients as – "Short Fat Fanny from Hikurangi and 2 Foot Bill from One Tree Hill!"

His skills as an exceptional advocate were assured.

Melinda secretly adored him. She had the last laugh always. Today's quip was –

"I always scream when having sex. Particularly when my boyfriend walks in on me."

While Richard and Wiremu were at Court, Melinda had taken basic details from each of six clients.

Richard beckoned Melinda and Wiremu into his large office. The outward wall was all glass with a magnificent view over Auckland and the harbour. The wall behind his desk was full of textbooks. The opposite wall had a very large screen hooked up to Richard's computer and the remaining wall was dominated by a large white board. A rectangular table and five chairs sat beside this whiteboard. The office was plainly high tech. Richard could flash files and sections of Acts of Parliament and anything from Google or his computer up on to it within a second or two. He had perfected this technique to include relevant case law, so his clients felt really included and cocooned by the legal advice given to them by the firm. Wiremu and Melinda had employed the same equioment.

Richard's main mantra to his legal staff was to "Prepare. Prepare. Prepare."

"Know your statutes almost off by heart. Know your subject off by heart. There is NO substitute for preparation. Usually, there is no lawsuit! It is a fact suit!"

Melinda and Mary came in and joined Richard and Wiremu. The door was closed.

"Morning, Boss," bounced out Melinda.

"Morning, Sir," said Wiremu with a little more deference.

Richard told them about his difficulties with Judge Christie and asked with a smirk –

"What do you call a lawyer with an IQ of only 20? Answer? Your Honour."

They both laughed. The pressure cooker pace of this office was lubricated with humour.

"Now, what have we got here?" asks Richard.

Melinda started with - "Three drink-drivers for tomorrow. One relationship property dispute. Three legal aid burglars for Tuesday and one rather distinguished-looking gentleman for a civil claim."

"Rightio. Willie, you take the burglars. I'll see them briefly before they leave."

"Consider it done!"

"Melinda, you take the drink drivers. Schedule the dates and I will see them all before I go. I'll take the civil man first, then the relationship property client. Wiremu, please get Janet in here for a minute."

"Will do."

"And remember. We're here to help people and our clients must be given the utmost respect. But we're not running a charity. I am not against pro bono work in the right case. We'll discuss that later. It's my decision if we use legal aid, but it's $2500 minimum for a plea of guilty from research down to sentencing, $3000 for a limited licence – No ifs or buts. No Banana – No Monkey."

"OK, Boss."

He added with a smile –

"Although there is no greater gift to your fellow citizen than to provide legal care and comfort for free."

They both nodded.

"But a blow-job is faster." Melinda could always be relied upon to come up with such an angle. Trouble is, she dropped these pearlers sometimes in front of High Court Judges.

"Melinda Cunningham!" gasped Janet who had just come in, barely suppressing a smile

"You're wicked! You will go straight to hell!" responded Willie.

"I talk to the Devil sometimes," added Melinda with a wink. "He says I'm OK … but you're stuffed!"

Richard tidied up. "Right! To work."

As they left, Wiremu made "Whoo Whoo!" noises, loping, crouching, scratching his armpits, pretending to be an ape.

Richard tried to kick him in the bum. Melinda giggled. They left and Janet paused for a minute.

"Janet, love. Willie will get the burglars squared away and Melinda will start on the drink drivers, I'll take the guy first. Give the relationship property lady the usual information forms to fill in. Look after her because she may be last in the queue."

"No problems."

They all swung into the large reception room and Richard addressed the clients.

"I'm so sorry, everyone. It's not usually like this. The Judge was in a filthy mood this morning and it took me some time to tidy up his behaviour."

They all smiled.

"We will start interviewing now and I will make sure that I will personally see everyone before you leave. Mr Stanton, come this way please."

Melinda and Wiremu could be seen choosing and shepherding clients into their respective offices. Mr Stanton followed Richard into his office. Richard closed the door. They shook hands.

"Good afternoon. How can I help?"

"Hi. Paddy Stanton. Wrongful dismissal. I owned a business called Stanton Engineering. A few months ago, I sold it and stood down as managing director and became a middle level marketing employee. But the new managing director was constantly criticising me."

"Tell me the main example, please."

"Only two days ago he rounded on me. I told him that I thought he was picking on me and being unfair. He raised his voice and, in front of a witness who will confirm this, shouted at me, and said – "Look, you're just a piece of shit and if I tell you to shit in the corner, you'll shit in the corner."

"I hope you hit the prick!"

"Well, no, but I wanted to."

"What happened then?"

"I went to the major shareholder the next day who was also the Chairman and complained and asked for an apology, but he would not give it and told me to sort it out with the boss."

"Did you try?"

"Yes, but he wouldn't help. I went back and told the new MD again that I thought I'd been unfairly treated. He told me to get stuffed! So I resigned. Can I do anything about it? Have I burned my bridges?"

Richard shook his head.

"You have been wronged. They will pay big time!"

"What can I do about it? Probably nothing?"

"Certainly not. Your resignation will be treated as a constructive dismissal. You can't lose. You will get three to six months loss of salary net and about $20,000 general compensation on top and then a contribution towards costs of about $5000. My fee would be $20,000.

So that would put a minimum of over $35,000 net in your pocket."

"As much is that?"

"It's not a lot. We're not the United States. How do you want to take it? I can't be certain about a full six-month loss of salary. The standard is usually three months. But even that would be getting close to $20,000. In addition, you would get an amount for humiliation and loss of dignity, and I think that could be $20,000 on top. Maybe more."

"Any chance of a loss?"

"If what you told me is all true then you will be successful."

"Is that all? It's a matter of principle. I'll pay you the $20,000 tomorrrow. Go for it."

"There's one thing a lawyer loves to hear and another thing he hates to hear. The first is "Shall I pay you now?" and the second is "Is that all?"

"I know your reputation is very good. And I've liked what you're told me today. Straight to the point. I know that the company's lawyers are MacPherson, Hale and Co."

"I think I've got everything I need from the information sheet Melinda filled out with you. Perhaps also the date when he swore at you?"

"Just on Tuesday, two days ago."

"Right. I'll dictate a letter from hell before I go home tonight, and I will email it to you for any corrections tomorrow. Try and get back to me tomorrow late morning and I'll forward it to the company. I will give it only three working days to reply."

"Thank you. I'll pay the receptionist."

"Thanks. If I don't win this case for you, I'll refund $5000. How's that? If they do not accept my terms, I will file in the Employment Authority immediately. I'll copy you in. I promise you we'll have a longer talk after we hear back."

"Thanks heaps. See you then."

Mr Stanton left the office. Richard closed the door and dashed off a letter on his dictaphone. He knew precisely what to do.

"Email to MacPherson, Hale and Co please, Janet."

> "Attention Mr Hale. Re: Graham Stanton versus Walrus Engineering Ltd.
>
> "I act for Mr Stanton. I raise a personal grievance on his behalf. His complaint is unanswerable. You will know the reason for my letter. On Tuesday of this week, without any justification whatsoever, the managing director said to him, "Look, you're just a piece of shit and if I tell you to shit in the corner, you'll shit in the corner." There can be no justification for this comment and language at all.
>
> On Wednesday, he sought some support from the major shareholder and owner of the business. He also requested an apology. He was told to "bugger off."
>
> On Thursday, my client returned to the managing director and again asked for an apology. On this occasion, he was told to "fuck off."
>
> My client has considered his position and has felt compelled to resign. I say the circumstances amounted to an unjustified constructive dismissal. Without a doubt.
>
> He is entitled to a minimum of three months' salary calculated at $25,000 but I reserve the right to claim for a longer period. He will clearly be awarded something in the vicinity of $15,000 to $20,000 by way of general compensation. Read the Timaru case of Irvine v. Wallace and Cooper. Six months loss of wages was awarded there.
>
> I seek an immediate settlement. Failure to reply to this letter or accept the settlement sought by mid-afternoon this coming Wednesday will mean that I will file directly in the Employment Authority and seek a mediation as the processes before the Authority unfolds."

He flicked the tape out of the machine, opened the door and tossed it to Janet.

"Please email this tonight if you can to the client for vetting. Thanks."

"Come in please, Mrs Fordyce."

He smiled at his next client and ushered her into his office. She was obviously an intelligent individual in her early 40s and was angry about a problem with her recent matrimonial property settlement.

"Good afternoon. So sorry to keep you waiting. I was held up by not just one but two Judges. May I call you Sienna?"

"Certainly. I have a relationship property problem. I've filled this in with Melinda. What a nice girl. She's very colourful."

'Yeah," muttered Richard. "Sometimes fluorescent!"

"Tourette's?"

"Just a touch. And employed to good effect. But it gets her into some sticky corners."

"Wonderful personality."

Sienna handed Richard a bundle of notes. He read them talking to her at the same time.

"Let's get straight into it. You separated two years ago and signed a formal property Agreement a year later?

"Yes."

"Your husband is a car importer and through his accountant's assessment at the time of the Agreement you were told the business had a value of only $50,000."

"Yes."

"You have now discovered with the help of a private investigator that your husband failed to disclose over 140 paid off imported cars in his possession concealed away in a warehouse with a combined net value of about $450,000 - $500,000?"

"Yes. That's right. My lawyer then told me it would not be worth questioning it and legal aid will not pay for it. At least, that's what she said."

"You got the house, the better of the two cars and $25,000?"

"Yes."

Well, that puts legal aid out of the picture."

"Yes. But he got the business, the holiday house at Taupo which was worth more than the Auckland house and $25,000. I calculate that he got at least $450,000 more than me when the undisclosed cars are taken into account, and he knows it was unfair."

"Is that your previous lawyer's folder?"

"Yes. She's seen the private investigator's report, but she says there's nothing I can do about it because we both had independent lawyers when we signed the Agreement."

"Have you raised the fact of the undisclosed cars with your husband?"

"I wrote to him and got this letter back." She handed over the letter. Richard quickly skimmed through the file.

"Apart from general abuse you will see I have highlighted the passage where he says –

"About the cars, you are too late to raise this now. You should have asked. You and your lawyer were stupid."

"Did he indeed? Great stuff for a Judge to read. Silly Boy! I see here the dispute began in the Family Court and you both filed affidavits."

Richard continued.

"In his affidavit, I see that not only did he not disclose the 140 cars in storage, but he positively asserted that no other undisclosed property existed."

"Well, my last lawyer told me I couldn't do anything. I just wanted a second opinion."

"That advice was wrong! You can do everything about it! Affidavits must be true, otherwise it's perjury. Any contract induced by fraud will be overturned by a Court. But more importantly, section 21J of the Property (Relationship) Act 1976 allows you to apply to set aside the Agreement if there is a serious injustice."

Richard pressed a direct link on his computer to the Property (Relationships) Act 1976 and flashed section 21J up on the large screen on the wall. He highlighted the relevant subsections in yellow.

"This section specifically permits the Court to set aside an agreement if serious injustice has resulted. Your claim for setting aside the Agreement is simply unanswerable."

He printed off a copy for Sienna.

"What do we do?"

"I will file an application to set aside the Agreement supported by an affidavit by you and an affidavit by the private investigator. We can file that tomorrow or early next week and serve your husband by Tuesday hopefully. Let's dump it all on him! No alternative to acting promptly. Let's light him up like a firecracker!"

"Love the sound of that."

"What I need to do is interview the private investigator and make a value judgement as to the strength of his evidence. I see from his letter that it looks cut and dried in your favour."

"Will it involve a full court case?"

"I very much doubt it. Do you like your former husband?"

"Why do you ask?"

"I think your ex has almost certainly lied in his affidavit. That is perjury. He will not understand that yet, but any good lawyer will have to tell him that the CIB will likely come knocking on his door. I will certainly use that to your advantage. He may well go to prison."

"Blackmail?"

"Well, I'll have to be subtle in the way I go about such things, but I'm used to that. He will settle. But such matters are all part of the expected dialogue between lawyers and pointing out the inevitable publicity is not blackmail. He brought about a settlement vastly in his favour, to your disadvantage, and he did so by lying on oath about the assets of the business. That's more than just naughty."

"I don't want to be a bitch. But that's his problem. How much can I claim?"

"That's simple. The net value of the cars divided by two plus interest at about 7% per year since the Agreement. In addition, because this was a deliberate fraud by him, he will be required to pay a hefty amount of legal costs. They won't cover all your costs but will come within $20,000 of my fee. Of course, I cannot estimate that yet because I do not know how far down the track we have to go."

"My God! My last lawyer charged me $66,000, and she obviously got it wrong. If you are prepared to limit the net cost to me to, say, $26,000, I can pay you in advance tomorrow and anything you recover by way of costs against Frank can be yours on top."

"That suits me. I'll draw up an undertaking to that effect and it will be available tomorrow morning."

"Anything else?"

"You come in at 4:30 pm tomorrow. Go through them carefully over the weekend and then come back at 8:30 am Monday and we'll get them all signed up with any changes you have made. I'll prepare a letter to your husband, and his former lawyers who will probably still represent him, and that will be a letter from hell designed to put real pressure on him. He'll settle!"

Richard shook her hand again and led her through the waiting room to the lift in the hallway.

"See you tomorrow afternoon."

"Thanks so much."

Richard left his office quickly and opened Wiremu's door.

"Rightio. Where are my three burglars? Or are you all innocent? Better still, can the cops prove that you are guilty?"

"Mr Locksley, I introduce Jimmy Costello, Hemi Ranui and Pete Anderson. All aged 19. They are charged jointly with breaking into a private garage owned by a person known to them. They admit breaking open the lock and taking a car."

The three young men were a little roughly dressed but clean and tidy and quite articulate.

"Did you do all that, boys?"

"Yes, Sir!"

"Why?"

"Well Jimmy owned the car. This bloke took it off Jimmy six weeks ago. He reckoned Hemi owned him some money."

"Did he take it with force?"

"He threatened to give me the bash if I didn't give him the keys."

"Did you tell the police this?"

"The cop didn't want to know. We wanted to make a statement, but he told us the case was open and shut. He said we broke open the garage door, which we did, and that was the end of the matter."

Wiremu butted in, "Mr Locksley. These lads pleaded not guilty through the duty solicitor a few weeks ago. The defended hearing has been set down for this coming Monday at 11.45."

Richard turned to Wiremu.

"Please get me the full police file by tomorrow morning. I'll need it for the weekend. Jimmy, what proof do you have that you owned the car?"

"I have the registration papers which show it's in my name. Here. I also have the finance papers which prove that. Here they are too."

"Right. Money. You are all working so you will not get legal aid. My fee for a case like this would normally be $15,000. There are three of you. I will defend all three for one fee but the fees have got to be $10,000 plus GST so that will come to $11,500 divided by three which comes to, say, $3900 each.

"OK by us"

"I have to be blunt. I need that before Tuesday. As we say in this job, "No Banana. No Monkey." But if we win, I'll apply for costs so you could get your money or some of it back. But costs awards in the criminal court are very miserable."

"Fine, Boss. We expected that. Pete will drop the whole lot in tomorrow for all of us."

"Good. Are your telephone numbers here? Yeah. Here they are. I'll ring you each over the weekend. Make sure you are available individually around teatime on Sunday. OK?"

"AOK. Yeah. Right."

"Thanks for coming in. You'll hear from me Sunday."

They all left. Wiremu remained.

"Here are the drink driving files. They're all in the waiting room. I have discussed all the fees from them. No problems."

"Thanks. Would you be so good as to shepherd them in one by one?"

Wiremu left and then came back. Richard was in his full stride.

"May I introduce John Stoddard."

"Good morning. Thank you, Willie."

Willie left.

"I've read the interview notes and I'm yet to peruse the police file but let's run through all the good things can be said about you."

In ten minutes, the interview was over, and Richard tidied his desk while Wiremu ushered in the next client.

"May I introduce Steven Hurring."

"Come in Mr Hurring. A spot of bother with teensy bit of drink driving? Come into the help parlour."

Richard finished three more similar interviews at pace and emptied the waiting and reception areas. Janet was answering the phone every two minutes and Melinda sat interviewing a client in her office. Wiremu was still escorting a new client into his office.

When Richard had seen all the clients and his staff had left, he turned out the lights and closed the office. He made notes, tidied the files and took some researched law home with him.

Driving home over the Auckland harbour bridge to his home overlooking the small urban Lake Pupuke on the North Shore district of Auckland, Richard scanned a check list he drew up for the next day's work.

- ✓ Friday District Court all morning.
- ✓ 6 afternoon interviews.
- ✓ Brief all staff.
- ✓ Prepare Stanton – employment dispute.
- ✓ Documents for Sienna – relationship property.
- ✓ Interview investigator.
- ✓ Prepare burglary case.
- ✓ High Court appeals at 3.00 pm.

Richard parked the car in the garage of his house, got out and walked to the front door and went inside.

Mary was waiting for him. She hugged and kissed him, but something was obviously troubling her. Something was wrong. Mary was the same age as Richard. She was a very bright and fascinating lady and well educated. She held a law degree but worked in advertising.

"Goodness. What's the matter?"

"It's Mum. She's had a bit of a turn. But she's not going to die. I think I'll have to fly to Queenstown tomorrow."

"Oh. Darling. I'm so sorry. Where is she now?"

"She's in Frankton Hospital but the general view is that she needs permanent rest home care."

How was your day? Mary adds.

"I'm absolutely buggered! I don't know how long I can keep this up. 15 years working 6 am to 9 pm sometimes six days a week."

"Perhaps it's time for a change? You know there have been many articles on mid-life "burnout" for professionals. You're doing extremely well but is it all worth it? You know how much we love the Southern Lakes District and Mum's home in Queenstown is beautiful. This just might be the time to up stakes and restart. It could be an adventure."

"You could be right. Roger and Alice still have a few years school left. Frankly, I find the Auckland scene a bit full on. Too much law society schmoozing and lawyers kissing Judge's bums. But I'm making $750,000 a year here. I don't know if I could match that in Queenstown."

"Does it really matter? We have only one life. This house is paid off. We have a healthy bank balance. Now that Dad has gone and me being the only child, I will get Mum's house when she passes on, and she's 86 now. I'm not being mercenary. Just pragmatic. I think we should now be focusing on lifestyle and early retirement. Why not?"

"It would be a massive lifestyle change."

"But for the better. And we wouldn't be burning our bridges. Mum lives in Frankton. It's walking distance to the airport. There are at least six non-stop flights to and from Auckland every day of the week. We certainly keep our house here in Auckland and don't consider selling it for at least 12 months in case we change our minds."

"I'm leasing my office in Auckland so there's is no problem there. Let me think about the idea overnight."

"I'd better get down to Queenstown tomorrow. I can get a morning flight. Let's talk tomorrow night. I'm just a bit worried about your future health. I don't like my job in advertising. We both love the South and know it so well."

"You go to bed. I'm stay up for about an hour and make a few notes."

"OK. Don't stay up too late."

Richard's home den was modest and comfy. The walls were lined with books. A side light was on, and a swivel desk lamp illuminated a small worktable. Richard was doing a lot of Googling and making notes. He occasionally made a phone call and prepared more notes. He finally yawned and walked up to bed upstairs and slipped into bed with his wife. She was barely awake.

"Find something?"

"Heaps. The Queenstown Court sits an average of two days a week in and there are other courts in Alexandra and Gore. That's a good thing because it allows for better planning for outside fun. For example, there is usually no Court on a Thursday and Friday which would allow us to choose long weekends for ourselves and the family. Trips to Melbourne and Sydney can quite easily be arranged. Heaven knows I can't do that now."

"Terrific. What about offices?"

"Well, that's the interesting thing. Not one, but two local senior lawyers in different offices have died within the last three months and another female lawyer has taken 12 months maternal leave. That leaves a huge gap to grab."

"This might all come together."

"The more I've been thinking about, the more I think we could have a really good lifestyle. We've holidayed there at least once a year for 15 years and have always talked about wanting to live there. We've always loved your mum's home and I might be able to pick up a legal practice on the cheap."

"I'm on a flight out of here at 8.20 in the morning but I'll try a late flight back on Monday evening, perhaps Tuesday morning. I rang the hospital and Mum is OK, but the social worker has already scheduled her for a wonderful rest home in Frankton about 500 metres away."

"Sounds great" says Richard.

"It could not be more perfect. I got to speak to Mum briefly and told her about the possibility of us shifting and she is overjoyed and volunteered that she would love us to take over the house."

"Do you believe in magic? Are we being told something here?"

"I feel the Loving Spoonful coming on," replied Mary with a rough attempt at singing a few lines.

"What have you got on this morning?"

"I need to analyse my caseload for the next three months. I'll have to make a few trips back from Queenstown if we do shift."

"Are you sure on what we're talking about here?"

"Actually, I am. Auckland's been great in our 20s and 30s. But I'm looking for a bit of a different lifestyle."

"Well think on this. Let's get your practicing certificate back. You had one six years ago, so it's only a matter of getting it reissued. Easy Peasy. I would love to work alongside you."

"I would love that too. Let's do it."

"OK. A few more positive steps forward. Get away early in the morning but we'll talk tomorrow night by telephone. I'll ring you after tea."

"What have you got on this morning?"

"Tons. High Court and District Court again. But over $30,000 in fees."

"Auckland's been great but I'm looking for a bit of a different lifestyle."

They gave each other a hug and turned over and fell straight to sleep.

The next day, early Friday morning, Richard was already in his office at 7.30 am. He was the only one present. He was speaking on the telephone to a land agent in Queenstown. Janet would be in soon.

"I'm ringing about the former offices of Mr Dave Thornton. Can you tell me something about them? Large office? Yes, four medium offices? Good reception space with room for three admin. staff. Five carparks. Are photographs on the website accurate?"

"Yes, Yes and Yes," replied the land agent. "It's a really nice suite with a possibility for expansion within three months or so."

"My wife will be in Queenstown late today. Could you see her on Saturday morning at, say, 10.00 am? Great. Thanks. Her name is Mary."

Janet arrived at work and put the coffee on. Richard greeted her.

"Good morning. Friday at last. Pop in here for a moment. Could you bring 2 cups of coffee."

Richard read the morning files until Janet returned with the 2 cups of coffee. He stood up and started talking.

"I want to tell you something. You are the only one other than Mary to be informed of what we are thinking. I'm starting to suffer a bit from burnout. It's not serious but yesterday Mary's Mum suffered a pretty bad relapse and is in hospital in Queenstown."

"Oh. I'm so sorry."

"Mary and I have been talking. Perhaps we're both going through the change of life, but we're rather attracted to the idea of simply shifting to Queenstown and setting up practice there. Mary will probably take up her practicing certificate and I think Willie and Melinda might be interested.

"Holy Heck! I love Queenstown and the whole Southern Lakes area. Can I come too?"

"Sure!" grinned Richard. "That's just what I wanted to hear."

Janet was clearly interested in the idea.

"Don't forget I was born in Gore and my parents are only in their early 80s and still live on the small farm 40 km on the Queenstown side of Gore. I could see them every weekend."

"What made you come to Auckland?"

"Chasing a man. Didn't work out. I've never told you that. I was 32 at the time, just a year before I came to work for you."

"Would you really consider moving back South?"

"Yes. I know I would love it."

"Well, Janet. I think this is where I get down on a bended knee. I would love you to come. I will pay removal expenses and your first three months rental."

"Don't forget I've got a fairly good house here in Auckland with no mortgage because of advances from my parents. Arrowtown, Closeburn, Lake Hayes, Fernhill would all be great by me. Goodness that's exciting."

"Well, it's not a done deal yet. But I think we will make a decision by early next week some time."

"I think I would be really interested. Like a new life."

Melinda and Wiremu walked in.

"Top of the morning to you two."

"Morning boss. Morning Janet."

"Good morning. Full day today but I'd like to take you to lunch today if possible. I have something important to tell you. All good. But now could you look out the files and folders for the court work and interviews for today, Monday and Tuesday. Be back in ten minutes if you can."

They both replied together – "Sure thing."

"Melinda, please grab the Sienna Fordyce folder and have a quick look through it. You saw her yesterday afternoon before me."

The pace in the office started to quicken. Telephones were ringing. Clients were coming into the waiting room.

The telephone rang. Janet answered it and called into Richard's office.

"Richard, it's the Ministry of Police in Wellington on the line for you."

"Jeez! Not those bloody parking tickets again?"

He picked up the phone.

"Richard Locksley."

"Mr Locksley, can you take a call from the Minister please?"

"Sure thing."

He placed his hand over the handset and muttered –

"Jeez! What have I done? It's the Minister."

The Minister came on the phone.

Richard beckoned Melinda in and motioned for her to be silent as he put the phone on speaker.

"Mr Locksley. Grant Brentwood here. We met once at a seminar about six months ago."

"Good morning, Minister. How can I help?"

"I'm in a spot of bother. I've been charged with drink-driving but there was no consumption of alcohol at all before the driving. The police came to my house hours later."

"OK, Minister. Happy to help."

"I had one of my staff pick up the entire file from the police and, as you know, my electorate is here in Auckland, so I'll be back for the weekend. Any chance of you seeing me tomorrow morning?"

"Absolutely Minister. Do you want me to come to you?"

"No. I know where you are. I just don't want to be standing out in the public if your outside door is locked."

"I'll make sure I'm outside at 9:45 am and if you turn up at 10 am I'll whisk you straight in."

"OK. I'll see you Saturday morning at ten."

"OK."

He hangs up and calls out through his open office door.

"Wiremu."

He came in on the double.

"You won't believe who that was on the phone. The Minister of Police. He's been done for drink-driving in Queenstown, and he wants me to defend him. It looks like it will be a plea of not guilty, probably set down for a fixture in about two weeks. Keep it under your hats."

"Holy Hell!"

"We're full up today but split the research between you and I want clear copies of the relevant sections of the Land Transport Act 1989 and all possible defences. Concentrate on the post driving consumption of alcohol case law. Justices Peter Mahon and Clint Roper wrote very good decisions against the presumption about post driving drinking. It's not an absolute presumption. If a defendant can show clearly that there was no pre-driving consumption, then he can usually avoid the presumption. The full police file will be dropped in here at lunch time. I want every potential defence considered. There must be no discussion about this with anyone. Anyone at all!"

"We will get it done by the end of the afternoon."

"Now, lunch with you guys today at 1.00? Melinda, will you also draft an application to set aside Mrs Fordyce's relationship property agreement and an affidavit by her and the private investigator? At this stage just do a short affidavit of the private dick, attaching his letter and confirming it as true. Both affidavits can be in alligator format – short and snappy. If Mr Fordyce doesn't settle he'll be off to prison for perjury. There'll also now be a memorandum of facts dictated by me on the file. Janet typed them up this morning."

"No problems. A serious misrepresentation of property assets? Section 21J as well as a bit of fraud?"

"Exactly. Right on the button. She's coming at 4.30 this afternoon."

Wiremu piped up.

"The High Court has advised that the two appeals against sentence can be heard this afternoon at 3 pm."

"Great!" said Richard. "I'm sorry to keep piling on the pressure!"

Wiremu tried to inspire confidence.

"No pressure at all. Pressure is a Messerschmitt up your arse at 300 miles per hour."

"Yeah, right."

"But Crown Law has advised they will not be taking a strong stance against the appeals. They think privately that Judge Christie needs a bit of a slapping."

"Good. I agree. And this morning?"

"You have four drink drivers and the prostitute up for assault. Four have paid the fees in advance but two require limited licences. I have quoted for those and started on the documents. And just to make your day, Judge Crusty is on the Bench."

"Lordy. Not again. Will no one rid me of this turbulent Judge?

"Bit of history there, Boss," said Melinda. "Henry II said something like that in 1170 to inspire his knights to kill Thomas Beckett."

"Good one. Not just a wind-up doll," joked Richard. "Rightio. To work everyone. We'll have some good clean fun at lunch."

That was too much for Melinda.

"What good is clean fun? Boss?" Richard thought he was ready for a snappy reply to her quip.

"I'll have you know, girl, that the word "fun" does not appear anywhere in any Act of Parliament, so the law is a pretty sorry world."

But she immediately retorted:

"If that is true, then the fluffy newborn chick of hope tumbles from the eggshell of life and splashes into the sizzling frypan of doom".

She was incorrigible.

CHAPTER THREE

Later that taxied at Queenstown airport, Mary's aircraft landed and taxiing up to the terminal. There was no air bridge. She alighted against the magnificent backdrop of the Remarkables mountain range and let out a sigh at feeling the whole atmosphere and walked through the terminal and straight out with a carry bag.

She climbed into a taxi. "Hospital please. What a lovely day!"

"Been like this for two weeks. Don't tell those bloody Aucklanders."

"Well, I suppose I'm an Aucklander now, but my family are thinking of moving permanently down here. We did live here many years ago."

"You won't regret it."

Frankton Hospital was just a couple of minutes' drive from the air terminal. Mary walked into the foyer and a nurse came up to her.

"Good morning. Can I help you?"

"I am Mrs McKenzie's daughter, Mary."

"Hello. I'm Nurse Jacinda. So nice to meet you. Your mum is doing well, although I think she will need permanent care. Come through here."

They walked together along the short corridor and into a single room. The Frankton Hospital looked over the beautiful arm of the same name of the huge Lake Wakatipu. Mrs McKenzie's room had a wonderful view over the water.

"Here's your daughter, Millie."

"Hi my dearest Mum. How are you? Oh, it's so good to see you."

She hugged and kissed her Mum and unwrapped some flowers which Nurse Jacinda took from her and put in a vase.

"I'm a bit feeble, dearie, but I'm feeling quite good. What a beautiful view!"

"I'll leave you two to it." The nurse left them.

"Mum. I'm here for a couple of days and I think I have some really good news for you".

"That's nice dear, but I'm fine. Just a bit old."

"Don't you worry about all this talk about going into a rest home. Richard and I have made some pretty serious decisions in the last two days. We are both suffering from Auckland burnout and it's almost certain that we're going to relocate here to Queenstown."

"Oh, that's so wonderful. That'll be so much fun. You can have the house. It was going to be yours anyway."

"We don't need to rush anything, Mum. We can all live together until the time to shift to a rest home becomes obvious. No hurry."

"The house is yours when you're ready. The rest home is only a few blocks away and I've visited friends there many times. I really like it."

"Plenty of time to discuss that. Is there anything you'd like?"

"I've been craving for a pineapple Fru-Ju. My throat is always a bit dry."

"I'll bring a box of them back soon. They'll be able to keep the extras in a fridge."

"Wonderful. How long are you here for?"

"Just for two days. I must look at some offices for Richard and the practice and I fly back Tuesday, or possibly Wednesday. But the plans are coming together very quickly, and I think we could be down permanently within two weeks."

"Well, I've been thinking very carefully. The social worker here says that the rest home will take me directly from the hospital and now that I know you and the family are coming down that's what I'll do. I would really like that."

Mary looked delighted.

"Let's take one day at a time. And if you go to a rest home, please know that you will come back every weekend or every fortnight if you wish and we'll look after you in your own home. The kids would love to see you in that setting."

"Lovely news. That settles that. No more talk. You hurry along and do your things today and come and see me when you can."

"I'll be back tonight and a couple of times tomorrow, probably with a lot of interesting news."

Mary kissed her Mum goodbye for the moment and left the room just as Nurse Jacinda brought in Mum's lunch.

"Mum wants Fru-Ju's. Is that OK?"

"No problems at all. Just drop them off at reception and we'll put them straight in the fridge. Millie, you just ask for one whenever you want it."

Mary left with a warm feeling in her tummy and full of love for her Mum.

The same morning in the District Court at Auckland. Richard was on his feet representing, in turn, four drink drivers and a prostitute up for assault. Judge Christie was yet again on the bench. He was in a foul mood this morning.

"Ah! The mercurial Mr Locksley up before me again. Will I ever see the back of you?"

Richard exploded.

"That's a quite inappropriate comment to come from the Bench! It makes me sound as if I'm a defendant and it's an improper observation for you to make!"

"Take it how you like."

"I'll take it right to the Judicial Complaints Authority. Your Honour, we must be on a better relationship basis that this. Please refrain from making those comments."

"I'll ignore that. Call the next case."

"No, Your Honour."

"What do you mean NO?"

"Your inappropriate comments today, Your Honour, together with your open display of bias yesterday, compels me to complain that justice will not be seen to be done to my clients by Your Honour today if I represent them before you! How can I assure them that you are a fair Judge?"

"You go too far!"

"No. It is you who goes too far! How can I explain to my clients that they will get justice before you? Justice must not only be done but be seen to be done!"

"Humph!" sneered the Judge in a deliberately disrespectful tone.

Richard almost disintegrated with rage, then put a check on his rising temper.

"Don't you Humph me! I insist that you recuse yourself. Otherwise, my clients and I will turn our back and walk out of this courtroom and report straight to the senior Judge on duty today."

"I'll cite you for contempt!"

"Try it!" Richard stuck out his jaw. The Judge sensed defeat.

"Oh, very well. But this is not the end of this matter."

He bent down to his clerk sitting in front of him –

"Send Mr Locksley's five cases next door to Judge Matthias in Courtroom No 3."

Richard and his drink drivers and prostitute clients walked out of the court and down the corridor to Courtroom 3.

"Good on you, mate. About time the big prick was exposed."

"I've got some wonderful stuff on that Judge. Buy me a drink after Court and I'll give you the tapes. They'll blow your mind away."

Richard took a very interested mental note.

He and his clients entered Courtroom 3. A court clerk walked in the side door and handed five court files to the Bench and said something softly, beyond hearing, to Judge Julia Matthias. She smiled and nodded. She was an intelligent, well-spoken 44-year-old appointed to the Bench four years previously. She was regarded as the best of the judicial bunch on the District Court in Auckland. As he entered the door to the Court, Richard turned to all his clients and whispered.

"Judge Matthias is a very fair and reasonable Judge. She does not like bullshit. I will keep my submissions very short and that will be to your advantage. Everything understood?

He whispered to Tyler.

"You're dressed up like a coloured feather duster. If you weren't just a sheila, people would think you look like a rooster."

"I know. Ain't I kooool? I actually think I look like a cocktail."

"Jeez, lady!"

The Judge greeted Richard.

"Good morning, Mr Locksley. Five of your files here? Will they take long?"

"Four minutes each, Your Honour. Baby alligators. Short and snappy."

"Thank you. Call the first one, Mr Registrar."

"Call **John Hendry Stoddard**."

Mr Stoddard walked from the back of the Court and stepped into the dock. A plea of guilty was entered by Richard. The prosecuting Sergeant read out the summary of facts.

"May it please the Court, the defendant was subject to a routine breath test two Mondays ago on Newton Road and recorded an excess breath level of 612. He was fully cooperative and has no previous convictions."

The Judge nodded for Richard to proceed with his plea in mitigation.

"The Sergeant has said it all for me. With a surprising amount of candour, the defendant has asked me to tell the Court that he is both very stupid and very sorry. He promises he will not see the inside of a Courtroom ever

46

again. There was no overt bad driving. His wife's birthday. A bit of champagne. Drove 300 metres to get some fish and chips. He has pleaded guilty at the first available opportunity."

The Judge was very brief: "Fined $600, disqualified for six months."

The next case was called.

Mr **Stephen Oswald Hurring** presented himself into the dock.

The prosecutor: "Almost identical circumstances, Your Honour. Breath alcohol level 593. One previous conviction for careless driving. Fully cooperative."

Richard stepped up again.

"My client is aged 52. The conviction for careless driving was when he was 19. He consumed some wine in his office before he left for home. He genuinely thought before getting into his car that he had not drunk too much. He is extremely sorry.

The Judge: "Fined $600, disqualified for six months."

Mr Hurring stepped down and proceeded to the back of the Court and out the door with a small "thumbs up" to Richard.

"Call **Patrick Jones Downes**."

Mr Downes stepped into the dock.

"Plea of guilty, Your Honour."

Richard stood up.

The Police sergeant read out the summary of facts.

"This defendant is only 17. The maximum breath alcohol level is therefore lower. He was apprehended driving on the northern motorway with a level of 158."

Richard was at his abbreviated best once again.

"Guilty. 1 pint of beer. Remorseful. In full employment. Specifically asked me to tell the Court he will never place himself in this position again for the rest of his life! Is that all made up? So easy to say. But I submit that you can rely on that undertaking as being firm and believable because it was the first thing he said to me before I even opened my mouth at the interview."

"Once again, a perfectly appropriate and short plea. It cuts straight to the relevant points," said the Judge.

She turned and addressed the defendant.

"I accept you know it was a wrong judgement to make and the law says I must disqualify you and fine you. But I will keep it to the minimum. You are convicted and fined $200, ordered to pay court costs and disqualified for three months."

Mr Downes stepped down from the dock.

"Call **Maria Rose Cunningham**."

Richard: "Guilty plea, Your Honour."

The prosecuting sergeant read out a summary of facts.

"The police accept that the defendant was not intending to drive this Wednesday morning.

A bicycle accident involving an 11-year-old boy cycling to school occurred right outside her residential property in Epsom. The lad collided with a full rubbish bin, and he badly cut his shins and abdomen. 22 stitches were required. Mrs Cunningham immediately applied complicated first aid and drove him to Emergency Care. She was breathalysed on returning home and showed a level of 401. She has one speeding conviction, although it was over 20 years ago."

Richard rose again.

"She was the proverbial good Samaritan, Judge. There was an alcohol build-up from her daughter's wedding barbecue on the Sunday, the day before. Her last drink was 16 hours previously. The child was badly bleeding from one leg. She thought it was broken as well. He was crying in pain. She did not consider whether the alcohol consumed the previous day would have put her at risk. I ask that you find "special reasons" not to impose the minimum mandatory period of disqualification. I submit the fullest of mercy can be extended to the defendant." Her Honour sentenced his client with a few remarks.

"Once again, a short but highly appropriate plea from Mr Locksley. The Court appreciates that approach. Mrs Cunningham, I do find special reasons and you will not be disqualified. I cannot bring myself to punish a good Samaritan. I am strengthened in this view by my belief that you would not have been driving had you not been presented with an injured boy. I'm therefore also prepared also to discharge you without conviction but on the basis, and please excuse the irony, that you pay $500 to the St John Ambulance Association."

"I am obliged, Your Honour," said Richard with a short bow.

"Call **Tyler Lesley King**."

Tyler advanced up the centre aisle like a sashaying model on a catwalk.

"Tone it down, girl," Richard whispered.

"A plea of guilty to common assault, Your Honour."

Tyler was a real trick. She was dressed colourfully and did look a bit like a cocktail with a bit of purple here, some shiny silver there and streaks of orange through her hair but she had a smile which could melt an iceberg. She smiled at Judge Matthias. The Judge seemed to melt just a wee bit.

The prosecuting Sergeant rose again and presented the facts.

"I must say I have some sympathy with the defendant. My recommendation was that this prosecution should not continue but the complainant would not accept my opinion. Technically, of course, there was an assault. I now read you the prepared Summary of Facts."

"The defendant is a sex worker. On Saturday, 13 August she was walking with friends near the corner of Victoria Street and Queen Street. The complainant, and his friends all of whom had been drinking to excess, approached her. The complainant said to her in a loud voice - "You're that slut who likes it up the arse!" She ignored him but he followed her uttering the offensive phrase several more times. He was drunk at the time. The defendant felt that she had received enough abuse and she turned around and slapped him hard once across the face. Unfortunately, his cigarette squashed into his mouth and his lower lip was burned. The police accept that this burn result was not intentional. She is aged 32 and has no previous offences or violence."

It was then Richard's turn.

"The Sergeant has said it all, Your Honour. She did commit an assault. But in the mind of the public, I say with some energy – "He got what he deserved!" It was one slap. It was made by a diminutive female against a much heavier, aggressive and alcohol-fuelled male. What on earth did he expect? I ask that you do not leave her with a conviction. She wishes to travel and had planned to do so this year."

The Judge paused and then said very carefully.

"I entirely agree. I must confess I even have difficulties in telling this defendant, as I must of course, that she should not have reacted in this way. Such words would stick in my mouth, even though I am a Judge. In the eyes of the law, she is guilty. But in the eyes of most citizens, he deserved what he got. Mr Locksley as usual has used the minimum of words necessary to put across your case succinctly. I have no hesitation in discharging you without conviction. Your name is also suppressed."

At that stage a man sitting up the back of the public gallery, obviously with his wife or partner, snorted and yelled out -

"Crap!"

Tyler signalled to Richard that the man was one the yob she had slapped. The startled Judge looked up. Richard butted in.

"The so-called victim's self-righteousness has no bounds, Your Honour. He was one of my client's customers. Several times."

It was clear that the victim's partner or wife was sitting alongside him. It was the first that she had heard of that!

"You bastard!" she snarled at him.

She then took her handbag and several books she had been carrying and threw them at him with great force. Both fled the courtroom chased by a constable.

"Don't worry constable. Any penalty I impose for contempt would be minimal with what he's going to get tonight. Mr Locksley, thank you for the usual theatre you create in my Court which has brightened an otherwise dull day. That's all, I think, for me this morning."

"The Court will rise." intoned the Court clerk.

And with that, the Judge stood up, gently bowed and winked at Richard as she disappeared out of a rear door of the court.

Reporters from the press bench descended upon Richard and Tyler obviously wanting the full story. Richard gave her strong advice.

"Tyler, you have now got name suppression. My advice is that you say nothing more. Sorry, ladies and gentlemen."

Richard and the clients left, and he split them up, one at a time, in the corridor. Each of the drink-driving clients were delighted. Each one had paid $2500 at the office. This had been the agreed fee. They left the corridor and Tyler turned to Richard.

"I am so grateful, Mr Locksley. I'll shout you a drink. I have something to give you."

"Struth. It's only 11 o'clock. Well, maybe one glass of champagne." They both left the building together.

CHAPTER FOUR

It was still only the morning. He had made over $13,000 already.

He walked along a side street with his client and down into a very dodgy looking basement bar. The clientele appeared to be the entire sex worker population of central Auckland. The sign outside read "Gentlemen's' Titty Bar"

"If she could only see me now," thought Richard thinking of Mary.

He recognised many of those present as his clients. Tyler moved to the bar and ordered a bottle of champagne.

Colourful characters came up to Richard.

"Hi, Richard. Remember me? Stage name was Miss Gay Abandon."

She appeared to be dressed in little more than a thong and two postage stamps.

"Of course. So good to see ya. Good to see you all."

A middle-aged man sashayed up. Richard knew him as Popeye the Pimp.

"Top of the morning to you, Richard baby. Howzit going?"

"Christ almighty! Popeye! If Mary could only see me now."

A bar tender called Patsy returned with a bottle of champagne and two glasses and Richard and Tyler both sat down at a corner table. At least Patsy was wearing a bikini. But it was an itsy bitsy teeny weeny one, with sparkles on it. "Lucky it wasn't windy" thought Richard wickedly.

People kept coming up to Richard and shaking his hand.

Seneca in a long, dotted gown.

Tilly dressed in a purple lycra 'not so much of it' something.

Monica with a miniskirt which seemed to start at her navel.

Serenity was wearing a see-through body stocking under a wispy "cover not so all."

"Hi. Great to see you" Richard spluttered.

"Must have a coffee some time."

"You're looking well."

"Bugger off, everyone. He's mine," spat Tyler.

Everyone then left them alone, but throughout the following conversation little waves were sent and kisses blown towards their table. Tyler opened up.

"That fat, bloated Judge Christie. I've always hated him. He's a womanising pervert!"

"I don't know if I would go that far," responded Richard.

"Well, I have a wee gift for you. It's a video from the Thunder Thighs Room at the Pink Pussycat Club three months ago. Store it away. It may come into good use one day."

"Don't even start to tell me what happens in the Thunder Thighs Room," sighed Richard.

Tyler opened her technicolour carry bag and emptied its contents on to the table. Tissues, condoms, lubricants, knickers. She may not have had the kitchen sink, but she certainly had the butt plug, and a purple one to spare. All the other detritus of her profession spilled on the table.

"Stone the bloody crows! Spare me the detail," smiled Richard.

"It smells like Granny's knickers drawer!" exclaimed Tyler with a laugh.

Richard pretended to gag and retch.

"Ew! Here it is." She handed Richard a USB pen drive.

"Get a load of this when you get a minute. You'll find it a scream."

"Thanks. I owe you one too. I'll put this in my War Chest. Sometimes I call it my Blackmail Box or my Dirt Tray."

Richard slipped the USB pen drive Tyler handed him into his pocket. He suspected it might contain dynamite. They finished the bottle of champagne, and he told her about the plans for Queenstown.

"I'm thinking of shifting the whole office and the family down to Queenstown. I'm starting to get tired of working 14-hour days. I can always come back to Auckland for cases, and you make sure you ring me for any help you need if I do go. I'll send you my card."

"I like the idea. This place is getting too big and becoming a bit of a shit hole. I might be following you down."

"Well, I'll be in the book. Give me a ring if you come down. Look. I better get a move on. I have two appeals in the High Court this afternoon and then some more interviewing."

"Well, thanks so much for today. Gosh. I got discharged without conviction and suppression! Oops! Money. Here's your $3500."

"Thanks. I'll be seeing you then."

"Do you want to know what I would do for $3500?" she added. "Several times!"

"Pass," he said with a laugh.

Tyler accompanied Richard to the bottom of the stairs and waved him goodbye. The rest of the clientele also waved and blew kisses like a flock of brightly coloured flamingo.

Richard smelled as if he had been violated by a dozen strippers. How would he explain this pong to Melinda and Willie? To say nothing of Mary.

He walked a block down Queen Street and into the Viaduct Harbour restaurant and bar precinct on the waterfront where he had arranged to meet Melinda and Wiremu.

Melinda and Wiremu were already there.

"Hi guys. Sorry I'm a bit late. I'm already had champagne with a client after Court. Want one?"

"I'll have a small one."

"I'll have two of his."

"You're a terrier! Let's order quickly. I have a few things to talk about. Melinda, any difficulty with Sienna Fordyce's documents?"

"No. Janet's putting the final touches to them at the moment."

"Willie. I've got the High Court at 3.00 and then Sienna is coming in at 4.30."

"The good news is that the Crown Solicitor's office has rung and said that they are filing a simple document for this afternoon's appeals saying that the Crown will "abide the decision of the Court," replied Willie.

"Terrific. That's polite speak for saying "We believe the Judge was wrong." You don't get that very often."

The waiter came across to the table and took their orders.

"The snapper and salad please."

"Chicken curry and rice please."

"Oysters. Thanks."

"... and a bottle of Moet," added Richard. He then opened up.

"I've got some pretty earth-shattering news I want to share with you to. It could change your lives a bit but hopefully there are some real silver linings."

Melinda and Wiremu exchanged glances.

"I think I'm approaching potential burnout. Nothing serious. Perhaps just a matter of seeking a change of scenery and pace. Just hear me out. Mary's Mum had a bit of a turn in Queenstown yesterday."

"We're so sorry."

"It looks like she will have to go into a rest home and Mary would like to be in a position where she can see her at least once a week. So Mary and I and the kids have almost made up our mind to shift lock, stock and barrel, the law practice and all, to Queenstown. But I want you to come. Please!

"Wow!"

"The local Courts sit only 2 to 3 days a week if I take in Alexandra as well and Mondays and Tuesdays always seem to be free. We are secure financially with no mortgage and Mary's Mum is giving her the Frankton house. So, we're not going to be worse off."

"You want both os us?"

"I want you to come. Definitely. I have the utmost respect for your abilities and your experience. I need you to come.

The waiter returned with the champagne.

"Here's the deal. You could remain here and take over my practice. I would not charge you any so-called goodwill, but you would pay something for the office equipment. OR, you could come with us! Janet has already agreed. Mary will take back her practicing certificate. I would pay your removal expenses, immediately increase your salaries by 10% and pay your accommodation costs in Queenstown for three months."

"WOW! You certainly don't beat around the bush," answered Willie.

"Hell! I like the idea. I love it," said Melinda.

"It's too early to talk about partnerships yet but both of you certainly fit the profile. However, within the next 12 months I will certainly look at a profit-sharing arrangement and even on two-thirds of my current figures that might mean a doubling of your current salaries."

"I'm on!"

"Me. Too."

"I'll take a quick pee and be back in a few minutes. That gives you a few minutes without me present to discuss the matter together. Oh, and I'll increase your annual holidays to 6 weeks a year and the office will be closed for four extra-long weekends per year. But I will ask for top performances and no clock watching."

Richard left the table and disappeared out the back of the restaurant. Wiremu and Melinda could be seen chatting and smiling and nodding their heads.

"I don't need to think about it. I'll go. I'm Ngai Tahu, I was born in Invercargill and went to Southland Boys."

"And we both met in the Law Faculty at Otago University. And let's not forget most of our families live down south."

"Will we miss Auckland?

"It's only a single flight away and we've now got significant added holidays."

"Well, I'm attracted to the idea."

"So am I."

Richard returned to the table, picked up his glass, and raised his eyebrows. Melinda and Wiremu were laughing.

"We'll come!

"Friends? Family? Social life? Sporting pastimes? Financial commitments here?"

"There's nothing to tie us."

"We can always fly back for a long weekend. And while you've been in the little boys' room, we each counted at least 10 close friends between us who live in Queenstown and Wanaka. So we're on!"

"That's bloody marvellous! Now let's eat and we will talk each day about the changes from now on. Wiremu, can you come with me to the High Court this afternoon and, Melinda, could you go back and double check on Sienna Fordyce's papers and keep the office running."

They continued eating and talking excitedly and positively. After lunch, Richard paid, and they all walked to a nearby taxi rank.

Richard and Wiremu caught a taxi to the High Court and Melinda walked back to the office a block away.

CHAPTER FIVE

Richard and Wiremu walked through the foyer of the High Court and up to Courtroom No 3. Terry Jenkins and Brian Grimsby had been brought from the prison to hear their appeals. Richard shook their hands and offered words of encouragement. A young lawyer for the Crown approached Richard in a friendly manner. Nick Brownston was a rising star in the prosecution service and just a little older than both Wiremu and Melinda.

"Good morning, Mr Locksley. You've got a milk run today. The Crown has been quite worried about Judge Christie. He seems to be quite inconsistent and a bit out of control. I can't quite put it that way to Justice Ellison today, but he will get my drift."

Richard joked, "It's cases like this where I can say an appeal is where I ask one Court to show it's contempt for another!"

"Lovely" said Nick. "You should tell Justice Ellison that one. He would love it".

"Better not push it" replied Richard.

"The Crown is happy with a fine for Jenkins for cannabis and three months home detention for Grimsby. We think he needs a bit of a shock."

"OK by me. Thanks for that. Let's see if we can both get the Judge to agree."

"Good luck."

The court clerk called everyone to order and signalled the arrival of the High Court Judge.

"All rise for his Honour, the Queen's Judge."

Justice Ellison entered the Court room quietly, bowed gently to both Counsel and sat down.

"Good morning, Mr Locksley and Mr Brownston. I have read the papers you have filed, and, in view of the stance taken by the Crown, I hope we could save time if both appeals were heard together. Do either of you have any objection?"

"No, Your Honour."

"No, Your Honour."

"Well then, Mr Locksley."

"May it please the Court, Case No 1. Terry Jenkins. Third conviction, but as the first two were well over 20 years ago I respectfully submit that such a gap mitigates very much against imprisonment. But it was the way that this District Court Judge approached sentencing. It's all on the written record. He completely shut me down. He showed no courtesy to me as Counsel and within 60 seconds of me starting he simply said, "Sit down! You're finished!"

Justice Ellison gently butted in.

"I've heard enough, Mr Locksley. The Crown does not wish to be heard. I agree with your submissions. I rarely rebuke a Court below, but the strongest comment needs to be made by me to prevent this sort of pre-determined judgment being pronounced by any Court of law."

The Judge paused and noticed that the press reporters were present.

"The District Court Judge's repeated comments fell below what is required of any independent judicial authority. I do not wish to see such conduct again. The sentence is quashed. The conviction will remain. Because the appellant has obviously had to pay for your services, and as a mark of my concern about the attitude of the District Court Judge, I do not intend to impose any financial penalty. But Mr Jenkins, another conviction for even simple possession of cannabis will become your fourth and there is every possibility that there will be a short-term of prison involved at that stage."

"Now, Mr Locksley, the appellant Mr Grimsby."

"Your Honour. I accept that my client should never have touched the girl in this way, but the District Court Judge did not wish to hear any analysis of the facts which he found "disgusting." But I needed to point out that there was no penetration, no under the clothing touching, no repetition of the pat on the bottom and no intention to take the matter any further. Those are quite standard submissions to make, however distasteful, in a case such as this."

"I understand," said the Judge. Richard continued.

"The District Court Judge seemed to imply that the submissions made by me were an attempt to justify Mr Grimsby's actions, and the Court process then went further downhill from that point onwards. I stated right from the outset, "I cannot hope to mitigate his offending out of existence." Those were the words I used. But once again, I was told in no uncertain terms to sit down. In short, Your Honour, my client did not get a fair go."

Justice Ellison waved at him to stop, but then smiled.

"You may think I'm just doing the same thing now but not at all. Not at all. The Crown seeks a short period of home detention. I do not argue against that penalty."

The Judge addressed Grimsby directly.

"Mr Grimsby. What you did was quite wrong. Being "impulsive" does not wash with this Court. But you were not given a fair hearing in the District Court. I have no hesitation in overturning the District Court Judge's sentence as being manifestly excessive and not appropriate. His remarks as recorded were out of order. He did not follow fair process in a simple sentencing hearing. The appeal is allowed. You are sentenced to three months' home detention."

"May it please the Court," Richard wound up.

Richard and Wiremu walked back to the office.

"Thank God for fair Judges. I've had a text from Melinda, and she is really excited about Queenstown. I must admit, I am too."

"Are you sure? Do you want more time?"

"Not at all."

"I honestly think it will be an adventure for all of us. I know Janet is also looking forward to it. I'm only worried that we will maybe moving too fast."

"Nah! Let's go for it, Boss. And we've finished the research for the Minister of Police. It's on your desk. Both High Court decisions are there."

Richard and Wiremu came into the office foyer. Wiremu went into his office and Melinda poked her head out of hers and handed Richard the papers for Sienna Fordyce.

"Here are Sienna's documents. She's rung and is coming in soon. Pretty short and tight."

"I don't think that matters. If we prove the undisclosed cars then he won't dare go near a Family Court. Plenty of time to file longer documents if he tries to defend his own lies. Mr Fordyce will crap his pants."

Sienna Fordyce came into the reception area.

"Hi Sienna. I'm just going over your documents. Please, come in."

They both went into Richard's room, and he closed the door.

"Just have a read of these for a moment. I'll get you a further copy of section 21 J."

"Thank you."

Richard pushed one key on his computer and fed the link into his copier. Out came one sheet and he handed it to Sienna.

"This is all fine. It's shorter than I thought it would be."

"The real evidence lies in the private investigator's report. At this stage, that's all that's necessary. Now, any other changes you want to make?"

"No."

"It must be sworn before an independent lawyer. I'll get Melinda to take you down two floors to Shipton & Co. That will take only a couple of minutes. You can then go, and I will get a threatening letter away with a copy of the documents to Mr Fordyce's lawyers tonight. In fact, I will get them hand delivered. They're under a block away."

"What next?"

"I'll contact you as soon as I hear anything, and I will start pouring acid on them in two days. It's always necessary to keep the accelerator pushed to the floor and the pressure on. He'll cave in. If he rings, don't engage with him at all! He'll be worried about a perjury complaint."

"Thank you so much."

"Come through and I'll put you in Melinda's hands."

Richard escorted Sienna through to Melinda's office.

"Melinda. Can you please escort Sienna down to Shipton & Co and get her affidavit sworn? I've already signed the application. I see you already had the private investigator's affidavit sworn."

"Yes, Mr Locksley."

"I'm grateful if you bring the papers back and put them with the letter that I will now dictate for Janet and then take everything down to the Family Court, get them processed and then to Mr Fordyce's solicitors. Of course, the Court does not get the letter. Let's bang them all on the counter tonight! Thanks."

"Thanks so much."

"I will contact you. T'ra. Janet, could you please bring your notebook in please."

Janet followed Richard into his office.

"Could you please type this letter to Mr Fordyce's lawyers, Johnson & Johnson and give it to Melinda when she returns."

He dictated to her:

"Your client - John Fordyce
My client - Sienna Fordyce

I enclose self-explanatory papers. My client's claim for one half of the equity of the deliberately undisclosed motor vehicles is simply unanswerable. I have not filed the enclosed papers yet out of concern for your client's palpable criminal liability for perjury. He has also committed a fraud on the Court.

149 vehicles have now been discovered and the equity independently valued at $501,000. We will settle upon one half of the above equity plus interest and $30,000 for costs. Your client was deliberately hiding up to a half million dollars of assets.

I expect the utmost urgency to be given to this file. It is of importance to my client and surely must be addressed with urgency by your client. You have received these papers late on Thursday afternoon. I expect your client to have made a decision by the end of the weekend and I expect a reply on Monday.

I will be available for a telephone call anytime from Monday 2.00 p.m. onwards.

Yours faithfully,"

"Thanks Janet."

"Richard, I just want to let you know that I'm very excited about Queenstown."

"That's great to hear."

"We're all being a bit adventurous, but I think it'll work."

"Willie and Melinda can't stop talking about it."

Richard was standing up at home that evening with a beer in one hand and the telephone in the other. The children were watching television. He was talking to Mary who was still in Queenstown.

"Mum's fine. She wants to go into the Rest Home. She's already said we can have the house. I've had time to have a look at the schools and I think they're perfect."

"Well. I've talked to Janet, Melinda and Wiremu. They will all come! Isn't that amazing?"

"That's delightful! And I've managed to see the office today. You had made an appointment for tomorrow morning, but the owner met me with key and he's keen to do a deal."

"What are the offices like?"

"I'm really starting to believe fate is taking a hand in our decision. They're simply wonderful. Within a block of the courthouse and beside the Lake. You will love them. He mentioned a rent. I sucked in my breath and looked horrified but, I tell you, the rent is only half our current rent in Auckland. He then said it was negotiable. He will give a three-month rent holiday if we sign up for two years and I countered with three two-year rights of renewal. He said he would accept that."

"Great news!"

"There's a large reception area, plenty of room for Janet and four offices. A large one for you. Two identical medium ones and a small one which can be for me but plenty of room to interview in. I've taken heaps of photos and emailed them to you."

"That sounds perfect. Janet, Melinda and Willie have friends and family down this end of the country, and I won't have to retrain anyone."

"So, it's the kids to tell now."

"When's your flight back?"

"First thing in the morning. My car's at the airport. I'll be home by teatime."

"So, are we getting close to deciding then?"

"Well, I'm already at this stage for a YES."

"Me too. See you for tea tomorrow. Bye love."

CHAPTER SIX

It was Saturday morning and Richard was waiting outside the office. A Government Ministerial limousine pulled up and out stepped Minister Brentwood.

"Good morning, Minister."

"Call me Grant. Bit of a bugger all this."

"Plenty of tricks left in my bag. Come on up."

Richard had already unlocked the door and they entered the lift and proceeded up to his office.

"Let's get straight into it. Tell me all about all the facts."

"I was at the golf club. I had nothing to drink whatsoever. I drove home and had two whiskies and then two glasses of wine with dinner. There was a knock on the door and two constables were there in uniform. They said they had a complaint about me not stopping for three seconds at a stop sign. I said specifically to them that I had not invited them on to my property and I wanted them to leave. I did practise law myself in a previous life."

"How did they react to that?"

"They arrested me and threatened handcuffs. I protested to them and when I got to the police station, I demanded to see the duty senior sergeant and conveyed my protest to him. I said I would be fully cooperative, but under protest and under duress. I gave a breath sample, and it was just over the limit."

"You have defences. Good ones. Have you considered potential political fallout from pleading not guilty?"

"Pleading guilty will have a bigger fallout, for God's sake. I'll be dismissed as a Minister of the Crown."

"No choice, then."

"I don't really want to call my wife as a witness.

"No need to. They cannot disprove your admission that you had the drinks when you got home."

"Is it as simple as that?"

"No. Not really. It will depend a bit on the Judge, and I will certainly give it my best professional shot."

"Now, you arranged your own fixture date and it's for Thursday week in Queenstown."

"I can come down the night before."

"I'll be down there setting up my new office. Here's the address. I'll arrange a backdoor entrance at the Court, just to avoid a whole horde of photographers and reporters."

"I have interim suppression of name. Will that continue?"

"If you are found guilty, no. But if you are found not guilty, as I see it, you have two choices. You would have a 50% chance of a final suppression of name order. But everyone in New Zealand will know soon enough that you were charged. If a not guilty decision carried with it a judicial comment that you are actually innocent of drink-driving, then you may think it beneficial to allow your name to be published. It would put to rest any unfounded rumour or innuendo."

"See your point. I'll give that some thought."

"OK then. You arrange to be in Queenstown the afternoon before the fixture date. I'll have dinner with you if you're free and we can go over the finer points then. It's an argument of law on the facts, so there will not be much for you to do."

"Thanks. You seem to have everything under control."

Richard accompanied the Minister down in the lift and to his waiting car on the street and waved goodbye.

The next morning, Richard was at home in the kitchen speaking on the telephone to the private investigator in Mrs Fordyce's case.

"Is that Simon Cameron? Richard Locksley here. I'm Sienna Fordyce's lawyer and I have read your affidavit about the discovery of all the concealed vehicles. Great work!"

"Thanks. Do you think it will help?"

"Help? It will blow Mr Fordyce out of the water! I don't think he will fight it out in Court. Send me a bill for, say, $1000. That OK by you?"

"Plenty. Is there anything else I can do?"

"Well, there is one thing. Have you any background information about a senior member of the Law Society, Magnus Denholm. He is giving me some strife at the moment."

"Do I ever! What a coincidence. He's a dishonest piece of work. Look, I'll send you something. Anyone else?"

"Well, I might be asking too much, but what about District Court Judge Albert Christie?"

"Dirty Bertie Christie!? I do indeed! He's getting a bit long in the tooth nowadays, but he still can't keep it zipped up. I'll send you something on him too."

"We'll discuss a fee. Anything would help."

"Well, I've been gunning for him too. He was vicious on the Bench to an elderly neighbour of mine, up before him on a stupid, misguided shoplifting charge which demanded a sensitive and understanding approach. He reduced my neighbour to a pile of tears and the doctor had to be summoned to the court. What a bloody bully! If I could engineer some payback for that disgraceful incident there is no fee."

"Great! Well, if I can construct something, I'll let you know. You can come and watch."

"That'll be fun."

"OK. I'll keep in touch. Bye."

It was now Monday morning, and District Court Judge Christie was perched on the Bench like a hungry buzzard. He appeared grumpy as usual. Richard was about to defend his clients, Jimmy Costello, Hemi Ranui and Peter

Anderson, on a joint charge of burglary. They looked nervous in the dock. Constable John Adamson had just finished his main evidence and Richard stood up to cross-examine him.

"Constable, your evidence is that my clients broke and entered."

"Yes."

"Where is the crime?"

"What, Mr Locksley?" the impatient Judge interrupted.

"Where is the crime? The crime is breaking and entering."

"No, it is not! Think again," snapped Richard.

"Stop asking questions in riddles, Mr Locksley. It is patently obvious."

"No, it is not! Please do not berate me in that manner. I am an officer of this Court. Once again, you are acting as a prosecutor!"

"Well, your clients broke into the house and have been identified as being inside."

Richard flashed a contemptuous frown and turned back to the witness.

"Constable, do you not understand? For the crime of breaking and entering to be complete there must be an intent to commit a crime within the premises. What was that crime?"

"To steal the motor vehicle."

"Perfectly obvious, Mr Locksley."

"Please listen to the evidence, Your Honour, and refrain from making such negative comments until you have heard the evidence."

"You are a disgrace to your profession, Mr Locksley."

"And you do the dignity of the judiciary no favours, Your Honour. You bring the judiciary into disrepute!"

"You will withdraw that remark!" snaps His Honour.

"I will not! Please listen while I continue my cross-examination. Constable, the defendant Hemi Ranui told you that the motor vehicle my clients took was owned by him and he offered to show you the papers. Yes or No!"

"Yes, I suppose so."

"And you refused to look at those papers and did not take them from him?"

"I thought he was lying!"

"But you could not form that impression unless you looked at the papers. And Mr Ranui attempted to tell you that his car had been taken from him by force by the complainant a week before. He was just taking it back!"

"Yes, I suppose so."

"Not, "I suppose so." Yes or no!"

"Yes."

"And I now have had the opportunity to see the police file. The next day Mr Ranui dropped the registration papers in his name into the Police Prosecutions Office asking them to be given to you as the officer in charge of this case! Correct?"

"Yes."

Why haven't you produced them in this Court?"

"It was for you to ask."

"No it was not! You know perfectly well you have a duty to this Court not to ignore relevant evidence."

"Yes, Mr Locksley. How is it relevant?" The Judge interfered again.

"Not you too? The crime of burglary is breaking and entering with the <u>intention</u> to commit crime. Here, the police had evidence, which they had not produced, that these three were recovering a valuable piece of property <u>owned</u> by one of them. That is not a crime."

"I suppose you're right."

"No "suppose" about it. That is the law. In fact, I now submit that there is no case to answer. There is no evidence of a crime. Put more accurately, there is no evidence of an intention to commit a crime. End of story."

Judge Christie thought long and hard and then pronounced grudgingly:

"I suppose I must follow the law."

Richard looked incredulous and shook his head.

"Don't you shake your head at me, Mr Locksley."

"But of course, you must follow the law, Your Honour. That is your job."

"Just sit down. I am reluctantly prepared to dismiss the charges even though I think the defendants were up to no good that night."

Richard interrupted sternly.

"You can't say that! There is no evidence at all to support that crack!"

"Don't interrupt me! Luckily for these defendants there is not enough evidence of an intention to commit a crime. The charges are therefore dismissed."

"I immediately make an application for costs under the Costs in Criminal Cases Act and Regulations 1987. The standard scale only allows for $226 for each client. I seek therefore $678 as a starting point. But section 13 subsection 3 allows you to exercise your discretion and make an order for costs order greater than that amount. I seek $4000 per client."

"That is ridiculous! This was not a case of special complexity or importance. You're not getting any more. In fact, your three clients can divide one payment of $226 between them. That is all."

"That is a derisory award. The complexity arose when you did not follow or understand the legal point on at least three occasions. Your decision reflects no credit to the Bench!"

"Leave this Court, Mr Locksley! You will hear more of this outburst."

Richard gave a cursory and almost contemptuous bow and turned his back and stalked from the court room and returned to his office. On the way, a man walked up to him.

"Mr Locksley? I'm Simon Cameron, the private investigator. We just spoke on the phone. Janet said you would just be walking back from the Court. I thought I would catch you and give you this information on that creep, Magnus Denholm. It's all in here."

He handed Richard a USB drive.

"Thank you so much. Have you got a card? I'm sure there are a number of other things I can use you for."

"Here. Happy to hear from you anytime."

"And you are prepared to travel?"

"Certainly."

Richard walked into the ground floor of his office building, caught the lift and entered the waiting room where six clients were seated. Wiremu and Melinda were interviewing in his office, and he greeted the first of the clients and ushered him into his office.

He interviewed all day and did further preparation well into the night.

CHAPTER SEVEN

It was a lovely balmy early evening in the kitchen at Richard and Mary's home. Alice and Roger were happily playing scrabble and watching television simultaneously. Richard spoke first.

"I'm now happy with everything. It's amazing when you put your mind to it. I think it will take only a couple of weeks to manage the transition between this Auckland practice and the new one in Queenstown." Mary spoke up.

"Well, it's certainly good news about Willie and Melinda being prepared to transfer. We can probably cut a deal with one of the airlines for cheaper flights for bulk flights back and forth, but how often do you think you may need to come back?"

"The focus will be on building up a Queenstown practice. I won't take any Auckland work unless it pays so well that I can't resist."

"Will our financial well-being decrease?"

"I don't think so at all now. We have to be able to capture the clients in the Southern Lakes District, but I'm experienced enough at rain-making and the Queenstown bar is very light on the ground now."

"Let's do it! I'm game if you are. If we find that we made a huge mistake and I think you could easily slot back here. The whole thing will be an adventure. A real adventure."

"OK. The decision is made! Let's get the kids organised and move quickly. It looks like we've got a fair amount of work in progress from me, two deceased lawyers' estates to start straight into.

"You wind up the lease on the offices here. They were getting a bit tacky anyway. If we come back, we just get new ones."

"So, we've made the decision. Have you said anything at all to the kids?"

"I have. They're keen. We've been so often that they know the area well and I think we will be left with far more free time to be with them than in the big city."

"When do you think we should shift?"

"If you can rearrange any outstanding fixtures and your Auckland clients, let's go on Monday week. The school term ends next Friday, so there are then two weeks holiday. I realise you have to return five or six times over the next six months, but you won't mind that will you?"

"No. Not at all."

"Well, let's do it."

The next morning. Richard was again in his office. He took a call from Bill Hale, a local solicitor.

"Locksley speaking."

"Richard, Bill Hale here. Ringing about Mr and Mrs Fordyce. I'll come straight to the point. I had no idea about these undisclosed cars. I'll be blunt. You have us over a barrel. I have told him straight that he has committed perjury. I think I am a straight shooter. I suspect there might be another 10 cars somewhere because I don't think he's telling me the truth, but I think you have discovered the vast bulk."

"Right. What's the deal?"

"If you can get a watertight confidentiality Agreement drawn up, we will settle for one half of the $501,000 figure plus interest for one year at 7% capitalised so that's $268.035 plus $25,000 costs That makes a total lump sum of $293035. There are some other vehicles, but no more than ten."

"PK, have a stab and round the figure up to $325,000."

"Done. I'll have an Agreement signed by my client around by early afternoon. Thanks for your co-operation. I will withdraw the proceedings. I will ensure that my client fully understands that a confidentiality agreement includes discussing the fact with anyone, including, of course, the police."

"Thanks. I'll return the Agreement signed by Mr Fordyce and make a payment of $325,000 into your trust account tomorrow morning."

"Fine. Must have a drink sometime."

Richard put down the phone and it immediately rang again. It was another phone call from a local solicitor, Gus Jenkins from MacPherson, Barton & Co. It was almost identical.

"Richard. Gus Jenkins. You've got us by the balls!"

"What for?"

"Your client, Graham Stanton. The one who was told to shit in a corner. I think you're a bit high, but my client company will pay you in return for a confidentiality agreement. There's no real defence and running it will cost them at least $30,000. So send round an Agreement for $45,000 all in and we've got a deal."

"Will do. You'll have it this afternoon. It would have been a fun one to run."

"Let's keep our clients out of Court. I look forward to the Agreement. Payment within 48 hours."

Richard hung up and called in Janet.

"Janet, please get Sienna Fordyce in at 3 pm and Graham Stanton in at 4 pm."

"On to it at once."

Janet left. Richard went to the store and beckoned in one of the waiting clients and closed the door once the client had taken a seat.

"Good morning. How can I help you?"

"Well, it's about my neighbour. He is a right prick! I need a good gunfighter.

You've come to the right place. Tell me all about it ..."

That afternoon at 3 pm. Janet ushered Sienna Fordyce into Richard's office. He told her the good news.

"The not-so-subtle blackmail has worked. Your husband certainly got the message that he had obviously committed perjury in his affidavit. We can settle at a very good figure, but it carries with it the usual confidentiality clause which means you can never report a police complaint or discuss the settlement with anyone else. Does that cause you any problems?"

"Not at all."

"He's accepted that there were 149 undisclosed cars and has accepted the valuation at $501,000. He's accepted that you're entitled to one half and will pay 7% for one year on top which will bring to you a figure of about $300,000. He will also pay some costs to me. I have manipulated figures so that this $300,000 figure will be in your hand."

"That's absolutely fantastic! I wasn't expecting half of that."

"I'll go to the figures again with you now and then I'll draw up an Agreement for you to sign but make sure you tell me if you require more time."

"I have no doubt that I accept the figure. I don't want to send him to jail. I don't want to appear greedy. I just want what I was entitled to in the first place."

"Great. Give Janet your bank account number and I will try and get $300,000 into your account tomorrow. Now let's look at this Agreement."

"I'm so grateful. I don't care what you get out of it. You knew what to do and tidied it up within a couple of days. That's worth your fee. I've never had that service from a professional in my life. Where do I sign?"

At the end of the interview, Richard ushered Sienna out of the office.

"See you again whenever you need assistance. Bye."
Richard's negotiated costs were $25,000, so he recovered $51,000 fees after adding in the $26,000 already paid in by Sienna after the first interview. He had a very satisfied client.

Richard beckoned in Graham Stanton. Graham sat down and Richard closed the door.

"Good news! They've accepted my figures so you will get $37,500 in your hand plus $7500 towards costs. It will help pay for the $15,000 you paid me before the weekend. You'll get $45,000 in a couple of days. Maybe we could have got more but I think there were some risks. You may well have got only about $25,000. Are you happy with getting $45,000?"

"Ecstatic! What fantastic service."

"Sign here. It's a confidential settlement so you can't race around bragging about it to anyone. Have you got your bank account number there! Payment will be made to your account within 48 hours."

"I can't thank you enough. Well worth it. Thank you."
Richard took Mr Stanton to the door and handed the signed agreements for Graham and Sienna to Janet.

"See you, Graham."

"Janet, please attach a short letter saying, "Settlement Agreement signed by client." Add details of our trust account please. Standard short bill prepared to each client please, "To my fee for knowing what to do and doing it immediately." Fee for Stanton $15,000 plus GST. Fee for Fordyce $51,000 plus GST.

A pretty good week, Eh?"

Richard knew what to do . . . and did it! It almost became his mantra.

CHAPTER EIGHT

A week later and the family were boarding at Auckland airport. The weather was bleak and wet, it was a good day for a departure.

The Air New Zealand 777 aircraft powered down the runway, lifting Richard and Mary and the children up into a cloudy sky. Two hours later they flew up the Kawerau Gorge from the Cromwell end and underneath the Crown Range Summit towards the Queenstown runway. Within the confines of the towering mountains all around, the plane resembled a magnificent bird showing off the proud Koru on its tail.

It was a gloriously fine day in Queenstown with clear blue sky when the aircraft landed. Richard and Mary alighted with the children, all chattering excitingly. They were met by Wiremu who was the first from the Auckland office to arrive. He was equally excited. "What a place. What a glorious position! We'll all love it here. I've got a van so I can take you and the luggage straight to the house. I'll pick Janet and Melinda up when they fly in this afternoon. We can work at the office tomorrow. I'll drive you home now."

"Fine by us. Thanks."

The next day, at 10.00 am, they all met outside the new office. Richard, Mary, Janet, Wiremu and Melinda all stood looking up at the three-story building which was to be their new workplace. It was an impressive structure with windows on two sides, both facing the lake. The discussion was snappy and pacey.

"Here we are folks. Ready for a new life?" exclaimed Richard, enthusiastically.

"It's fantastic. The whole look is exciting."

"Sure is. I'm ready."

"I've already checked out the police station and the new Court building. They're just up the road from the offices."

"How has your new accommodation worked out?"

"It's fabulous. We may want to get an extension on the term if possible. It's a large two-bedroomed unit overlooking the lake. Walking distance to the office."

The lift whisked them all up to the second floor and double glass doors to the new office faced them as the lift opened. They excitedly entered their new office.

"Fantastic!"

"I said you would like it."

They all started chattering over each other.

"Look at that view."

"Look at my office."

"We've all got wall screens in each office."

"To work, everyone," ordered Richard.

"First things first," contributed Melinda. "But not necessarily in that order. I will get the champagne."

She was a right trick. Richard pretended to kick her in the bottom. He upped the stakes and looked directly at her.

"As God once said, and I think, rightly, Richard's the Boss. Remember that."

She giggled. Richard continued.

"Gather round. In a minute, you're to go to your own offices and within half an hour I want you to make a list of everything you need. You each have the best personal printers and copiers. But I want everyone set up by lunchtime. Warehouse Stationery delivers this afternoon."

"Yes, Boss. What work have we got set up? How do we share the load?

"I've done a deal with the estates of the two deceased lawyers. What's left of their many clients will be transferred to us on the basis that we bill out uncosted work and transfer to the estates 25% of any recovered amount."

Mary added, "Richard and I have calculated that there are at least 80 scheduled criminal and traffic cases from those two firms alone. Plenty of civil and family court work as well."

Richard took over.

"Willie, could you please draw up a two-year schedule of the Court dates for the Queenstown and the Alexandra District Courts and fill in the scheduled cases we have inherited. Oh, we better have the scheduled High Court sittings in Dunedin, Timaru and Invercargill as well."

"Shall I do a laminated list of the contact details for those courts, police stations, probation officers and all that stuff?"

"Good idea. One for each of us and a couple of spares. An electronic copy on each computer. We need pin boards in each room, Janet."

It was Mary's turn.

"The Family Court cases include care of children, relationship property, maintenance and domestic protection matters. And a lot of protection orders. You should see the files. I've also counted at least 80 civil cases. All seem to be runners."

"Right. Willie does the full schedule. I think we need to have the schedule as well as a whiteboard in an alcove in Janet's area, but out of sight of the waiting area."

"Mary, you please analyse each of the Family Court files and schedule priorities. Willie, you do the same with the criminal cases. Leave the civil cases to me. Melinda, you sift through all other cases. We will have a further meeting at the end of play today. I think we all need to work this weekend."

"What would you like me to do?" asked Janet.

"You arrange the waiting room and your reception room as you want it. Then double check all the office equipment from the major printer behind your desk through to the individual office screens."

"There is a 60-inch screen in my office and 40-inch screens in your own offices. I want our individual computers able to be switched on at a few seconds' notice on to the wall screens. Hunt down a local computer geek who will come to the office regularly at an hour's notice if we need him. We'll pay him well."

They all started to move.

"Right. To work. Janet, could you please arrange a local cafe to bring in coffee and lunch at noon. We'll have another short meeting over lunch and another one at 4 pm. Oh, and please arrange individual business cards and letterheads for the office."

They all scattered to their own offices. Richard left to inspect the District Court. On the way he made the effort to stop and talk to local people and introduce himself.

As Richard walked up to the District Court, he stopped and had a chat with a friendly uniformed police sergeant who had just come out of a local coffee bar.

"Richard Locksley. Goodness me. Do you remember me? Tane Fleming. I was with you at the hostel at Otago Boys High, what, over 25 years ago?"

They shook hands.

"Of course. Tane! Great to see you. I knew you joined the force, but I did not know where you were stationed. We'll have to catch up sometime."

"That would be great."

"What about late this afternoon? What time do you get off duty?"

"I'll meet you over at that bar across the road at, say, just after 5 o'clock?"

"Great. See you then." The Sergeant spotted a grim looking man approaching.

"Oh, God. Here comes that whining sod, Bernard Brinsley. Watch him. He's a very unpopular senior lawyer here in Queenstown. Just between you and me, the police think he's a bit dodgy."

A 50's something, rather sour-faced lawyer in a suit walked up. He looked the sort of man who would practise giving limp wrist handshakes.

"I take it you're this new boy, Richard Locksley. I'm Bernard Brinsley, local Law Society watchdog. I've been warned about you."

"Don't be so pompous. Watchdog? Ruff Ruff," retorted Richard cheekily.

"You'd better watch your step around the town. We don't like bloody usurpers."

"I'd better go. See you tonight." Tane touched Richard on the shoulder and walked away.

Richard asked Mr Brinsley, "What do you mean?"

"The Law Society has had enough complaints about your disrespectful courtroom behaviour, and we won't put up with that that type of Auckland behaviour here."

"Well so much for a pleasant introduction and welcome to Queenstown! What's your beef?"

"You've been warned. And don't pinch clients."

He stalked off with nothing further said. Richard shook his head to himself. He continued walking to the District Court.

He chatted to court staff and was shown around the three courtrooms, the adjacent cells and the interview rooms.

Richard then walked back to his office in sunshine through The Mall. Bustling locals and tourists filled the area, the footpaths and the shops and bars.

He noticed four Mongrel Mob members lounging in the sun on a seat near the village square. They all wore their distinctive patches – Mongrel Mob Queenstown. One recognised Richard.

The first Mongrel mob member spoke up.

"Jeez! Mr Locksley? What are you doing down here?"

"Good to see you, Hemi. When did you get out?"

"Mt Eden let me go a couple of months back and probation recommended I come down here. I'm trying to go straight."

"Three months? That's a record."

Hemi (laughing), "These are me mates – Jimmy, Hone and Rangi. Where's your office?"

"Hi, guys. You keeping him out of trouble? There's my office over there. Here are some cards."

"Top bloke, this lawyer. See him right and he'll see you right."

"Hang loose, Bro."

"Thanks, buddy. Here are some of my new cards."

They touched knuckles and smiled. Richard continued on his way.

❧

One hour later. Richard and Janet and Mary were in the reception area of the office. They had obviously been busy because everything was tidy and squared away. The telephone rang non-stop, and Janet made appointments. Wiremu and Melinda were interviewing in their offices and Mary was talking to a rather posh-looking woman sitting down in the waiting room.

The double doors crashed open and the Mayor of Invercargill, Sir Tim Shadbolt, bounced in with his customary energy and hugged Richard almost squeezing the wind out of him.

"Ritchie! Great to see you fella. How long has it been? I haven't seen you since we judged that Dunedin Festival Queen competition.

"Well, there was the Hollies concert at Millbrook since then. You certainly put up a show then!"

"And then there was that wee chat with the Inland Revenue. Jeez. You handled that well. How's Mary?"

"She's just in there interviewing. That was her behind you just a minute ago. Come on in."

Richard ushered Tim into his office and closed the door. Loud laughter emitted for several minutes. In the meantime, Melinda finished her interview and saw her client to the door and then returned to Reception.

"That was the Mayor of Invercargill, Sir Tim Shadbolt. He's just like he is on television. All smile and teeth. And lots of laughter as you can hear."

"Is there anybody Richard does not know? We've only been here a day."

Tim and Richard sat in his office like old friends.

"What can I do you for, Sir Tim? Apart from go for a beer, mount a soapbox in the Mall, slip into a massage parlour and smoke a joint."

"Ah! All those days are well behind me. I haven't done anything naughty since the last Century." Richard laughed.

"It's really good to see you. When can we do a bit of socialising?"

"I'm here to see you professionally. I gotta get back tonight but the family and I will be up the weekend after next and would love to see you and Mary then. I see from your advertising that you have come down from the big smoke and set up here. Great move! The boys have kept me in touch with your exploits in Auckland. But Auckland's loss is the South's great gain."

"How can I help you?"

"Well, I've been defamed. And I think seriously. You remember when I was Mayor of Waitakere there was some innuendo spreading round that I had lost or stolen the gold chains of office. The whole thing seemed to blow over and the only embarrassing thing was that I may have been careless although I still think one of the staff lost them."

"Yes, I remember that. I remember both of us having a beer in Vulcan Lane discussing it."

Tim laughed, "Yeah. I seem to remember forgetting the last half of that session. But the National Spotlight weekly tabloid only last week effectively accused me of stealing the gold chains as well as several other things. It's a nasty article. Look, here's a copy.

Tim pulled out two copies of the offending pages and showed them to Richard. The clear accusations of dishonesty stuck out in bold type on page 1.

"YOU'RE ALL BULL, TIM. YOU KNOW WHERE THE GOLD CHAINS ARE!"

"It's front-page stuff! The tabloid also goes so far as to say that I asked the police to stop their inquiries into the missing regalia two weeks later. The rest of the comments on page 5 clearly accuse me of theft. But the comments go further. They say that as a Mayor I completely dropped looking after Waitakere's environment. That is so untrue."

Richard butted in. (You must butt in with Tim.)

"They have no defence unless they establish the defence of truth. But they must establish that you did steal the chains. The defence of honest opinion won't work because they can't get away with saying they had an honest opinion that someone was a criminal. The defence of qualified privilege also won't work because it does not give a publisher a blank sheet to write anything like this."

"What can I do?"

"Defamation cases can be very expensive. Particularly if you lose. If you lose then you could be ordered to pay very huge costs to the other side. I mean, something in the region of more than $150,000 but there are some tricks we can play if you are not too greedy to minimise that risk."

"I'm all ears", said Tim craning forward.

"If we sue in the High Court then the costs could be phenomenal. It would ruin you if you lost. Even if you win, the costs award might not be as high as you would like. But the limit in the District Court has only recently been increased from $200,000 to $350,000. It gives the District Court a lot of leeway. This is not the United States. You are not going to get millions, so that is why I asked if you were greedy."

"I'm not greedy. I would be happy with, say, $75,000."

"OK. If that's the case, then we sue in the District Court. You must realise there is no jury in a District Court case civil case."

"What are my chances?"

"I think very good indeed. I can't guarantee 100% until I see what actual defences they put up. You can't expect them simply to send you a "cheque in the post" next week. My advice is that we issue proceedings without even entering the tedious few months of correspondence back and forth. When I was admitted to the bar at 22, I had a great boss who had a little figurine on his desk of a barrister with a sign saying, "Sue the Bastards." I like following that advice."

"I love your style. Always have. There is one small catch. Money. You once did a deal with me on that breach of privacy case. We did a "split the returns" deal. I'm happy to do that again. 50/50."

"We must do it correctly now. I'll type up an authority and you pick it up in 20 minutes. You take it to a lawyer in Invercargill and then scan it back to me."

"That's good. Obviously, you don't have to pay anything if I lose my case and have to pay costs to the tabloid."

"OK. I'll go a step forward. When you win, I will apply for a hefty award of costs. We'll then add the award and costs together and divide that amount equally. So, let's say if you got an award of $100,000 and I got costs of $40,000 we would split the $140,000 equally. That is to your advantage."

"Great with me."

"You can pick any Court in the country because the tabloid is published all over New Zealand. I think Invercargill is too close to your home. Why not here in Queenstown?"

"Good idea."

"Right. That's settled. Come back in 30 minutes and pick up the signed authority. But before you go fill in these details and give them to my office manager. Her name is Janet. It's just a few details such as full name, address, your desired occupation, contact details etc. and leave all those documents with me. I'll complete and hopefully file within the week and get the tabloid's registered office served immediately."

"That's what's so energetic about you. Your reputation is for doing accurate things quickly. I remember you sent me a bill once simply saying "My fee for knowing what to do and doing it." You arrogant bastard. But I loved it!"

Richard smiled and shook Tim's hand, showed him out the door and introduced him to Janet in the waiting room.

"I think we're cut from the same cloth, Tim. See you in about 2 weeks for a barbecue and some beers. Here's my card. Janet, when you've taken the basic details from Tim, could you come because I want to dictate a short document which Tim will pick up in 20 minutes."

Mary came out of her office.

"Shadbolt! The devil incarnate himself! Don't you lead my good husband astray."

Tim laughed until tears roll down his cheeks.

"I think it may be the other way round, Mrs L. We're having a beer and a barbecue in a couple of weeks. Anyway, better be off. See you in about 10 days. Janet, I'll be back to pick up Richard's document in 20 minutes."

Sir Tim left the office. You could hear him talking to people all the way to the ground floor. Richard laughed.

He then returned to his office and worked on a notepad with a pencil for a few minutes. Janet knocked on the door and came in with her pen and notepad.

"Just a simple A4 document please. Two copies. Give Tim one when he comes back."

CONTINGENCY AGREEMENT
To: Richard Locksley.
From: Timothy Richard Shadbolt.
I have asked you to represent me on a contingency basis. If you are prepared to represent me on the basis that you are not paid if I do not win my case, I agree to the following conditions.
You represent me free of charge.
If successful, you apply for costs.
Any award of damages is added with any award of costs and then divided equally.
I am very happy with this arrangement. I have taken independent legal advice.

Signed . . . .
I,   , have independently advised Mr Shadbolt about this arrangement and I certify that I believe he has entered it fully understanding the intent of the award and costs sharing agreement.

. . . .

"Janet, remind Tim to get it signed before an independent lawyer in Invercargill and sent back to me ASAP."
"Certainly, Richard."
"Right, Willie. How's that schedule coming along."

"It's only the criminal cases at this stage. We've inherited a fair few. In the next three weeks, there are nine days of sitting time in the Queenstown Court and four in the Alexandra Court. There are defended fixtures."

"Good. Anything major?"

"It's a bit worrying that there are seven serious assault charges arising from three incidents of mayhem in the Mall at night. You have the Minister's case on Friday and a not guilty plea has been entered on a charge of arson for another client. I estimate the fees just from these cases over the next three weeks will be over $100,000."

"A very good start. Mary, what about Family Court matters?"

"A whole heap. I have counted over 60 so far and most are relationship property disputes. There is potentially such a huge amount of fees involved that I suggest I spend the next two days personally contacting each of the clients to see if they wish to engage this firm. But the clients I've spoken to so far want to and I am seeing three this afternoon."

"Splendid. Just sing out if you need any help. We want to hit this town running and be the best legal firm in town. We must get our brand up and running. Southern Lakes Law is a great start but use Team Law as well from time to time. Janet?"

"The cards are being printed as we speak. I will deliver some to the police station, community corrections, doctors and accountants and put them up on every public or commercial noticeboard I find."

"Some advertising in the local rag?"

"On to it already. I'll have a draft by lunchtime for you. The office screens are all working very well."

Melinda contributed her thoughts. "I've noted many, many company, commercial and conveyancing files which I think are worth working on. You, Mary and

Willie can handle the Court work. I will always be available. But I have a particular interest in the company and commercial side of things, and Janet is qualified as a legal executive, so why don't we have least put a bit of effort into those files and see what comes of it. I think there is at least $300,000 worth of work in that lot now."

"Yes, I'm happy with that. We'll get you an assistant clerk or young lawyer if necessary. All right. Let's all get into it. Janet, everything OK at your end?"

"Fine. Everything is working and a big delivery is coming from the stationery store this afternoon."

"Mary, I'm having an introductory drink with a local Sergeant at 5.00 but I'll be home by 6.00. Willie, can you gather together the court files for this week and next week and see me in 10 minutes and we'll go through them one by one."

"Splendicious. 10 minutes it is."

"And everyone, advertise our presence in the region in every way you can. We're here to stay. We're here to provide the very best service possible. I get the feeling that the two local lawyers who recently died were pricks like that Brinsley I met this morning. This region might be ours for the taking."

"Will do."

"Now remember. Our service must be Top Gun and accurate. We can charge big fees, but the client must know the level of fees in advance. But it must also become known that we will do pro bono work and legal aid work when we can. Only that way do we build a credible law practice. I am the boss at the moment and the buck stops with me. But we will try and make every decision on a consensus basis."

Melinda took a small black round plastic object out of pocket with a large red button on top. She pressed the button, once, twice, 3 three times. Each time a loud voice and a different accent loudly uttered the word "NO." Every time this small machine uttered the word NO, they all howled with laughter.

Each one of them cried,

"I want one. I want one. I want one."

"My Uncle Mike finds me this sort of stuff when he's overseas. I'll have a word with him."

"I want one for the front counter. I wonder if I can also hook it up to the telephone."

"Better try and lay your hands on another four Melinda. Tell your uncle Mike you can have two free drink -driving cases on the firm."

"I think he's already had three."

"Oh, he has not. He's a nice bloke. You're wicked, Melinda!"

"Have I shown you the fart gun? Wait until you see that."

There was a lot of laughter.

Later that afternoon. Richard went into the Coronet Bar in the Queenstown Mall and met up with his police sergeant friend, Tane. Tane was not in uniform.

"Gidday, Mate."

"Hi. So good to see you in town. What the hell was up with that bastard Brinsley this afternoon?"

They each got a beer and retreated to an alcove by the window overlooking the Mall.

"I have no bloody idea! I've never met him."

"Well watch him. He's a nasty piece of work and not very popular with the locals or the police. He's got some sort of chip on the shoulder. Apparently, he's put his hand up a couple of times to become a Judge but has been turned down. That's made him bitter and jealous."

"Ah. That explains a lot. Anyone who applies to be a Judge probably isn't up to the job."

"I've got a bit of dirt on him. Three of his clients saw the CIB here a couple of weeks ago about him. They said he fraudulently overcharged by claiming work for a former partner, who has been incarcerated as a senile patient at the rest home in Frankton. Apparently, the old geezer is still on the letterhead as a consultant. Brinsley still charges him out at $395 an hour plus GST. That's fraud!"

"Holy hell! Was he charged?"

"No. But, look. I understand he has not paid the clients back, and that stinks. I'll suggest they come and see you about what can be done."

"OK. I'm all for building up a war chest of that kind of information, particularly for someone who insults me on my first day here in the main street."

"Done. Now, some essential information. The police force here is very good in my opinion. We have a dedicated CIB and a very competent inspector who has a law degree. I don't think there's one bad apple among them except for a couple of lads who need a bit more experience in court. You can knock a few rough edges off them."

"What about the Judges?"

"We don't have a resident Judge. There is some talk of a resident designated Central Otago Judge being appointed in the future but in the meantime, we get serviced by Judges from Invercargill and up north."

"Who are they?"

"The best is Tony Bradshaw who has a really good legal brain. He's a very fair bloke. It is rumoured he likes a pint and a poke."

"Don't we all?"

"Then there's Judge Lorraine (legs apart) Langham. She was a senior student when I was at university. She used to joke herself about having to be buried in a Y-shaped coffin. She's a very good Judge too and a bit of a dag. 'Nother beer?"

"You need a bit of that on the District Court Bench. I love the old saying that the District Court Judge is "quick, courteous and wrong" and the High Court Judge is "slow, rude and right.""

"That's about it, but I think you'll find that Bradshaw and Langham get it right most of the time. But we have other visiting Judges as well."

They remained chatting for another half hour. Occasionally members of the public came up and Tane introduced them to Richard. Richard handed out a few cards. Finally, Richard looked at his watch.

"I'd better get back home. Plenty of plans still to be made. It's been a big move in my life, but my family and I are looking for a life change."

"Okey Doke. Give me a buzz if I can help in anyway. We lock 'em up. You let 'em out. That's OK with me."

See ya. Let's make this a regular gig?

"To be sure. I'll send those disgruntled clients of Brinsley to you. See ya."

Richard left with more of a spring in his step than was the case in Auckland.

Not long after. Richard drove his car into the garage of their well-appointed house overlooking Frankton Arm. He walked in and was greeted by his excited wife and two children, Alice and Roger.

"Hi kids. Hi love. Everyone settled in at school?"

"Cool, Dad. I met a few friends I made when I was down here on the holidays. The school has skiing on Wednesday afternoons for its outdoor sports' class. I'm really going to enjoy it here."

"I'm missing some of my friends in Auckland, but I like it better here and it will be good seeing Grandma and more of Mum."

"Let's all go out for tea. What would you like to try? French or Spanish?"

"Spanish!"

Mary spoke tp Richard.

"Are you happy me doing six hours a day for the first few weeks just so that I help them settle in?"

"Sure. No problems at all."

"That'll work well."

It didn't take long to drive into Central Queenstown.

CHAPTER NINE

Elsewhere that evening, a large crowd was thoroughly enjoying comedy acts in a popular mid-town bar and grill. The sign above the front door said: "Lakeside Comedy Bar and Grill." Sandwich board signs inside and outside announced the proceedings as "Offensive Humour Night" and "Don't Come If You Don't Want to Be Offended." There was much laughter and whistling and everyone seemed to be enjoying themselves.

It was clear from other signs that members of the public were invited to present short and humorous monologues and there were no shortage of interjections and heckling from the boisterous audience. So it was a bit of an Amateurs' Night.

Young Tom Finlayson was on stage finishing his monologue. Some people had tears of laughter running down their cheeks. His humour was of the explosive kind.

Tom was 22 and a final year law student at Otago University on holiday in Queenstown. He had an impish appearance and a cheeky face and long curly hair which made the audience want to laugh without hearing a word from his mouth. He was dressed like, and rather looked like, a ventriloquist's dummy. He was a very talented mimic and able to speak realistically in the dialect of many countries...

". . and of course, do you know why Maori men don't get AIDS. They don't get off their bums long enough to catch it, eh?"

The audience hurt with laughter, including a table of Maori labourers and their Wahine. They laughed the loudest.

To the faint-hearted, Tom was offensive, but he laced his jokes with a continual monologue about the dangers and pitfalls of banning free speech, particular in comedy.

"I might seem offensive. But should I be banned or cancelled? That is the question."

He invoked the words of his idols, Rowan Atkinson, John Cleese and Ricky Gervais, within a limerick he had made up which had the audience thinking.

"Atkinson, Cleese and Gervais
are right on the button when they say -
Comedy's broke,
When you're censored by WOKE
And the speech cops you're told to obey".

"I'd better go soon. I'm having a seven-course dinner with an Irish girl I met at the bar. That means a six-pack and a potato."

"Mind you, it's better than the Eskimo I went out with last month. To her, a 13-course meal meant a dozen stubbies and a plate of whale blubber meal."

You could see that Tom was not one of the Woke Folk.

Nobody objected. Everybody laughed. Tom was spending more time for the laughter to die down that he was presenting his monologue.

"Look here. I'd better go. It's getting really hot in here. I'm sweating like a Jew at a money machine."

There was another round of uproarious laughter from what appeared to the entire audience was were packed right to the walls.

But this time two fiery-looking members of the audience stood up and started shouting angrily. They held up signs of protest.

"RACIST" and "HANG THE LOT OF YOU!" and "LOCK THEM UP!"

"How dare you! You're going to get a punch in the head you potty-mouthed prick!"

"Let's lynch him! I've called the cops!"

Tom was ready for these hecklers with a jokey put down. It just further inflamed them.

"Excuse me! I am trying to work up here. How would you like it if I stood yelling at you down the alley while you were giving blowjobs to transexuals!?"

The crowd roared with laughter. But it was not at transexuals, but at the put down uttered by Tom. The incongruity of the humour was obvious. But there was one anti.

"I'm a transexual" said a rather butch-looking woman with a beard in a dress up the back. How dare you!"

"Oops!" said Tom "I misjudged that one. I didn't see the lady with the cock. You're not that weightlifter are ya?"

There was another roar of laughter.

The protestors with the signs advanced on the stage while everyone else in the audience laughed and applauded Tom. Two uniformed police officers came from the back of the bar and promptly took Tom into custody.

Outside the bar, Tom was pushed roughly into a patrol car.

"What have I done wrong? What are you arresting me for?"

"Breach of the Human Rights Act, son. Hate speech! Just come quietly."

The patrol car drove away with Tom in the back seat.

The next morning, in Willie's office, he was interviewing Tom Finlayson who had engaged the firm. Tom was now well-dressed but very sombre.

"What can I help you with?"

"I've never been in trouble before, but I was at the Comedy Shop Bar and Grill last night and members of the public were asked to get up and do an impromptu two-minute monologue. I had prepared something before I left home. Everyone was pretty shickered and most of the humour involved a fair bit of racism and offensiveness. Actually, the evening was advertised in the local newspaper and outside the venue as "Amateur Politically Incorrect and Offensive Joke Night."

"Have you been charged by the police with something?"

"Yes. And I spent a night in the police cells. I was telling some rather offensive jokes and then I finished by wiping my brow and saying, "I'd better finish. It's really hot in here. I'm sweating like a Jew at a money machine." There was a roar of laughter all around the bar but then two females and one weedy-looking bloke started to scream and yell at me, and things turned rather ugly."

"What happened then?"

"I apologised over the microphone, but these three people came up and threw their drinks over my head and then they were booted out by the security guards. I took off to go home but as I went to go out the door two police officers grabbed me and said, "You're under arrest for hate speech.""

"We don't have a hate speech law per se in New Zealand. Let's have a look at your police bail papers and your summons."

Willie spread out the papers. Tom handed to him a printout and then flashed up section 61 and 63 of the Human Rights Act 1993 on to his wall screen.

"The keywords are "threatening, abusive or insulting" *coupled with* "likely to incite hostility against or bring into contempt any person on the ground of the colour, race or ethnic or national origins of that group of persons." That's a pretty hefty allegation to justify a charge. Note that proof of intention is not specifically part of the charge."

"But this was a comedy night! I was clearly only joking. They may have been offensive jokes. They may have been in bad taste. But as I will explain to you in more detail, I wove into my monologue the tension between offensive language in public and the rights of free speech under the NZ Bill of Rights Act."

"Then that's your defence. I need to do a bit more research. I want you to write me a detailed statement describing the evening at a bar. Approximately how many people were there? Was the whole crowd against you? I need to know everything. Every bit of detail."

"OK. I'll drop it in tomorrow afternoon."

"I'll complete my research and arrange a date for a defended hearing. Do you have notes of your monologue?"

"Yes, I do. I was pretty nervous, and I thought I might forget my words, so I still have that, word for word. I had memorised it."

"Drop me in a copy and I want you to practise privately delivering the monologue again. I want to polish it up with a few ideas which I will discuss with you next week. The senior partner in this firm, Richard Locksley, will likely handle this case. It will be a gutsy defence and his skills will be invaluable. But I'll be sitting alongside him."

Wiremu escorted Tom to the lift and shook his hand.

Over in Richard's office, he was interviewing the three men who had been referred to Richard by his friend, Sergeant Tane Fleming.

"Morning, gentlemen. I understand Sergeant Fleming suggested you contact me."

"Yes. I'm Jim Henderson. These good folks are Bruce Scurr and Clem Sinclair. We were all individual clients of Mr Brinsley. But we know each other from golf, and we recently compared notes, because we thought Brinsley was dishonest. I had seen him about a dispute with a fence."

"He drew up a new lease for me on a commercial building for my panel beating company."

"He provided me with a pretty full opinion about a franchise business and the company formation."

"Have you bought your individual bills in?"

"Yes. Here they are with the important parts highlighted in yellow. And we also prepared a statement of facts signed by us all. We did this for the police. We think he should be refunding us at least 50% of each bill. It's not a lot but it's an average of $7500 in each case."

"We found out that the consultant at the top of his letterhead is now in a senility ward at a local Rest Home and has had a stroke. But he was charged out at $395 an hour plus GST for approximately 20 hours work on each of our cases. He also charged out for an associate lawyer who now lives in Australia. He wasn't working at the firm when Brinsley did our work so that's fraud too."

"We've discussed our complaint with the police, but they are a little reluctant to turn it into a criminal charge."

"OK. Leave it with me. It's this firm's policy not to charge for these matters when a complaint is made against another practitioner unless there is a financial recovery. I'll get to the bottom of it."

Richard escorted the clients to the lift doors."

"Thanks for coming in. I'll contact you within the next seven days."

"Thanks, mate. We're grateful."

At the same time, Melinda was interviewing two parents in their early 30s. Hetty Jones was looking very worried and her husband, Andrew was gently holding her hand.

"What's the problem? How can I help?"

"I've been charged with assault on my four-year-old son. He's a lovely boy."

Hetty burst into tears. Melinda went to a side table and got a glass of water and a box of tissues.

"Just take it slowly. Did the police give you a discovery package with a statement of facts in it?"

"Yes. Here it is."

Melinda read the police allegations, checked the Act under which Hetty was charged and flashed the section up on her wall screen. Section 59 of the Crimes Act 1961 filled the screen with the heading "Parental Control".

"The basic statement of facts say that a social worker was at your place about another matter and saw you pull your four-year-old son into the bedroom while he was kicking and screaming."

"Yes. But she doesn't say that wee Paul had stabbed the cat once and went to stab it again after I told him to stop. He then stabbed the scissors at me. I was bleeding slightly so he hit me with them. I ordered him to his room. He refused and told me to get fucked. I had never heard him use that language before. I said, "Right young man, I'm going to put you in time out until teatime." He knows the score. I had to drag him, but I never hurt or harmed him."

"It says here there were red marks on his wrists."

"But the social worker then grabbed him very roughly and took the wee fella out of the house and down to the medical centre. I followed her protesting. When we got to the medical centre, Paul was crying at the force applied to him by the social worker and the redness was put there by her force. It was quickly going away."

Melinda looked at section 59 of the Crimes Act 1961 on the screen on her wall.

"Here is the section under the Crimes Act 1961. There are two points in your favour. You can use reasonable force to prevent Paul from engaging in offensive or disruptive behaviour. That's the first thing. But it also affirms that the police have the discretion not to prosecute complaints which are very minor."

"What should we do then?"

"Will you need legal aid, because you must pick a lawyer off a list, and I cannot pick your own lawyer?"

"I had a legal aid lawyer once and they were hopeless. They demanded that I plead guilty, and they were not very good at all. My mum says she will pay, and she has the money available, provided the fee does not exceed $7500."

"Well, it will cost $6000 if we plead not guilty and I think you have a defence. But it won't cost any more. I don't think you have an option. It's not a very pleasant thing to plead guilty to assaulting your own child."

"I'm in Court tomorrow."

"I'll be there, so meet me at 10.00 am up the back of the Court and I will arrange a fixture date which will be a few weeks away. I can also get interim suppression of name."

"Thank you so much."

"I've got all your details here, so I'll contact you in about two weeks and we'll have another meeting before the final Court date. You ring me straight away if you have any questions or concerns at all."

Melinda led Hetty to the door of her office and Janet stepped forward and accompanied her to the lift.

"Very nice to meet you. You're in good hands. We'll look after you."

Richard was now interviewing the local newspaper's Court reporter, Jennifer Stockton.

"Good morning. We haven't met but I'm the main Court reporter and we'll get to know each other. I'm in a spot of bother. Please call me Jenny."

"Goodness. I thought I'd been rumbled. I hate press interviews."

"No. I want your professional services. Court lawyers around this town are hopeless and the two recent deaths have decimated capable court advocates. But in any event, I made some inquiries from my colleagues up North, and they all speak so highly of you."

"That's very nice to hear. But I am a bit of a rogue, and I am sure there's plenty of room for improvement. How can I help?"

"My husband and I own a renter. It's a nice little property only a block or two away from our house up the Gorge Road. We let it out each year during the ski season for a set period of up to three months to coincide with the ski season."

"Do you have a written tenancy agreement?

"Here it is. It's straight to the point. It's expressed as a fixed term tenancy from 1 June until 31 August. It strictly specifies only two tenants, no dogs and no parties of more than eight people including the tenants."

"They both signed it?"

"Yes. But there are three problems. We have now found out that two other people have been living there from the start and there are three large dogs going in and out of the house and they obviously stay there."

"Well, there are two breaches for a start."

"There have also been six parties where over 80 people have been present, and the police had to be called three times."

"Another breach!"

"We then carried out a routine inspection at the weekend and found damage far greater than normal fair wear and tear. The front window has been completely broken and boarded up. There is the very strong smell of dog urine throughout the carpeted areas of the house."

"The toilet bowl has been cracked in three places - three bloody places, and parts of the woodwork throughout the house have been ripped off and burned on the fire. I have given them in writing three Notices to Remedy the breaches and the 14 days' time frame has exported on each."

"Have you discussed it with them?"

"Yes. They just shrugged their shoulders. How do we get them out? They now say that I must give them three months' notice."

"Absolutely wrong. It's a fixed term tenancy but we can prove serious breaches and damage which in my opinion justify an immediate eviction order, perhaps giving them 24 hours, but no more."

"That's really heartening. The law can provide a remedy?"

"You sign an authority to let me deal with the Residential Tenancies Tribunal and leave me a copy of the tenancy agreement and provide me with a three-page statement setting out in some detail the facts and an accurate description of the damage and the cost of repairing the damage. I'll file an immediate application today, if possible, certainly tomorrow morning, for an urgent hearing before the Tribunal. We won't get a hearing this week, but we might get a telephone hearing early next week."

"What will it cost?

'If you give me a clear, typed statement properly laid out the main work is done. Clients generally leave that to the lawyer and that's where the hours mount up. But words are the stuff of your profession, so you do a really good statement and have it back to me tomorrow. "I'll keep costs to an absolute minimum. Probably $2000 maximum but I will try and bring it well below that figure. I will also apply for costs against the tenants, but that is rarely granted, and even then, not for legal fees. But we may be able to pick up a thousand dollars."

"OK. The rent was $700 per week so the bond money was $2800. They are now in arrears with weekly rent to the tune of $2100."

"I see the tenancy runs out in four weeks so if we act quickly, we might get a hearing with urgency during that time."

We can ask for damages, an order for immediate eviction and will have a go at getting some more rent for the two other tenants. $200 a week from each of the should do it."

"That's really reassuring. I'll email you a statement tonight and check my email every hour tomorrow in case you want me to make any amendments."

"I'll just get Melinda, an associate lawyer in here, to assist."

Richard telephoned Melinda who picked up the phone immediately.

"Melinda, could you pop in here for a minute please."

He hung up and within a few seconds Melinda came into his office.

"Hi. Jenny, this is Melinda. Melinda, this is Jenny Stockton. She and her husband own a rental property up the Gorge. Bad tenants. In arrears. We have the bond of $2800. The usual old facts. Two non-permitted tenants. Two large dogs crapping and piddling all over the place. Some pretty serious damage."

"... and you want an emergency application to the Residential Tenancies Tribunal?"

"Yes please. Jenny's a journalist and will do a full statement and email it to us tonight with all the facts and a cost for repairing the damage. Please draft an application for an emergency hearing for eviction, all outstanding rent and damages and in this case we will ask for costs as a special case. You can take Jenny to the lift but give her your email address. Jenny, send the statement also to my email address. Here's my card as well as Melinda's email. Between the two of us we will get on the job straightaway."

"Anything else?"

"The extra hook in this one is whether we can craft into an application a request for an assessment for rental for the extra two non-permitted residents. I think now $225 per week minimum for each one for nine weeks should be enough, but Melinda will search for any precedents we might be able to find."

"On to it. Jenny, would you come this way please."

"Thank you both. Your speed and efficiency is very much appreciated."

"See you soon. In fact, I'm in Court this afternoon."

"Oh dearie me. The Minister of Police?"

"There's really a story there. There will be some big fireworks I think. Do you know who the Judge is?"

"Some old geezer Judge from Auckland called Christie. I haven't seen him before, but he was really laying down the law in an unpleasant way this morning."

"Oh God, No! He's following me around the bloody country like an old fart. There might be some fun and games this afternoon. See you then."

Melinda escorted Jenny out. Richard called in Janet.

"Janet, love. Could you go and unlock the War Chest folder and create three shortcuts on my computer for folders 137, 138 and 139 and label the shortcuts accordingly. I won't need them today but may need them any time tomorrow. I feel it in my bones. What's the time now? 1.00 pm. The Minister's case is set for 2.15. I'd better get cracking. I think I'll be out all afternoon."

"Yes, Boss."

Richard placed a file and two textbooks into a leather satchel and walked into the reception area.

"Willie. Are you able to come with me this afternoon? I might need some assistance."

"No problems."

The two lawyers left the office and walked to the Court house.

"We have that buffoon Judge Christie. He's come down for 10 days to sit here in Queenstown and for a week in

Invercargill. He's following me around like a bad smell. Something's up."

"What do you want me to do?"

"Take notes very carefully of any fireworks between the Judge and me. Don't be too obvious about it but you should be sitting next to me so you could be taking notes about anything. But I may need a witness."

They came up to the Court building.

"Right. Here we are. Christ! Look at all the reporters! I'm going to sneak around the back where I've arranged to meet the Minister. You go inside and check that the back door is open for us."

"Will do."

Richard quickly walked down the side of the building and around the back and was greeted by the Minister with two diplomatic protection police officers.

"Good afternoon, Minister."

"Good afternoon."

"Come with me. Be ready for a crowd, but at least the press cameras will not be able to be used in Court."

"I've got no real problem with that. I don't care about name suppression now. Stuff them all! Who is the Judge?"

"Bad news! Crusty Christie from Auckland."

"I've heard of him. The Attorney General's embarrassed by this Judge and would relieve him if he had the chance."

"Well, the Attorney General stands behind me in line. I have several scores to settle."

Willie opend a back door and they entered the building and climbed the stairs to the side entrance of the No 1 Court.

"Here we are."

Richard opened the door to the Court. It was 2.10 pm. The case was set to start at 2.15. The public gallery was far more full than normal and there were clearly at least 8 reporters and media personnel present. Willie came forward and joined them.

"Minister. You sit here beside Willie and me. When the Judge comes in, we all stand. Willie and I give a short bow, but not you, and then we sit down. When your name is called you stand up and walk up to that dock. I then stand up and announce myself. The Judge will allow you to sit after a few seconds."

"All understood."

Another side door opened, and the Court clerk came in.

"All stand for his Honour the Judge."

Judge Christie entered from the left and took his seat without the customary and cursory bow to Counsel.

The press bench was full and headed by Jenny Stockton, who Richard had just recently interviewed about her bad tenants. Mary had also slipped in the back and was sitting in the gallery.

Richard also noted that Bernard Brinsley was sitting up the back as well, notebook in hand. Prosecuting Sergeant Neville Richardson and a constable were seated at the prosecution table immediately across the aisle from Richard, Willie and the Minister. The clerk announced the case.

"Call Grant James Brentwood."

The Minister stood up and walked up to the dock. Richard and Willie rose to their feet.

"May it please your Honour, I appear for the defendant with Mr Pihama."

"I don't know if does please me, but I suppose I'm stuck with you."

"Here we go again! That is a most improper remark to make before the case even starts! I protest!"

"Protest all you like. Let's get on with this case."

"I put you on notice that my client cannot be seen to get a fair hearing from Your Honour just on that remark alone."

"Proceed with the case, I said."

"I ask that my client be seated."

"Granted. You may start, Sergeant."

Before he started, Richard had decided to set the Judge up for a bit of cheek. This was a case where it was a reasonable tactic to unsettle the Judge from the start.

"Before you start, Your Honour, my client is wrongly described on the charge sheet as a Minister ..."

He was abruptly interrupted by the bad-tempered Judge.

"Oh stop it! You know very well that his occupation is not relevant to the charge. He could be called anything!"

"Anything?" retorted Richard, with a cheeky jaunt. He was obviously about to be very cheeky.

"In that case, would the Court now refer from this point on to my client as an Anglican Archbishop!"

The Judge turned purple and could be seen biting his lip with rage.

Richard was playing to the audience up the back who were already grinning.

The Sergeant stood up with a barely concealed grin.

"This case is relatively straightforward from the police point of view. The defendant was ultimately asked to give a sample of blood which returned an analysis of 81 over 100. He is charged with driving with an excess breath alcohol level."

"What is your defence, Mr Locksley?"

"I do not have to disclose that at this stage, Your Honour. You know that! Let's hear the prosecution evidence first."

"Oh, very well! Trouble as usual."

"Only for Your Honour". Richard managed to get a crack in first.

The Judge wisely did not respond. But he sneered.

"Proceed Sergeant."

"I call only one witness, Constable Smithells. The relevant certificates he produces prove the basic chain of evidence."

Constable Smithells walked to the witness box opposite the well of the Court from Minister Brentwood.

"Please place your hand on the Bible. Do you swear that the evidence you are about to give will be the truth, the whole truth and nothing but the truth?"

"I do. On Saturday 26 March last I was informed that the defendant had attended a function at the golf course club rooms on that afternoon. I knew him to be the Minister of Police. I knew that there had been some excessive drinking at the club and the licensee has been warned. I warned him myself. He told me that the Minister of Police had been at the function and had driven home about 2 pm. Because of the state of intoxication of other patrons, I ascertained where the Minister was staying, and I drove to that residence at 7.30 pm. I was shown into the house by someone I did not know.

I confronted him in the dining room and told him clearly that I wanted him to undergo breath and possibly blood testing procedures under the Land Transport Act."

"Did he comply?"

"Yes. He did. He accompanied me down to the police station and the subsequent blood sample indicated through the certificate that he had an excess blood alcohol level. I produce the relevant certificate."

"Just answer any questions defence counsel puts to you."

The sergeant sat down. Richard powered to his feet.

"Your turn, Mr Locksley."

"Constable, surely other matters were discussed between you and my client?"

"Not really. Just inconsequential chat."

"Inconsequential chat!!?? You are not telling the whole truth!"

"I am."

"I suggest my client strongly denied to your face that he had consumed any alcohol whatsoever before driving home from the function. He emphasised that by repeating "none whatsoever."

"He may have."

"He may have"? Is that your answer? Did he or did he not say that?"

"Yes, I think he did."

"That's not inconsequential chat! Did you make a note of that response?"

"Yes, I think I did."

"Constable, I put it to you that you are prevaricating. In my first five questions you have replied in a manner of "he may have" and "I think he did.""

"So what, Mr Locksley?" growled the Judge, clearly impatient.

"The issue goes to the very heart of the lawful right for this Constable to instigate the breath and blood alcohol procedures. You know that!"

"Don't take that tone with me. I've warned you before."

"I regret to submit that once again you are acting as a second prosecutor and not as a Judge."

"I warn you ... "

Richard somewhat rudely butted in.

"In the words of the late, great Justice Speight, this prosecution has chosen its statutory battleground and picked its evidentiary weapons. I am entitled, indeed it is my duty, to test the evidence against that formidable thicket."

"Proceed. But don't take all day."

"I will take until hell freezes over if it is necessary to pursue my defence!"

Judge Christie looked furious but did not say a word. Richard continued.

"Constable. Can we take it as a fact that when you first spoke to my client at his house and before you requested any procedure to be followed, he told you to leave his property?"

"Yes. He did."

"He revoked your licence to be there?"

"I suppose so."

"You actually put it to him that he had consumed alcohol at the function before driving home and he denied strongly consuming any such alcohol at the function?"

"Yes."

"And can we take it is a fact that he left the function at 2:00 pm and you first confronted him at 7:30 pm."

"Yes."

"Five and a half hours later!" Richard raised his voice.

"Yes."

"And can we then take it is a fact that he told you that on arriving home he consumed approximately three small bottles of beer, some wine and two whiskeys."

"Yes."

"And as you walked up to his house, you were able to observe the adults drinking at the dinner table."

"Yes."

"And you informed him that you would arrest him if he did not comply."

"Yet none of this information is recorded in anything on the police file? Why not?"

"I took those notes off the file because I thought I was entitled to rely on the presumption in the Land Transport Act 1989 that the alcohol level at the time of taking the sample was conclusive proof of the alcohol at the time of driving."

"You removed relevant notes from the file!!?"

"Yes."

What? After a formal request for full discovery from me."

"I suppose so."

"Did you remove anything else?"

"I may have. I can't remember."

"Have you provided full discovery of the police file in this case?"

"Yes, I have."

111

"And the provision of that file carries with it a letter certifying that it contains all documents?"

"Yes."

"And that certification was written by you?"

"That certification was false?"

"Yes. I apologise."

"And you have sworn to tell the whole truth in this evidence you give today?"

"Yes."

"So even with the extra concessions I have drawn out of you at this early stage, you did not tell the whole truth?"

"Well, that's your interpretation."

"Do you confirm that at the time you went to my client's house you had no evidence of poor driving by him."

"There was no such evidence."

"And you had no evidence of any accident?"

"No such evidence."

"And you had no evidence of my client drinking alcohol at the function six hours earlier?"

"Well, I had been informed that everyone had been drinking, and drinking to excess."

"For goodness sake, Constable! There is a note from you on the police file saying that between 250 and 300 people were at the function."

"Yes."

"And you identified at least a dozen of your own police colleagues there."

"I agree that I made that note."

"And do you agree that the only house you visited of the citizens at the function was the house of my client, the Minister of Police."

"Yes. But one of the barmen had told me that I "might be able to score the Minister of Police that night."

"Oh, did he, Constable? I ask you to look at this document. In preparation for this event, I asked the Commissioner of Police to intervene personally into the deficiency of discovery to the defence in this case. And I found this document which had been stamped, signifying that it had been on the police management file for this case. Read it please, and then I will ask you three questions."

Richard signalled to the court orderly who took a page from Richard's hand and passed it to Constable in the witness box who reads it. The Constable paled.

"Where did you get that note?!"

"Never mind that. I have it! Did you type that note and is that your signature at the bottom?"

"Yes."

"Did you remove that note from the police file some time before the commencement of this hearing? You are under oath."

"Yes."

"Read out aloud what the note says."

"I can read it, Mr Locksley," whinged the Judge.

"No sir. This is a public Court, and the evidence must be read by this witness in public."

"Oh, very well."

The Constable, reading the note, continued.

"I visited the house where I believe the Minister was staying, because I thought he needed to be taken down a peg or two for ignoring the Police Association's complaints over the last 18 months."

"Constable. How can that note be read other than it is expressing an intention by you to take the Minister down a peg or two."

"I don't know."

"I have no further questions, Your Honour."

Richard sat down.

"That is the end of the police case, Your Honour," said the prosecutor.

"Your turn, Mr Locksley," growled the Judge.

"I do not intend to call evidence. I raise four defences. The facts to support those defences have been conceded by the Constable."

He raised his voicew deliberately.

"Firstly, good cause to suspect is still the fundamental requirement by any Constable to start the breath or blood testing procedure in facts of this very kind. He must suspect an accident or an offence or pre-driving drinking of alcohol. There is no evidence of any of these grounds. The prosecution fails fundamentally on that submission alone."

The Judge glaced impatiently at his watch.

"Secondly, the so-called conclusive presumptive test must be read against the factual matrix of the drunk driver. In this case there is clear evidence that there had been not one drop of alcohol consumed by my client before driving and it is a simple inference to draw that the Constable knew that fact."

The Judge could be seen checking some airtickets.

"Thirdly, the Constable was on private property. Before he required my client to accompany him for a breath or blood sample, my client clearly revoked the Constable's implied licence to enter his property. And quite clearly this was not a fresh pursuit case. The requirement to accompany was therefore not lawful. End of story."

The Judge idly stared at the clock on the wall.

Richard's teme was rising.

"Finally, the actions and the evidence of the Constable are so flawed that the charge should be dismissed on those grounds alone. He deliberately omitted discoverable documents. He presented a false declaration as to the truth of that discovery. But most importantly he has displayed a bias against my client as disclosed in the note I produced to the Court."

The Judge appeared not to be listening. He was drumming his fingers on the Bench.

"He actually admitted that his enquiry was a chance to take the Minister down a peg or two."

Richard lowered his head and paased for a full 20 seconds and then looked up.

"Your Honour. During my important submissions, you have looked at your watch, stared at the ceiling, looked at air tickets, watched the clock on the wall, druumed your fingers on the Bench and appear to have deliberately ignored what I was saying. I place you on notice that I will be complaining strongly to the Judicial Conduct Commissioner."

Before the Judge could respond, the Sergeant stood up and waved Richard down with a kindly wink.

"If I may be heard briefly. The police will prosecute citizens only in an honourable manner and that has not occurred in this case. I had no idea that the points drawn out by Mr Locksley existed. Considering the answers given by the Constable, I seek leave to withdraw the charge. NO. I go further. I support Mr Locksley's application to dismiss the charge outright. On behalf of the police, I accept that there is not a jot of evidence that the Minister had been drinking before driving."

"Thank you, Sergeant. I make no application for costs. The name suppression order can now lapse."

"But I have not had my say yet. I am the Judge."

"But there can be no contrary argument to my submissions!"

"They sound a bit of slick trick to me."

"That is an appalling comment to make! You lower the good reputation of this Court."

"Don't you dare speak to me like that!"

"I am an officer of this Court! I must not be treated like this. Your comment is a direct slur on me and carries with it the inference that my client is a drunk driver who has somehow got off on some form of clever trick. I demand that you apologise to me and then apologise to my client.

"I won't!" snapped the truculent Judge.

"You must dismiss this charge immediately and tell him and the public that the facts you have heard today establish beyond any doubt that he was not a drunk driver. I demand that."

"Nobody demands anything of this Judge!"

"I do! Dismiss this charge and declare that my client was not a drunk driver on this day! If you do not, this case will be referred to the Minister of Justice as well as the Chief District Court Judge."

The Judge's face reddened, and he moved to say something. Instead, he did not. He closed the textbook in front of him and banged it down. He half rose to his feet.

"Case dismissed! You did nothing wrong, Minister. Perhaps I went a bit too far, Mr Locksley. This Court will rise."

The Judge left through the side door and the Court remained silent for five seconds. What had they just heard?

Jenny, the chief reporter came up to Richard first.

"Bloody impressive! I hope you can be as big a bullying, shouting, arrogant prick for me!"

"Thank you. I haven't had anyone say anything so nice to me for a long time."

Minister Brentwood came up with his hand outstretched.

"Holy Hell! You got me off without calling me to give evidence? What a skilful performance! We need a few more bastards like you in politics."

"Thank you, Minister."

"When are you going to teach me how to be such an abusive sod like that?" asked Willie, admiringly.

"He needed a good kicking," was all Richard could say.

They all laughed. He was kidding.

The courtroom cleared and Richard, Willie, Minister Brentwood and his private secretary and a diplomatic protection squad detective and Mary walked out into the sun. They were surrounded by at least a dozen media representatives all baying for a statement.

Richard whispered to his client and steered him away from the press throng with his arm.

"Minister. My advice is simply to say, "This case proved that I had nothing to drink at all before driving home from a function. I thank the police for the sensible stance they took when the prosecutor heard the full evidence. I thank Mr Locksley for establishing the evidence very quickly that I was totally innocent of this charge. I will make no further statement.""

The Minister did just that and they then walked quickly to the Minister's limousine.

"My flight leaves in just over an hour. Can you join me in my car?"

"Sure. Willie, can you pick me up from the airport in, say, half an hour?"

"Sure."

Wiremu and Mary started to walk back to the office. The private secretary and the detective got into a police car and followed the limousine along Frankton Road to the airport. Frankton Arm's blue water sparkled and the Remarkables Mountain range towered, 5000 feet to the right.

"Thank you again. Nice touch about the costs and the suppression of name."

"I had to think on my feet. But the limit of costs is set at $226 for a half day and I made the instant decision that you do not need this charge dismissed on a mere technicality but needed a finding that you were 100% innocent. That finding will be to your advantage."

"Right decision! Now, is there anything I can do for you."

"Well, obviously pay me. And before I hear any moaning, my fee is not based on the number of hours but on a lifetime's experience. $22,500. OK by you?"

"Cheap. Send the bill. I'll pay by return."

"There is one other thing. There is some rumour that a resident Judge might be appointed for the Central Otago region sometime in the not-too-distant future. That would involve servicing Queenstown and Alexandra and assisting occasionally back in Auckland from time to time. I would merely like to be considered. No more."

"Noted. I will certainly sing your praises to the Attorney General. Rightio. Here we are. God, I feel a weight is lifted from my shoulders and I have you to thank."

On the airport forecourt, they alighted from the car just as Willie pulled up behind. Richard shook the Minister's hand, and the Minister joined his private secretary and his protection officer and walked quickly into the airport terminal. Richard got into the car driven by Wiremu. They returned to the office.

CHAPTER TEN

On returning from the airport, Richard and Wiremu walked through the doors of the office to a buzz of activity. Willie met a young female client and took her into his office.

Mary was interviewing new clients.

A middle-aged man dressed like a cow cocky flashed a big grin at Richard and introduced himself. He stuck out his hand.

"Mr Locksley. Joppy Watson. I tried to catch you before you went to court, but I missed you. However, I followed you up and I saw you represent that Minister bloke. I thought to myself, "If I am ever caught with the dismembered body of a prostitute in my suitcase then you're the bloke I need to ring."

Janet and Melinda looked up a bit startled.

"No need to worry, ladies. I've burned the body parts."

Richard laughed.

"I found that my ex-partner's bones need to be burned twice. Bastard!" exclaimed Melinda.

"I'm calling the police on you. You are one wicked lady," said Janet.

"My sense of humour, mate," Joppy said to Melinda.

"Come on in."

They moved into Richard's office and Richard closed the door.

"I've got a wee problem. I farm a lot of cattle. Well, over 22,000 to be precise. I own a 20,000-acre farm in Southland and one three-quarters of that size on the way up to Mount Cook.

"What's the problem? Better get your full name too."

"James Peter Watson of Fantail Ridge Downs, Eastern Southland. Joppy to all."

"OK. Just the basic facts first before we explore and record the detail."

"I'm looking at a larger spread in South Australia and I've been away for six weeks. I had a farm manager called Sparky Robinson, or Theo Henry Robinson to be precise, and when I returned home a few weeks ago he was nowhere to be found. His sleepout had been cleared out, many of my tools worth five grand taken and the $55,000 4x4 nicked. But when I checked the stock, Crikey, I found that the bastard has stolen 419 prime cattle, sold them to a major stock firm, National Agricultural Trust Ltd in Invercargill, and he managed to divert the money and transfer it to a bank in Jakarta and he has now disappeared. He must have engaged a fleet of stock trucks working the best part of 5 days. But he got away with them all!"

"And this is all fairly simple to prove?"

"Well, I think so. The manager of the stock firm identified Sparky and confirmed the sale price at $523,750. The average price per head was $1250. North Invercargill Motors confirmed it paid $55,000 for the vehicle. I'm happy with those figures. As I said, the tools were worth $5000, so the grand total of what he nicked comes to $583,750."

"What have you already done about it?"

"I've seen two firms of lawyers in Invercargill and one here in Queenstown and I was told that it would cost me $100,000 to "chase a ghost" with only a small chance of success. I would be willing to spend that just put the prick in jail."

"But he could be anywhere in the world. What's the more important to you? The money or the body?"

"I don't really worry about the money. I will track him my own way and break his kneecaps."

"OK."

"I loved your style in Court. I have a proposition. I am a rich man, but I don't want to throw good money after bad. If you're prepared to chase the money on my behalf, I will pay you one half of what you recover. No questions.

No complaints. I would be happy with that. Three of your colleagues have told me I can't win. They have told me it will be almost impossible to find him but, even if they do, he will have had the money hidden away and will declare himself bankrupt."

"I think they're wrong. I'll represent you. But you won't question my fee and how I get the money."

"No problems."

"OK. No win. No fee. But I want no moaning if I recover the lot and pick up a fee of over a quarter of a million."

Joppy grins.

"No problems. I'd be delighted because I would be picking up the same amount whereas now, I have nothing."

"I'm obliged to refer you to an independent lawyer to advise you on a contingency fee."

"Stuff that! You're the fourth lawyer I've seen. I'm happy to sign a waiver."

"OK. I'll draw one up now."

Richard picked up the phone and called in Janet.

"Janet, could you bring your notepad in please."

He introduced her.

"Janet, this is Joppy. More particularly, James Peter Watson of Fantail Ridge Downs, Eastern Southland to be precise. Could you immediately type up a Contingency Agreement? 50/50. Same as Sienna's, but add at the bottom: –

"Mr Locksley has told me I must sign this before an independent lawyer, but I have declined. I do not want to do that. My agreement with Mr Locksley is well thought through by me and has been sealed by a handshake."

"That's fine by me," confirmed Joppy.

"Janet, if you can do that now he will sign it on the way out."

Janet left the office.

"You're obviously into Court work. What else does the office do?"

"My wife Mary is a lawyer, and she handles most of the Family Court work although I keep my hand in. I do civil disputes and criminal law. A bit of everything. Willie is following my kind of work.

Melinda is concentrating more on company, commercial, rural and planning law. Both youngsters are pretty nimble on their feet in Court though."

"And you say you came here for the lifestyle?"

"Yeah. But we all came from down here originally. The setting here and the atmosphere from Stewart Island to Mt Cook is just so stunning."

"Hey. In about 10 days, I'm choppering 'round my properties. It'll take only two or three hours. Would you like to come? We usually stop for a barbecue up the top of a mountain."

"Too bloody right!"

"OK. Give us your number and I'll firm up times and dates."

Janet returned with the document.

"Fine. Ah, here's Janet. Ah, that's right. Have a read and sign only if you're happy."

"Let's have a look. Yes . . . I'm happy with that."

He signed it and handed it back to Richard.

"I'd better be off. See you Monday."

"Really nice to meet you. I'll get on to this right away."

Joppy left, calling out to everyone in the office –

"Goodbye. Sayonara. Auf Wiedersehen."

He disappeared into the lift. Richard turned to Melinda.

"Melinda. Can you please look up the law of the tort of conversion?

"The law of perversion? Right you are. A little light home reading, Boss? Do you want me to spice it up a little?"

Richard laughed, "CONVERSION! Not perversion. You are one sick lady."

"I seem to be hoving tribble with my worms."

Richard drew his finger across his throat before her next joke tumbled out.

"I'm looking for the pages in Todd's "The Law of Tort in NZ." There is clear law that even the innocent handling of someone else's property amounts to civil conversion and damages can be recovered against the innocent party. You don't have to prove intent."

"Tort?" replied Melinda. "Do you mean as in "I tort I saw a puddy tat?"

"Attention please! You don't even have to prove carelessness. The law is well settled. Every recent case please and a copy of the relevant texts."

"Anything else?"

"Yes please. The full contact details and the names of the managers of National Agricultural Trust Ltd and North Invercargill Motors. I need to write a letter within the hour."

"Consider it done!" Melinda quickly left the office.

"I tort I saw a puddy tat?" mused Richard to himself. "Not bad!"

In the bar across the road from the office old friends had gathered. It was 5.30 pm. Richard was enjoying a beer again with Sergeant Tane Pihama who was out of uniform. They were talking about the Minister's case.

"So Judge Christie looked extremely peeved when he felt he had no option but to dismiss the charge. The turning point was when I was able to produce that note which the constable had taken off the file about "taking the Minister down a peg or two."

"Was that useful?"

"Damned right it was. It just turned up in the mail. Wonder who sent it?"

"You mean the one in the grey envelope? The young cop will not make that mistake again and nothing's on his record."

"You jammy bastard! Tell me, would you like to go straight from Sergeant to Commissioner of Police? I can arrange it."

They both laughed.

"Let's have another beer first."

❧

Later that evening the family were all at home. Richard, Mary and the children were sitting in the lounge. Grandma was sitting in her favourite chair. She had come home for two nights. A large fire burned in the fireplace. All were smiling.

"So are you really happy in the Home, Mum?"

"It's lovely, dear. A real luxury to have my food cooked and served up and I don't mind having help in the shower. Perhaps the best thing is the outings they take us on. Every second day. In the last week I've been to Arrowtown and the Gardens. I'm out and about more than when I was living on my own.

Do you want to play Scrabble, Grandma?"

"I'll get it."

"OK. Hot chocolate, anyone? And it's Saturday tomorrow. What say we go on a family trip on the Earnslaw? Grandma can come and we'll have a nice lunch at Walter Peak and see the animal displays."

"Yes. Yes. Yes."

"I'd love that."

Mary and Richard smiled at each other.

"I don't think we've had a weekend off work for a decade."

"Yes. I've no doubt we made the right decision."

On Saturday, the family boarded the Earnslaw Steam Ship on Lake Wakatipu. It was mid-morning. The sky was clear and almost dark blue. The lake was very calm. On the foredeck, Grandma was in a wheelchair smiling broadly. Her favourite red tartan rug purchased from the Royal Mile in Edinburgh was wrapped around her legs. Her smile was as broad as the Remarkables mountain range behind her.

Richard and Mary were holding hands. The children were running up and down the deck squealing with laughter. The Earnslaw proceeded out across the lake to Walter Peak Station. The vessel, now well over 120 years old, was belching its trademark black smoke. The Wokes were already trying to ban the 'Old Lady'.

"Balls!'" grumbled Richard.

On the way, a couple, Wanda and Chris Copeland, tapped Richard on the shoulder.

"I do hope you don't mind, but are you that lawyer we saw in Court the other day?"

"We were really impressed, and we wonder if we could talk to you about a little case."

"Certainly. We can have a full interview on Monday at the office, but briefly what's it about?"

"We've just had a kitchen fully renovated by Lake Kitchens Ltd. It cost us $70,000 and we have paid half of that, but the workmanship is so bad that you can see gaps in a couple of the drawers and another three are falling apart and we specified real wood and not chipboard."

"What's happened," asked Richard.

"He's threatening to come in and rip bench tops and taps out because he says there's a clause in the building contract which allows him to do so if the account remains unpaid."

"Oh," said Richard. "It's called a Romalpa clause, but it's only enforceable if the work is satisfactorily completed."

"Can we do anything?"

"Look, we have to work fast if he is likely to come in on Monday. We need a letter sent by email tomorrow to him warning him to stay away under the Trespass Act 1980 and a letter to the police. This is so we can gain their assistance if he comes to your property. Can you both be at the property all day Monday?"

"Yes."

"I'll see you tomorrow at 10.00 am at my offices. Here's my card. I'll do the letters myself."

"But tomorrow's Sunday. Is that OK with you?"

"All part of the service. See you then."

"Thanks so much."

They walked away smiling.

"Gosh. You can't help yourself, can you?" said Mary, smiling.

"Gotta build up the business, love. Our team is going to take over this town!"

The Earnslaw burped another large plume of black smoke and sounded its whistle. A small "sod off, greenies" was acceptasble for this grand old girl to declare.

"Paradise!"

The regular pianist on the rear of the vessel started up on the ivories. He played this regular gig four times a day.

It was a real delight to listen to over 30 Chinese tourists full of bonhomie, linking arms and singing along to merry old English Music Hall songs.

With Chinese gusto they sang out energetically –

"I ruv a rady, a weally rubbery rady ..."

Richard almost laughed out loud.

"Hush," said Mary.

"Don't dirry darry on the way..."

Even Mary had to try hard not to laugh.

"Hurro! Hurro! Who's you're rady fliend..."

Richard stood up and, with the consent of the parents, picked up a delightful three-year-old girl and danced gently with her swaying in front of the piano.

The tourists all clapped and sang along.
Richard and Mary joined in with equal gusto. But they almost wet themselves with happy laughter.

They were not so Woke today but their kids would soon sort them out.

CHAPTER ELEVEN

Lake Wanaka at first sight from the Cardrona Valley Road end was a sight from Heaven to behold.

A police car came over the small rise at the end of the road and confronted the beautiful expanse of Lake Wanaka stretching out to mountains to the left, the right and at the end.

Constables Sally Eldridge and Mark Hannagan were on a daily patrol around the outskirts of the township.

"I always find that view amazing!"

"I know. Bloody fantastic."

They drove straight on down to the lake and turned right along the lake front and passed the sign erected, warning motorists of crossing ducks. Many ducks nested among the lakeside trees and frequently waddled across to forage in Pembroke Park opposite. The police officers slowed down for the full family of one father, mother and five ducklings.

Over on the Park, they saw elderly Wanaka identity, Grandma Marjory Jenkins. "There's Grandma Bo feeding the ducks."

"She's a nice old duck herself. Been doing it for years."

They passed Bo, slowed down and Sally wound down her window.

"Good morning, Granny Bo. Keep up the good work."

"Thanks, dearies. But less of the Granny, please, or I'll knock your heads together."

The police car travelled on towards the township. At the same time a family of ducks crossed the roadway - Daddy Duck leading followed by Mummy Duck then Huey, Louie, Dewey, Freddy and Minnie.

Suddenly, a large four-wheel drive people carrier roared up with two adults and two children in it. Grandma Bo watched in horror as she observed the vehicle descend upon the ducks. About 20 metres from them, the vehicle sped up and intentionally ran them over. She saw most of the occupants laughing and she turned red with rage.

Bo knew her ducks. The mother and three ducklings were killed.

She shook her arm angrily as the vehicle accelerated away. Her keen eyes followed the vehicle up to the lower township and she saw it slip into an angle park outside the Urban Grind Coffee Café.

"Bastards!" She again shook her fist angrily.

She then ran over to her car, revved it into action quickly and tore off in pursuit. Bo parked close to the Café and jumped out and ran into the building. Her stride and purpose of mind would have done Boadicea proud almost a Millennium ago. Boadicea was her middle name. It was her parents' little joke, but it turned out to be a prophetic nickname!

Inside this popular coffee and cake Café, three staff were behind the counter. The popular venue was three-quarters full and the family which she had recognised in the car which had run over the ducks were seated at a table not far from the front door. It's the one by the large Banksy prints on the wall. They were laughing.

Bo rounded on the family and yelled at them.

"What a disgraceful way to have fun!"

"What are you talking about?"

"You know damn well! You deliberately ran over those ducks, and you killed the mother and three of the ducklings. It looks like the father is injured. I saw you all laugh, and you just drove off. Blood, feathers and duck guts smeared across the road!"

"Oh, for God's sake. They were only ducks."

Not the right answer for this indefatigable grandma!

"I'll show you "only ducks!"

Bo leant forward and with her left arm and swept all the coffee cups and plates off the table. The children, aged about nine and 11, started whimpering. The daughter was a truculent little Ginger. The older child looked like that annoying fat boy that is always the front of the queue at McDonald's. Bo then brought back her right hand up and delivered a firm slap across the face of the grinning man and the smirking wife. She then took out a camera and took a photograph of the family.

"You deliberately drove at those ducks. I saw you grinning and laughing. I can't put you in the stocks, but I can put your ugly mugs up on the notice boards 'round the village."

"Don't make such a big deal about it, Granny."

"Don't you Granny me! Squashed mother duck! Injured father duck! Three flattened ducklings! Duck blood and flesh all over the road! Your kids won't stop crying for a month!"

Two police officers arrived and spoke gently to Bo. One got her to accompany him up to the police station in her car and the other took full statements from the family who turned out to be holidaying Aucklanders.

The anagram JAFA was well known to the Wanaka community. It is not difficult for gentle readers to figure it out.

Grandma Bo was in custody and the Aucklanders were allowed to continue on their way. Story ended? Certainly not!

The next morning in the new Southern Lakes Law Offices in Queenstown, Richard was standing up with a very small microphone and mouthpiece attached to his head. He was using his voice recognition equipment, which was highly sophisticated and entering dictation as words flashed up on his screen. Melinda came in.

"Good morning, Boss. Here are the addresses you wanted about the stolen cattle and here's the tabbed textbook with the latest cases. The claim is unanswerable. You could use the summary judgment procedure here."

"Thanks. Hang around and I'll do the letter to the stock firm first and then you can do a similar one to the vehicle company. Let's attack the letters so we can get them away by email today. I'll do the guts of the letter. You add in the addresses if you will."

Richard dictated.

"Dear Sir,

I act for Mr James Watson whose nickname is Joppy. He owns Fantail Ridge Downs, Eastern Southland. Until recently his manager was Sparky Robinson. Approximately four weeks ago Mr Robinson stole 419 prime cattle and sold them to your firm for $523,750. Mr Watson accepts that was the correct value. I accept that your firm was duped into believing that the cattle were Mr Robinson's to sell. But they were not.

The law does not afford you a defence. You cannot claim that you were not negligent. I do not allege negligence. The tort of conversion governs the situation. Your firm's involvement amounted to civil conversion, however innocent the firm may be. I enclose a copy of the relevant parts of the leading textbook and three Court of Appeal and High Court decisions on point. We can get summary judgment on this.

This matter must be settled. I will not allow it to grind on with letters seesawing back and forth. The claim is so unanswerable that I am 100% certain that I could obtain summary judgment in the High Court at Invercargill within three months. I'm ready to issue proceedings at once.

I asked that you confirm within a few days that you will pay the sum of $523,750 plus interest and costs into my trust account on the basis it is accepted as being an end to the matter. My client will offer to forego any claim for interest and any claim for costs. The tort of conversion will mean that all direct costs can be recoverable. If the matter is not settled within, say, four days, then those concessions come off the table and interest will accrue at 7%, direct costs will likely be in the vicinity of $40,000 and you must take into account probably a similar amount to come from your lawyers.

Yours faithfully,"

"Terrific. Send it through to my screen and I'll have a letter to the car firm done in a jiffy."

"Melinda, please do a similar to the car dealer who purchased the 4x4."

The telephone rang as Melinda left.

"Sergeant Tane here, Ritchie. I've got a client I think you should represent. She's at the Wanaka police station now. She's 78 and pretty upset about a bit of a mess she got herself in. Everyone in the station sympathises with her."

"What happened?"

"She saw some bastard Aucklanders deliberately run ducks over on the road. She chased them down and gave them bit of a slapping."

"Good on her."

"But they won't agree to a diversion and want the poor old dear put in stocks in the middle of town. She needs the best. She says she'll drive over."

"No. I can take a bit of time off now. I'll get there in the car in 60 minutes. Can you let Wanaka know I'll be across in, say, one hour 10 minutes?"

"Sure. They'll bail her to later in the week in Alexandra District Court and she'll go home now to 25 Wiley Road in Wanaka. A couple of houses off Beacon Point Road and through the archway in the hedge. She's a tough old stick but she's still upset. I'll get the station to tell her you're coming. She is good for a fee."

"I'm on my way."

He hung up and called out to Janet.

"Janet. I'll be away for three hours in Wanaka. I have my cell phone with me. I'll be back by 4.00 pm."

Richard grabbed a pad and a pen, his cell phone, I-Pad and a dictaphone. As he got ready to leave, Janet put a large coffee in his hand and Mary came out of her office. Richard flashed a smile at his wife.

"Can you spare three hours? I'm off to Wanaka to see a 78-year-old defender of ducks. Grab a coffee at the Cardrona Pub, or a beer on the way home. We'll be back by later in the afternoon. We'll have some fun in the country."

"Count me in. I'll grab my jacket."

Richard held the lift and was then joined by Mary, and they descended to the basement carpark.

Their car sped to Wanaka through beautiful scenery – Frankton Arm, Lake Hayes, the zigzags at the start of the Crown Range, the summit of the Crown Range looking north to Wanaka, past the Cardrona Pub, through the Cardrona flatlands and over the small hill to the expansive view of Lake Wanaka that the two constables had remarked upon only two hours earlier.

The vehicle drove along the front of the lake and to its left into Lakeside Road and up to Beacon Point Road and 25 Wiley Road. Richard and Mary walked around to the front door and were met by Mrs Jenkins. She was a real sweetie but also a tough cookie at the same time. She held all her marbles, Mary instantly observed to herself.

"Cup of tea, dears?"

Mary spoke up first, then Richard.

"It's a pleasure to meet you. Milk, no sugar please. This is Richard. He specialises in court work."

"I'm here to help," said Richard. "The police in Queenstown briefed me and have now sent me a summary of facts on my iPad. I see you've never been in trouble before and are still heavily involved in community work. I also understand you pack a fairly powerful slap."

"The adults bloody well-deserved it."

;

133

Richard continued, "We've picked up the whole police file. You had been charged with assault on each of the parents and wilful damage in respect of the crockery."

Mary added, "The owners of the crockery now know who you are and after the story about the ducks they have been only too ready to withdraw that charge and provide the police with a glowing reference for you." Richard spoke up.

The Aucklanders won't be so accommodating. They're demanding their pound of flesh and their day in Court. But I'll be ready for them. Technically, you're guilty, but there are so many good things that can be said on your behalf that I am confident it will all work out well."

"I suppose you've looked at all possible defences? I don't like giving in too easily."

"I avoid pleas of guilty where I can, but there is no option in this case. Self-defence and provocation don't apply. I can look at the temporary insanity but, hey, I'm only joking."

Bo's eyes twinkled. She obviously had a sense of humour.

"Could I say I am psychotic? But I suppose they'd tell both of us to sod off!"

Richard laughed.

"I will put the right perspective on for you in Court. It's Thursday week at the Alexandra Court. OK for you? I'll meet you there at, say, 10.00 am."

"Yes. I'm fine for that."

"Can you e mail me? Do you run a computer?"

"Yes, a wee beauty."

"Well could you draw me up a couple of pages listing your community work in the last 50 years and particularly in the last 10 years. Send it to me and I might ring you for a couple of extra questions."

"No problem."

"I'll ring you a couple of days before the case."

"Thanks. I'm 78. Shall I come dressed as Joan Collins or Grandma from the Beverly Hillbillies?"

"Somewhere in between. I'll see you then."
Bo waved goodbye to them until their car drove out of sight.

❧

Richard and Mary started their trip back to Queenstown.
"What do you think?"
"If we get the right Judge, it will be a breeze. If we get a shocker then we may have a problem."
They drove over the Crown Range summit and started down towards to middle plateau area and gazed out at a huge field of long growing straw grass with a small nest of green trees 100 metres into the field. A wonderful old-fashioned haystack resided at the far end. It was a hot day. The sun was shining.
"I'm feeling a bit frisky looking at all of the hay in that field," Mary said quietly.
"Horny as a mountain stag!" replied Richard.
"Well, I might not go that far. But we couldn't do this in the middle of the day in Auckland. We might be seen."
Richard had a yarn ready.
"Did I ever tell you the story of having to cross-examine that Irishman who was giving evidence for the girl in a paternity case? His evidence was meant to be about witnessing the sexual congress of the couple in a field not to dissimilar to this one. It was meant to be the necessary corroborating evidence.
I had to break him down and prove him an unreliable eyewitness. I didn't do it very well."
"Tell me, Paddy.   You *assumed* they were being intimate?"
"Oi."
"Have you ever lain down with a lass in a field of straw just to talk?"
 "Oi"

135

"And a casual observer seeing the straw rustle in your case might conclude you were having intercourse?"

"OI .... AND THEY'D BE ROIGHT TOO!!!" was the loud reply from the witness.

Mary laughed out loud.

"Classic case of me asking one too many questions."

"C'mon. We're off! Before you keep yapping more."

This loving couple parked the car, hopped the fence and ran bent over through the long grass. They could have been seen by any interested passing observer shredding the occasional item of clothing.

The Southern Alps may not have moved, but the haystack certainly shook over the next 20 minutes."

"We'd better not put these 20 minutes on Grandma Bo's bill!" said Richard.

They held hands for the rest of the trip back to Queenstown.

CHAPTER TWELVE

The next day was Willie's turn to fly the flag for the newest law firm in the Southern Lakes. He walked into the Court accompanying his Asian client, 28-year-old, Heng Lee. Mr Lee was charged with careless driving causing death on the Crown Range. It was a tragic accident.

Judge Tony Bradshaw entered from the side door at the same level of his Bench. The Judge was an energetic young, recent appointment with a pleasant face and bright mind.

"Silence for his Honour the Judge. This Court is now open for defended fixtures. Call Heng Lee."

Mr Lee entered the dock.

"May it please the Court, I appear for the defendant."

"Thank you, Mr Pihama. How long will this fixture take?"

"About an hour, Sir."

"All right. Proceed Sergeant."

"May it please the Court, the facts will show that a car driven by the defendant was seen driving on the wrong side of the road between the airport and Lake Hayes. Conditions were good. It rounded a bend and collided with a vehicle coming the other way. The driver of the other car was killed instantly. The Police say the driving of the defendant was careless. I call the officer in charge of the case."

A callow constable climbed up into the witness box. He was sworn in and started his evidence.

"On arrival at the accident site at 2:10 pm on Sunday 29 October a hearse was present with the deceased body of the driver of one of the cars in the back. The defendant admitted to me that he was the driver of the other car. He was very upset. He told me that he had been informed that the right-hand side of the road was the correct carriageway. He said the car rental company had told him that. I told him I did not believe him and charged him with careless driving causing death."

Wiremu rose to cross examine.

"For the record, the accident took place well under one kilometre from the airport?"

"Yes, he had not driven very far."

"No."

"Constable. Did you interview anyone at the car rental firm?"

"Yes. They denied saying that he should drive on the right-hand side of the carriage way. The next witness will be the relevant employee."

The rental car employee, Rose Winters, then entered the witness box. The sergeant led her evidence from her.

"I can recall speaking to Mr Lee at the time he hired our car. He had a limited grasp of English. I gave him a pamphlet about New Zealand driving conditions. I did not tell them he could drive on the right-hand side of the road."

"Just answer any questions please."

Willie rose to his full height.

"Miss Winters. Do you accept that the pamphlet does not specifically say that New Zealanders drive on the left-hand carriageway?"

"I hadn't considered that. Let's have a look. No. I can't find anything in writing to that effect."

"There is a small diagram on page 6 which shows a two-lane carriageway with a simple sketch of a vehicle with what was presumably intended to be the front of the car illustrated with a curved end."

"Yes. I can see that."

"And that was the only thing in writing given to my client."

"That's right."

"My client told the police that he said to you, "Do I drive on the left-hand side of the road?"

"Yes. I can recall that."

"And you signified your agreement by saying "Right.""

"Yes. I think I did. I was meaning to convey to him that he must drive on the left-hand side of the road."

"What? By saying "Right?"

Miss Winters flashed a look on the face as if the penny had just dropped.

"Oh my God!"

"Thank you for being so honest, Miss Winters. Has something just dawned on you? Do you accept the real possibility that there could have been a dreadful misunderstanding?"

"Yes, I do now. It's just dawned on me."

"That is all."

"Do you intend to call any evidence?" asked the Judge.

"No, but I have some strong legal submissions."

"I thought you might. Let's hear them. That High Court of Australia authority, I suppose?"

"Yes, Your Honour. This was a most tragic accident. But the law does not treat every accident as necessarily involving carelessness."

"I agree," said His Honour.

"In this case, we have a tourist with a limited grasp of English, no previous experience of driving in this country and imprecise advice given in the brochure and a confusing response by the staff member set up the foundation for a terrible misunderstanding. He thought he was entitled to drive on the right-hand side of the road. He drove for under one kilometre so there is not even room to say that he had time to observe other vehicles driving on the left-hand carriageway."

"And your legal precedents?"

"All here, Your Honour."

Willie handed them up to the court clerk.

"Again, I submit again that not every accident means there has been careless driving."

"I accept that as a principle of law."

"The issue has been examined by the highest courts of this country, the United Kingdom, Australia and Canada.

It is not necessary to prove intention to commit careless driving. Indeed, if that was the test then a charge of dangerous or reckless driving would usually be the allegation."

"Granted."

"I submit that careless driving must inherently have an element of knowledge. Every first-year law student knows most offences have an element of actus reus (the act) and mens rea (the mental element)."

"Well, that is certainly true for reckless driving."

"I put it this way. If the driver of the vehicle knows that the circumstances could likely amount to carelessness, then an inference can be drawn of mens rea. But the facts in each case must be relevant. A driver who accepts a risk must inevitably be guilty of careless driving if an accident occurs."

"What do you say are the important facts in this case?"

"My client was effectively told that cars drive on the right-hand side of a two-lane carriageway in New Zealand. This was not simply misreading a brochure. He had dialogue with the representative of the car rental firm. There was clear ambiguity."

"And that fact seems to have been accepted now by the rental firm," observed the Judge.

"Yes, Your Honour."

"I think I have to agree. I'm going to dismiss this charge now but in view of the importance of the issues raised I will deliver a written decision through the registrar within a week. I want to consider all these cases you have submitted to the Court. Thank you very much for your very professional attendance to all these questions of law."

"May it please the Court. I am obliged, Your Honour."

Mr Lee stepped down from the dock. Willie bowed to the Bench and left the Court. He shook Mr Lee's hand outside.

"All the best of luck for the rest of your trip. I am, here is the receipt for the $10,000 you paid to my office together with a note of my fee."

"Thank you so much. In my country I might have been taken out and shot in the back of the head."

"We don't do that in New Zealand. But some people think we should."

They shook hands again and Willie returned for his next case.

A few minutes later, Willie was in the same Court before the same Judge. He was now defending a carpenter charged with unlawfully presenting a firearm.

"Call Norman Peter Standring."

Mr Standring walked from the back of the courtroom to the dock.

"I appear for the defendant, Your Honour. This is another defended fixture. May the defendant be seated in the dock?"

"Certainly. Proceed Sergeant."

"On 27 August last, two off-duty policemen heard a number of shots ring out from a forest in the area approximately halfway between Queenstown and Glenorchy. They thought they heard a voice cry out. They walked on to the private property and approximately 200 metres from the main road they were confronted by the defendant with a 22 rifle in his hands and this man called out to the constables to leave his property because they were trespassing. The constables feared that a shot may have been fired towards their vicinity. I call Constable Tulloch to the witness box."

Constable Tulloch walked to the witness box and picked up the Bible and held it up, somewhat theatrically. The Court clerk intoned -

"Do you swear by Almighty God that the evidence you are about to give touching the matter now before this Court shall be the truth, the whole truth and nothing but the truth?"

"I do. On Saturday 27 August last, Constable Tompkins and I were off duty and cycling in the vicinity of what we subsequently know to be the defendant's sheep and cattle farm bordering the Queenstown/Glenorchy public road. We heard approximately 8 shots and then we heard someone appear to cry out. We quickly got off our bikes and ran towards the noise of the shots. As we came around body of large trees approximately 200 metres from the road, we were confronted with the defendant holding a rifle. He accused us of trespassing. He held a firearm. We arrested him and charged him with unlawfully presenting a firearm."

"Yes Constable. Just answer any questions please."

The Sergeant sat down. Wiremu stood up.

"Constable. Demonstrate to the Court please how my client was standing."

"Like this."

The constable demonstrated by holding the rifle across his chest with two hands and then swinging it down with one hand so that it pointed to the ground.

"As he swung it to the ground, he warned us about trespassing."

"Thank you, Constable. No questions, Your Honour."

"That is the case for the prosecution."

"Yes, Mr Pihama. Only the one question?"

"Yes, Sir. The defence will not call any evidence. I have submissions to make."

"Short and sweet. I think I can anticipate your submissions."

Wiremu started his short submissions.

"The charge of unlawfully presenting a firearm has unusually not been the subject of High Court or Court of Appeal interpretations. It appears that everyone seems to rely on the Magistrates' Court 1926 case of Police v Hanlin which is only reported only in an out-of-date copy of Maxwell on Police Court Law."

"And, let me guess, that case deals with the definition of "presenting." I can remember it. Do you have the old textbook there?"

"Here it is, Your Honour. In a nutshell, "presenting" means "pointing." For the offence to be complete there must be an actual pointing of the firearm at the victim. The constable's own evidence graphically shows that this did not occur. This was not a public place. An offence of "unlawful possession" might have been available in that situation. But the alleged offence took place on private property. There were no words uttered to suggest some form of verbal assault. The only offence potentially available was one of unlawful presentation . . . I submit the facts here do not stack up. Particularly to the standard of proof beyond reasonable doubt."

The Judge paused for about 30 seconds and read from the textbook handed up to him by Wiremu.

"I agree. Shortest defended case I have heard this year. The charge is dismissed. There was no presentation under the existing legal definition."

"May it please the Court."

His client stood down from the dock and Wiremu bowed and left the Court with his client.

Outside the Court house after the case Wiremu and his client talked.

"Wow! Well done. I thought it was going to be a lot more difficult than that. Can I now use you as my lawyer? I was wanting to change anyway."

"Sure. Happy to help in any way."

"Oh. Here's the $6500 we agreed on. Well worth it."

"Thanks. I'll send you out a receipt. Bye. I've got a client waiting."

❧

Back at the office, Richard was hard at work on Tim Shadbolt's defamation papers in his office. The telephone rang.

"Richard Locksley."

"Good morning. Darryl Platt here. This is urgent!"

"What can I do?"

"I'm on my cell phone, 20 metres away from a vehicle crash on a country road near Dalefield. He came 'round a corner straddling the centreline then suddenly his back door flew open and he hit my car. We both went off the road. I've heard the Police are on their way. Trouble is, I have had a few drinks. This'll be my fourth. I'll go to jail."

Richard was fast and professional in his responses.

"Listen to me carefully. The quick, truthful answers to my questions are vital! Did you stop?"

"Yes."

"Did you clearly ascertain if there was any injury?"

"Yes. There wasn't any."

"Did you render all practicable assistance?"

"Yes. I helped push the other guy's car to the side of the road."

"Did you identify yourself?"

"Yes. I gave him in writing my name address and telephone number. Oh no! I can see the cop car coming but it's a long way away."

"Good. You have fulfilled your legal obligations. Now DISAPPEAR. This instant! Keep away from the Police. Hide if you must. Call me in 30 minutes and I will explain my advice. But don't get caught or they will breathalyse you!"

"What! Are you for real?"

"Yes. No time to explain in detail now. Just do as I say. I can shield you from a drink/driving offence and you have a good chance of avoiding a careless driving charge as well. You are under no legal obligation to stay. My initial questions and your answers have shown that you fulfilled your legal obligations."

"I suppose this'll cost me."

"Yes. You will get a bill for a lifetime's experience. Not just a few minutes."

"Ten grand? It's worth it to me.

"Yes, but no more. There will be follow up work. But if you avoid any conviction then $10,000."

"OK by me."

"Head down and away you go. Fast. Ring me tonight."

CHAPTER THIRTEEN

That afternoon an Employment Mediation was in session. Melinda and her client Christine Cook sat together across the mediation table from her employer, who had his lawyer present. Mrs Purvis, the Mediator sat at the end of the table. She was a formidable woman, exuding plenty of professional confidence.

"We'll start this mediation. I see both parties are represented by lawyers so you will have explained to them the process. The papers disclose that Christine's employment was terminated within 90 days of commencement. Everyone accepts that, don't they?"

"Yes. So what's the beef?" asked the employer's lawyer.

"Don't you know? It was in my personal grievance letter?" retorted Melinda.

"Where?

Right here! I told you she was employed for a week during the previous Christmas period."

"I don't get your point!"

"Well section 67 A (3) makes it clear that the 90-day trial period provision does not apply if Christine had been previously employed by the employer. She was employed for two weeks during the last Christmas/New Year period. End of story. No other reasons were given for the termination. The termination is therefore unjustified, and my client is entitled to at least three months' wages, plus let's just take the average award of compensation of, say, $7500, plus there must be an allowance towards costs because of the blatant breach."

"What! Where does it say that? I don't do much of this type of work."

The mediator piped up with an uncharacteristic jolly laugh.

"Well, you are having a very fast and steep learning curve, Mr Catchpole. Melinda's submission is unarguable. I'll take a five-minute adjournment. If what she says is correct, then her claims are sustainable."

"The average awards before an Employment Authority are 3 months wages, $7500 compensation and some costs."

She stood up and left the room and Melinda and her client went outside into the sun. Mr Catchpole and his client remained in the mediation room.

"You never told me that!" whined the client.

"You never asked!" Mr Catchpole's response was weak.

"Now we're swimming backwards upriver. We have to settle."

"That sucks. How much will it cost me?"

"You'll be up for three months net wages, which is $12000. You will be ordered to pay a minimum of $7500 for general compensation but can't really argue the point if they want $7500 because it could be $8000 - $12,000. And if this case goes through to the Employment Authority you are paying my fees plus $4300 to them. We may be able to round the whole package down to $17,500. Can't see you getting away with anything less than that as a full hearing before the Employment Authority and at that stage your own legal costs will be over $10,000. But I think you must offer $4000 by way of costs to seal the deal."

"So we must settle?"

"I'm afraid so."

The lawyers got their heads together for no more than five minutes. The deal was done. $22,000.

Janet heard singing as Melinda bounded up the stairs.

She opened the office doors and Melinda came in elated. No clients were in the waiting room. Janet and Willie looked up.

"Whoopee! $22,000 to be paid within seven days. 30 minutes work. We get $5500." Willie gave her a hug. She registered her pleasure.

Richard came out of his office.

"Excellent work. There's no substitute for knowing the law and quick preparation. You knew how to do it and you did it! My shout across the road. Anyone want to join me?"

They all agreed. Mary came out of her office, and they turned out the lights, locked the door and walked across the waterfront to the nearest bar.

❧

Their favourite bar at the end of the Mall in Queenstown was humming. Richard, Mary, Willie, Melinda, and Janet were enjoying a few diesels. Melinda had been persuaded not to dance on the tables . . . but it was hard work.

"Hit me with your rhythm stick!" She sang off key.

Richard tried to ignore her, but he harboured a desire to dance on the tables himself. Janet remained within grabbing distance of Melinda and office talk abounded.

"The phone's been going all day! I've made at least five appointments for each of you."

"I've picked up at least 3 extras myself," Willie added.

"I think I've now got most of the Family Court files into order and there are a lot!" said Mary. "I also had a visit from the local Community Advice Centre, and I think we're going to receive a steady feed of domestic violence and interim childcare work. Janet and I better get the legal aid machine into work."

"This is all good news. I have two great contingency fee civil cases settled with Mr Stanton and Joppy which might kick start the finances with the thick end of half a million dollars. But everything counts, people."

Tane Fleming came into the bar.

"Hi all. I thought you guys might be here."

"Tane. I'd like you to meet my wife, Mary and my two rising star lawyers, Willie and Melinda, and Janet, a legal executive and foundation rock of the office."

"Nice to meet you all. Crikey, you have really started your Team Law brand with a right roar. Everyone is talking about you all and your approach to the law. Well done."

"I'll get you a beer for that."

Janet explained some organisational matters.

"I've made sure your business cards are with the night shift." Tane replied.

"I also notified a specialist family violence squad that your firm also specialises in broken relationship disputes."

Mary commented, "I seem to be spearheading that line of work. You can let it be known that there is no cost whatsoever for a first interview. There will also be a percentage of pro bono work for the right cases. Very noble of us, but it's also very good advertising."

"We're all having a bit of the knees up in the office Friday week at the end of play for Tim Shadbolt and a few new clients, so you are most welcome and bring anyone you want from the Station."

"Don't mind if I do. Thanks."

An hour later, Darryl Platt rang Richard.

"I'm at my uncle's place. I won't go back home until tomorrow. The police have not contacted me. They won't know where I am."

"Well, when they do, play down the amount you had to drink. I am not going to tell you to lie but keep it to a minimum. Certainly under 4 stubbies."

"Understood," replied Mr Platt.

"Then emphasise the fact that the other driver was on the wrong side of the road, and that his door flew open and hit your car."

"Do I have to say anything else?"

"Well don't look as if you are being uncooperative. But that is all. Put the cops off the scent of drink driving and careless driving. Place all the fault on the shoulders of the ther driver because that is the truth. You have already given your name and address."

"OK."

"All of this means that the police almost certainly cannot prove drink driving, careless driving or failing to report an accident. If there is no injury, your only duty was to report the accident to the other owner, and you have done that. The only issue then becomes the other driver cutting the corner and the debris on the road will show that. It's worth going back and taking a sketch plan and a few photographs but wait a few hours and no more drinking."

"Great advice. Thanks so much."

"Keep in touch," said Richard.

Another large fee was paid into the office the next morning.

ॐ

Mary was telephoned the next day by a client wanting to finalise her marriage break-up. The next afternoon Mary met Mrs Shirley Harrison in her office.

"Mrs Harrison, what can I do for you?"

"My husband and I have just separated. We need to sort out our property issues."

"Let's get the basic facts first. Are you legally married and how long did you live together? I ask that because the first three years of a de facto relationship is treated differently."

"Yes, we are legally married. We lived together for 22 years. Three children. The oldest is independent and at university. Two younger ones are at High School."

"Have you got a list of your property?"

"Here it is. It's in digital form. We own a manufacturing business which we think might be worth over $1 million.

It was established after the marriage. We each own 50% of the shares and are both directors. The valuer's assessment is attached."

"Houses? Cars? Furniture and chattels? Savings? Other investments? All here?"

Mary scanned it into her computer and flashed it up on to the screen.

"I see there is no mortgage. Are there any large debts?"

"No. We agree that I will take the house which is valued at about $750,000. We can divide between ourselves the furniture and chattels. We will need some assistance on the valuation of the business. He will take the business and pay me in cash one half of the difference between the house value in the business. At least, that's what I say."

"Ah Hah. But what does he say? I've seen all this before."

"He says that all his effort and talent has gone into the business and therefore he is entitled to a bigger share than me. But I brought up three children, worked in the business at least 20 hours a week and he conveniently forgets that I put $50,000 from my Dad's inheritance into the business. But that was 15 years ago."

Mary re-assured her client, "Quite simply, there cannot be any other result than equal sharing. Is there anything that you have missed?"

"No. Nothing."

"OK then. It now becomes a matter of tactics. This firm is sick and tired of tricky lawyers who try and wear the other one down by raising all sorts of defences, hoping that delay after delay will lead to a result in their favour. It's the oldest trick in the book and we are on to it! I cynically say that 99% of lawyers give the other lawyers a bad name."

Shirley smiled and Mary continued.

"The law is quite clear. After three years of living together, everything is split down the middle unless, and I quote section 13 the Property (Relationships) Act 1976, "If the court considers that there are extraordinary circumstances that make equal sharing of property repugnant to justice" then the Court can allow one party more. But it's extremely rare for a Court to do so. Hardly ever is that section used."

Mary flashed up the section on her wall screen.

"Nothing in these facts would get past even square one, but his lawyer may try and bluster and bluff, so our tactics are to be immediate and strong and not give in. I take it you are strong enough to do that?"

"I certainly am."

"The only other thing I need to ask is whether there is any property owned by a trust or a company because sometimes that ownership can become a little tricky. But there are several ways in which the Court can bust those trusts and break the companies and give to you an equal share."

"No, nothing like that. So you think this should be easy?"

"Under the law, you are safe as houses. But he might think that he can wear you down psychologically, so let me be the bully – only if I must. A solid letter from us now will make any competent lawyer that he instructs advise him to "pull his head in", if he continues to demand more than 50% of the manufacturing business."

"Thank you. I feel relieved already."

"I'll have these lists you have given me reformatted so that I can attach them to my letter. You drop back this time tomorrow to check the letter I'm going to write on your behalf. I'll get you to countersign both the lists and my letter just to show we mean business. OK by you?"

"That's really heartening. I'll see you about mid-tomorrow afternoon."

Mary accompanied her out to the waiting, gave a small wave goodbye, and beckoned in her next client.

Melinda was interviewing Evan Thornton. His nickname was Thug. He was what not-so-polite people call a bogan. He had an unkempt mullet hair style and two rings in his left ear and brass looking nose pin which only made him look like he had a large hickey. Melinda was not impressed

"Hello. Melinda's my name. How can I help?"

"I'm being done for being the father of a child. I don't want to pay child maintenance."

"Tell me about it."

"Well, me brother and me cousin picked up this hitchhiker and she stayed with us for the weekend. She was real easy and a bit of a slut and hit up each of us. I mean, she hasn't made any complaint, it's just that we all knocked her off on the same weekend. She's a slut."

Melinda opened the top drawer of the desk and pulled out what was not so politely known as a fart machine shaped like a cartoon pistol and she pulled the trigger. Fart noises come out of the trumpet-like barrel. It came from the "Warehouse – Where Everyone Gets a Bargain". Uncle Mike had bought it for her as a gift for someone who has everything.

"PPhhallarrttt!!"

It was really a kid's toy owned by adults. Melinda was that sort of adult.

"This is a gift from my favourite Uncle Mike. When I use it, you drop the potty-mouth language! Now, start again. What's happened?"

"Well, me brother got these court papers from the Family Court and he went to Court and she was there and admitted to the Judge that she had sex with all of us that weekend. The Judge got her to name all of us and then he made an order that we all have medical tests to establish who was the father of the child. Do I have to do that?"

"There are a number of things you can do. I might be able to give you some good advice which protects you from having to pay maintenance. But I need to know that you can pay the fees of this office first."

"How much will it cost?"

"$3500. Up front."

"Fuck me!"

Melinda sounded the fart machine again.

"PPhhallarrttt!!"

By this time the whole office was standing outside Melinda's office, gagging with supressed laughter. The interview exchanges were muffled, but the fart machine punctuated the muffled conversation every minute or so.

"As soon as you resort to lavatory humour, the writing is on the wall," quipped Richard. "But that's the way I would like to conduct all interviews."

"Stop the potty mouth!" cries Melinda again from through the door.

"Sorry! OK. I've got the money with me with me now. Eftpos?"

"All right then. You go out and see Janet at reception and pay her the money and bring me back the receipt and we will continue the interview. But I have my gun here and will use it if necessary."

Evan left Melinda's room and was back within a minute holding a NZ Law Society receipt for $3500.

"Now, have you got the court documents served on you?"

Evan gave them to Melinda.

"As I thought. It's not actually a formal court order. If you disobey a court order you could go to prison for contempt of court. This is a Judge's <u>recommendation</u> that you undergo what is called a parental test. But section 57 of the Family Proceedings Act 1980 says that if a man refuses to carry out that recommendation, that only allows the Court to draw an adverse inference against that man.

"What's that?"

"It usually means in "the girl against one boy" paternity case that a refusal will likely make the Court to say you're the father."

"Is it different in my case?"

"Well yes. Don't you see? I assume that the Court has issued a document against all three of you <u>recommending</u> that all of you take blood or saliva tests to establish your DNA. But if you all refuse then no Court could make an order establishing who is the father. In that way, you all avoid your financial responsibility."

Evan went out and danced a bit of a jig and yelled in delight.

"Yeh! Thank God!"

"Well just a moment. I want to talk to you about your actual responsibility and whether you should recognise that a child knowing who it's real father is very important."

"I don't give a fucking toss!"

Melinda employed the fart gun again with great effect.

"PPhhallarrttt!!"

Evan immediately modified his language.

"Perhaps you should. I'd like you think about it," advised Melinda.

"Right. Let me think. Three seconds pass."

"OK. I've thought about it. No way am I admitting that sprog is mine."

"OK. I'm not here to pass judgement on you in any way. I just wanted you to know the options available. Please tell the other two boys what I have told you and ring me before the afternoon is out with the names of their lawyers, if they have any. I need to explain to all three of you what the law says about recommendations and what you can do."

"OK."

"You must realise that if the other two give the tests and are excluded from being the father then a refusal by you to cooperate will almost certainly lead to the Family Court making a paternity order against you. But if you all refuse then you all get off."

"Best advice I've had all day."

"You must keep in touch with me at all times because the advice I've given you has to be carefully managed so that all three of you are protected."

"I understand. I will see the other two boys within an hour and ring you before 5 o'clock tonight. Thanks, Missus."

He almost skipped out of Melinda's office. She went out into the reception area and whispered to Janet.

"I'm not escorting that little sod to the lift. I don't want to touch him. He's like an Australian. I don't know where he's been. I've just deprived a poor little baby the right to know its father."

"You have your sole duty to your client. And you've got $3500. Not bad for one interview." Janet knew her legal ethics.

"I've still got some follow-up work to do, but perhaps you better formalise the receipt with a bill of costs. Let's take a leaf out of Richard's book and simply say, "My fee for knowing what to do and doing it." Make it GST inclusive. I had to blitz him with my fart gun."

"I heard. We all heard. We all want one of them!"

"I'll speak to Uncle Mike. He is a cool dude!"

CHAPTER FOURTEEN

At home that evening, the family was sitting around the dinner table having just finished a wonderful meal. The telephone rang.

Richard answered it.

"Richard Locksley."

"Mr Locksley. Constable Sonia Hemmings here. As you know there's been an All-Black's training camp in Queenstown for the last four days. The boys got up to some pretty bad hijinks last night. We had to detox four. But we also locked one up and charged him with disorderly behaviour. He is calling for you."

"Thank you. Put him on."

"His name is Jono Mattson."

Jono came on the line.

"Hello? Is that Mr Locksley? My dad knows you from Auckland. He is a lawyer on the North Shore. I rang him and he gave me your name."

"Yes Jono. I know him well. What the hell have you been doing?"

"Me and the boys had a few diesels too many and we were clowning around down at the waterfront, and they told me about the big salmon, trout and eels which hang out down there outside the underwater viewing tank. I swam out towards the viewing tank to have a nosey. I was still about 5 metres away when a cop yelled at me to get out and I obeyed him immediately."

"He came up to me on the shore and I was a bit abusive and I argued the point with him. He said he would let me off with a warning if I donated $250 to a local charity."

"What else," asked Richard.

"I said I didn't believe I'd done anything wrong, and he said, "Right. If you're going to be like that, then I'm arresting you for disorderly behaviour and you'll be up before the Court on Thursday.""

"I've got all I need. I'll be down at the station in about 10 minutes," Richard answered.

"Don't give any interview at all until you have seen me. If I can get police bail, where can you stay until Thursday? The police will not look kindly on you going back to stay with the boys because they think you'll only get on the booze again."

"Luckily my uncle and aunt live here. He's a teacher and she's a nurse."

"OK. Be ready to give me their names, address and telephone number when I get there."

He hung up, grabbed his car keys and turned to his family.

"Sorry guys. I've got to go and interview and bail out an All Black. He's been a naughty boy. Jono Mattson. Do you know him, Roger?"

"Sure bet! He's got to be the fastest runner the All Blacks have ever had. Try to get his autograph for me will you?"

"Would a police mug shot and fingerprints do?"

"Would they what! Cool! I could trade them for a genuine Ritchie McCaw jockstrap. At least that's what Melinda told me."

Richard laughed.

"I'm going to have to have a serious talk with that girl in the morning!"

A few minutes later Richard bounded into the Police Station reception.

"Good evening, Mr Locksley. You want to see Jono."

"Yes, thank you. Please always call me Richard. Tane calls me Ritchie."

"What's good enough for Tane is good enough for me."

Richard was led to the rather cramped windowless police cell. Jono now looked a rather scared young man. He was still wet, shivering and clad only in shorts and a wet T-shirt.

"NO! This is not good enough Constable. Please arrange for some dry clothes, a blanket and a hot drink. You may be busy. He may have given you a hard time. But I will not have my clients treated like this. And the Police

Complaints Authority will agree with me. Please just bring me what I ask for and that will be the end of the matter."

"Certainly, Mr Locksley."

She hurried off. Within a minute Sergeant Tane Fleming returned with clothes, a blanket and a large mug of hot, steaming coffee.

"Sorry about that, Richard. Our boys thought he needed a bit of quieting down. But enough's enough."

"Thanks Sergeant. No harm done. I've got my cell phone with me. Any problems if I use it? I'm not sending out for drugs. He can stay at his uncle and aunts with a strict condition that he does not leave their place. You might know them. He is a teacher. She's a nurse. Also, could you see if we could agree upon a statement of facts before we go, because I might have a crack at a defended case this Thursday. It'll only take half an hour. I am sure he will agree to everything the police say he did."

"No problem. I know his uncle and aunt. They are OK for a bail address. I don't think an All Black is going to skip bail."

"Thanks."

The Sergeant left the room. Richard smiled and turned to Jono.

"That looks like bail is done and dusted. Now, you little, no, rather big sod. What have you been doing?"

"Just what I said over the phone. We were all full of hijinks. But I didn't swear at anyone. I was not violent. I got out of the water as soon as being ordered to do so by the cop. I was fully cooperative. If anything, their behaviour was worse than mine. As two of them put me in the police car they pushed me roughly and one of them said, "You smart arse. We'll teach you not to act the fool in our town."

"OK. There are a couple of good legal cases which suggest that your hijinks did not reach the standard for a disorderly behaviour charge."

Jono looked relieved.

"I'll try and arrange a defended hearing this Thursday if the Court can squeeze it in. I am sure we can draw up an agreed statement of facts, although I might not be able to get the abuse from the police into that agreed statement of facts."

"OK by me. I don't want to turn it into a major case."

"Leave things with me then. I'll ring your uncle, arrange bail and I can drop you up there or he can come down. Here's my card. Be at my office at 9.00 am Thursday morning."

When Richard arrived home that evening Mary was in bed.

"Hi love. Big day. It's getting a bit like Auckland."

"But don't you love it! I think I'm much happier and I really like practising law. And it's good to be with Mum."

"How do you think the kids are liking it?"

"Absolutely fine. The school had its first skiing afternoon today and they are taking to it like ducks to water."

"Goodness me. Don't use that analogy with Marjorie Jenkins, our ducks' lady. It seems like a week ago that we interviewed her in Wanaka and it was only this morning."

They had a kiss and a cuddle and almost immediately went to sleep.

The next morning, Richard was sitting in a coffee shop with Mary having a pleasant conversation. His cell phone rang. It was Janet clearly quite agitated.

"Richard, that unpleasant Law Society man, Magnus Denholm rang. He's in Queenstown. He demands to see you today and wishes to bring that creep Bernard Brinsley. He also wants to bring another person. I put them down for 3 pm. Is that OK with you?"

"That's OK. Oh, have you loaded those War Chest clips on to my computer desktop?"

"All done. The shortcuts are in the top right-hand corner. Each are named. Oh, and I've put an easy set of instructions on your desk. You I just need to push a number to start whichever piece I want. Jeepers. I had a peek, so I have entered the password GRUESOME. Get it?"

"Great work! Patch me through to Willie please."

Willie came on the line.

"Willie. It looks like I got three antagonists coming in at 3 o'clock. Please make sure you are in your office uninterrupted. You know what to do with recording. Listen in. Be ready to come in when I buzz you. Make sure my office camera is on."

"I'll be ready."

Richard put his cell phone back into his pocket. Mary looked interested.

"Join Willie at 3 pm in his office if you want to have some fun."

"What's up?"

"Let's just wait and see."

Before they could say more a robbery took place right in front of them outside the coffee shop. A man in his 60s was being pushed and swung round by a young lowlife and his satchel was grabbed from his hand. The lowlife ran off, but Richard and Mary were heartened to see two uniformed constables race past the window in hot pursuit.

"What were you saying about being a bit like Auckland?"

At 3.00 pm that afternoon, Richard was back working in his office. His door was closed, but he heard the waiting room doors open and some muffled conversation between two men and Janet. Janet opened Richard's door and ushered in Magnus Denholm and Bernard Brinsley.

"Good morning, gentlemen. What is this all about?"

"I think we should wait for Judge Christie."

"Judge Christie? So this is a social visit?" Richard's tone was sarcastic.

"Is he bringing prostitutes?" Richard spoke with a grin. He was softening them up. He could see precisely what was likely to happen.

"That's a disgraceful remark! You will deeply regret that!"

"I think you will be the ones to regret it. Take care, Gentlemen."

"You should know that he has laid complaints against you. Ah. Here he is."

Judge Christie entered the room.

"OK. I will see you all. But I want it on the record that you gave me 15 minutes notice that two of you were coming and now you spring a District Court Judge on me with no warning. How dare you ambush me!"

The two lawyers coldly ignored Richard's comment.

Wiremu was listening in and sensed the tension. He knew about the Warbox and, thinking quickly, he phoned Tane and asked if he would drop around.

"It's a professional request from Richard," he explained.

He then double checked that the links to the Warbox were on Richard's computer with the names – Brinsley, Denholm and Judge Christie.

The two Law Society lawyers geared themselves up. They thought they had the upper hand.

"Judge Christie has complained that you have been offensive, abusive, disrespectful and unprofessional to him on many occasions. I have seen it myself. The Society has asked us to report as to whether there should be disciplinary proceedings. In our view, your behaviour would justify you being struck off the Roll."

"Rubbish!" responded Richard. Their faces tightened.

"Only the other day I saw the same thing happen when you were appearing before this Judge."

Richard jumped in again.

"Well not to put too fine a point on it, Judge Christie is regularly an extremely offensive, abusive, disrespectful and unprofessional Judge on so many occasions. I also say that most of the practicing bar think he should no longer be sitting as a Judge. And several High Court Judges agree! Now, what do you think of that!"

The Judge exploded.

"That is preposterous! How dare you! Gentlemen, I demand that you take disciplinary steps to strike this man off the Roll of barristers and solicitors."

"Upon what grounds?" snarled Richard.

"Upon the grounds that your actions show that you are not a fit and proper person to act as a lawyer," said Stoddart.

"And upon the grounds that your conduct in my Court is seriously unbecoming a member of the profession."

"And what are you asking me to do about it?" Richard showed his contempt. He was setting them up.

"We are here to see if you will voluntarily hand in your practicing certificate and undertake not to practise law again. If you do not do just that, we will all make complaints that, in our opinion, you are not fit to practise law and that you have made threatening comments to us today of a criminal nature."

"You're just pissed off because you know I am the best advocate in the country and you're jealous." Richard was rising to his arrogant best.

"We will say you have directed threats at us all."

"I beg your pardon? That last allegation is simply not true and what you have just said amounts to blackmail! Is that the view of you all?"

"Yes."

"I go along with that."

"Yes, if it comes to that."

"But you have just admitted, at the very least, to conspiring to pervert the course of justice!"

"We'll deny it and it's the three of us against you."

Richard answered incredulously, "And you will all do that? Deny what you just said?"

"Yes. We'll win. You'll lose. Three of us. One of you."

"Too right."

"I didn't think it would be this simple," said Richard. That was not the answer they expected.

They looked uneasy. Richard continued. He pressed down on the accelerator.

"You two had better both start think about resigning, and you Judge, retiring within the next five working days!"

They all looked startled. Richard was just getting warmed up.

Richard picked up his phone and pushed a button and spoke to Wiremu.

"Willie? Can you come in pleaseWillie. If Melinda and Mary are there, please bring them in. Janet too, I think. Close the front door with the "Back in 30 Minutes" sign and put the telephones on answer phone. Oh, and is the Sergeant there? Ask him to come in as well please."

He turned to the three men who were looking decidedly nervous. Judge Christie was twitching.

"Feeling a bit twitchy there, Judge? It is only going to get worse. I have had the camera running! See there. All of what has just gone on is on video and audio tape."

Judge Christie, Mr Brinsley and Mr Denholm turned pale.

They looked very worried. They had not realised they were facing the most brutish attack-dog in the legal profession. And it was only just starting!

Melinda and Willie opened the door and came in followed a few seconds later by Mary. Then in came Sergeant Tane Fleming in full uniform. Then Janet joined them. Richard directed them with authority.

"Just stand by the window please people. Sergeant, please sit down there near the Judge. I may be making a citizen's arrest. Did you hear all of that?"

"Yes. And it's all recorded," said Wiremu.

"Same for me," added Tane.

The others all nodded in agreement. Willie handled a remote which instantly turned on the large screen on the wall in Richard's office and he hit the fast reverse button. He stopped 10 seconds later and pushed PLAY. The whole part of the conversation in Richard's office was replayed. Every word and every facial expression was faithfully recorded. What stood out was clear evidence of blackmail and an expressed intent to pervert the course of justice.

> "That's enough for me to arrange that all three of you hear the lock of a cell door turn behind you! I don't break any privacy laws because I am part of the conversation. You know that.'"

The three men sitting down turned pale. The blood had drained from their faces. They realised they were confronted with taped evidence of those crimes. They could not erase it. Denials would not work.

Richard rose as if he was in the High Court. He was looking down on them. He maintained the dominant position. He was rather like a hawk pecking at roadkill.

> "It's now my turn! You might try and argue that what you have said to me is not blackmail, but you would have nine months of hell waiting for it to be tested by a jury. But what you have definitely done is admit to conspiring to pervert the course of justice. Isn't that so, Sergeant?"

> "Seems open and shut to me, Mr Locksley. It is also clearly blackmail in my opinion."

> "Too right it is!" Richard was just getting started.

> "Things are serious. The Crimes Act 1961 calls it 'conspiring to pervert the course of justice'. But looking at you three now it should perhaps be re-worded to say "PERSPIRING to defeat the course of justice!" And I have only started!"

The three men moved to stand up as if to leave.

> "SIT DOWN!" roared Richard in his most stentorian tone. Otherwise, I will execute a citizen's arrest myself. Right here! Right now! I can deliver you into the sergeant's custody. That's how it works for a citizen's arrest under

the Crimes Act 1961! While you are in the police cells tonight, ask to be shown section of the Act!"

"But ..." stammered Denholm. It's the only word he could get out.

Richard maintained the momentum. He revved up the accelerator. Vroom! Vroom!

"You haven't seen the rest of the footage yet. These claims you make against me of "conduct unbecoming" will involve you three being witnesses. I would therefore be entitled to attack your own fitness and credibility and allege your own conduct unbecoming. Here is how I will do that!"

Richard pushed two numbers into his computer. The material came from his War Chest.

First of all, up came a graphic and highly pornographic video of the Judge dressed in a schoolgirl's uniform having oral sex performed on him by a prostitute, obviously in a brothel.

"Now, you cannot get much better than that!" mocked Richard.

The Judge spluttered and appeared to suffer a medical event. Mary offered him glass of water.

Richard raised his voice at him.

"Keep watching the screen, Judge! There are another 20 minutes. We see you totally nude soon and then we hear you telling the prostitute that you love her and would like to take away for a weekend to Taupo. Oh, how your wife will love learning about this event! And you are accusing me of conduct unbecoming simply for some criticism of your judicial actions in Court? You won't get off first base against me."

"Turn it off! Please turn it off!"

"Nah! I'm quite enjoying it, Boss", says Melinda.

Melinda could be counted upon to turn the knife in the right case. And this was it.

"And Judge, I've seen the last 20 minutes and it's gross. It gets worse," added Willie.

"Now they're all off to prison!" added Richard.

"I'm so sorry. I'm so, so sorry. I withdraw everything." Judge Christie wailed.

"I have not finished with you yet, but let's move on."

He turned to Mr Brinsley.

"Brinsley. You're a right opportunist prick! You barely know me. I don't think you know how many friends and clients I have. It was a prostitute client who gave me that video of the Judge barely three weeks ago in Auckland."

"Stop! Please!"

"No, Bernard, I'm going to call you Bernard, I've had three clients come to see me about your double and triple billing. I have the documents! Here they are on the screen."

Click. Click. Click.

"You charged one $22,500, the second $15,100 and the third $19,000. But you will see that between one half and one third of each bill related to consultations you alleged you had with a retired senior consultant in your law firm as well as a formal legal associate did not work at your firm. You cheated!"

Brinsley gulped.

"The police know that the consultant has been in the dementia ward at a Frankton Rest Home for over five months. He's completely Ga Ga. And the associate left to work with another firm in Australia over six months ago. All my information comes from the clients and the police under the Privacy Act. Yet the bills refer to work within the last three months. Now that's fraud, false pretences, criminal deceitful conduct or call it what you like. Crimes have been committed. You're off to prison too."

"At the very least you will never be allowed to practise law again. And you talk to me about conduct unbecoming and not being a fit and proper person to practise law? You bloody hypocrite. I'll return to you in a minute."

Richard then turned to Mr Denholm.

"Denholm! You've been a pain in the arse since Adam was a cowboy. Pious. Pretentious. Sanctimonious. A hypocrite. You say that I am guilty of conduct unbecoming. But I know a certain private investigator in Auckland who has been investigating you. He's my client! Look at this marvellous piece of video. Let me click on this link. The Show's only beginning."

Click. Click. Richard pushed another two keys. A video started playing showing Mr Denholm coming out of a South Auckland house in daylight pulling his pants up and then kissing a woman who was holding an 18-month-old child.

"Who is this, Denholm? It's your mistress of three years. Her name is Cynthia Darlinghurst. That is your child. None of this is known to your wife."

"What the ..." started Denholm.

"The kid's name is Donald and he's only 18 months' old. Adultery is not enough to establish conduct unbecoming, although your wife and family, brothers and sisters and mother-in-law might well disagree. But there is a crime here. WINZ has been defrauded and you have been a party to that fraud. I know from the private investigator that you prepared and witnessed the statutory declaration by Cynthia knowing it to be untrue."

"You advised her to swear that she did not know the father of child. And you have given her money and advised her how to hide up that money and assets you have purchased for her in order to maintain the Domestic Purposes Benefit. You thereby intentionally shielded yourself from a regular weekly Child Support assessment of over $150."

Mr Denholm was by now sickly white and shaking. Richard continued to turn the knife.

"Those actions amount to crimes. How do I get this information? I have personally acted for the private investigator professionally on several occasions. So you will go to prison as well and certainly will not be allowed to practise law again."

Mr Denholm appeared to gag and retch on to the carpet and then attempted to say something, but nothing came out his mouth.

"Now gentlemen. We have a problem. The Sergeant here has seen and heard everything, and he may feel obliged to take the matter further on his own initiative. And I have a duty under the Solicitors' Client Conduct Rules to report any suspicious or wrongful conduct. So neither of us can offer you a deal here. But I might be prepared to consider not reporting all of this upon the following conditions."

"What?"

"Anything." They all spoke at the same time.

"This is what is going to happen. You will shortly leave my office and I am never to hear of these complaints again. I warn you. Even if another Law Society officer raises them, it will be disastrous for all of you! You now bury them for ever."

The three men nodded in agreement.

"Bernard. I hope we might have a pleasant and professional relationship in the future and put all this behind us. One week is too short to make a lifetime enemy. I do not want that. But within one working week you will pay back all the fees charged to my three clients. Not just the double billing. All of the fees. I expect to check my trust account for the total of $55,000 which includes a fee component to me of $10,000. All that will be deposited by the end of play tomorrow."

"Agreed."

"OK. Agreed, " spluttered Bernrad, very meekly."

"Denholm. I never wish to hear from you again. But mark me. All the information I have on you will be kept under lock and key. That goes for you too, Bernard. A copy will also be kept with my will, with an Instructions Memorandum to my executor in case a dirty trick is played on my name after my death. I shall reach out to you from beyond the grave and you will all be destroyed!"

"Agreed."

"Judge. You're in a different category."

"Have you ever heard the term "splenetic"? It's a great word to look up in the dictionary. Bad-tempered, ill-tempered, angry, wrathful, cross, peevish, petulant, pettish, irritable, irascible, cantankerous. Oh, there's more! Tetchy, snappish, waspish, crotchety, crabby, querulous, rancorous, bilious, bitter, liverish. My God. They all describe you perfectly."

The words all rattled off Richard's tongue like a machine gun.

"What do you want me to do? Please. Please."

"You will resign from the Bench within this week. Cite health or family reasons, you will never sit again. You started all this!"

"But . . . But . . ."

"No ifs or buts about it. You deliberately brought a potato peeler to a gun fight, and you have lost. You had the cheek to accuse me of conduct unbecoming. I also warn you that my sex worker client believes she can find video footage of you right on top of a 15-year-old. I must get that video! So you have NO wriggle room. Neither did the 15-year-old girl, I might add. I expect to read of your resignation sometime next week."

There was dead silence. Richard waited a few seconds.

"Right. That's it. Now piss off the three of you!"

Melinda's and Wiremu's eyes were agog! You didn't get taught this at Law School.

Tane's face was beaming. This was his puny old mate at High School who he used to beat at Rugby in High School.

The three men slowly stood up and shuffled silently to the door. Richard waited until he heard the lift doors close. He checked the waiting room. No client was waiting. Janet had rescheduled them.

"Yo! Whew! You're a bastard!" said Janet.

"Nice one, Boss. The best bastard I know," added Willie.

Melinda chipped in with her contribution:

"Yea. Though he walks through the shadow of the valley of death he fears no evil for he is the biggest bastard in the valley!"

"But they were coming at me," said Richard. "They were going to use all their collective energy to get me struck off. I had no option."

"And did you notice the Judge's very small dickie? Like a pink jellybean." Of course, it was Melinda who made this contribution."

Janet admonished her, but with a laugh, "How do you notice these things? You are one evil lady."

"Yes," added Wiremu. "A real case of de minimis non curat lex. The law does not concern itself with trivialities."

Mary piped up, "Enough you two. Any chance this could backfire on you, Richard?"

"Only if they each want to go to prison, get struck off and have their reputations ruined for the rest of their lives. Fat chance."

"Champagne. Melinda, will you do the honours?"

She scuttled off grinning to herself. They did not teach such tactics at Law School.

"Now. What's the schedule for the next week?" Richard was back to work.

CHAPTER FIVETEEN

At home that evening, Richard and Mary were having a drink in front of the fire.

"Holy bananas. I can't say you are not interesting to live with. How do you maintain the pace?"

"You identify the problem and then work out the most effective way to solve it. If you have doubts, then don't act. Prepare, prepare, and prepare again!"

"You were pretty impressive."

"But those three were coming at me with hand grenades and I had to go nuclear. It was either their careers or mine!"

"Don't get me wrong. I'm very proud of you."

The next day, Saturday again, and Richard, Mary and the children were on the shores of the Shotover River and climbed into the famed jet boat ride. Off they went, everyone squealing with delight along with six tourists.

Another weekend. The kids really seemed to be enjoying themselves.

"And I don't even have to go to the office for two days. Far better than Auckland. I'm starting to feel relaxed. Where will we eat tonight?"

"Thai! Thai! Thai!"

"Thai it is. As long as you don't poo your pants."

"Just like Judge Christie," laughed Mary.

❧

It was once again a beautiful early morning in the Queenstown Gardens. The trees soared into the sky like rocket ships and an early Summer was well in the air.

36-year-old Nurse, Miriam Whiting, walked her beautiful, caramel-coloured 18-month-old German shorthaired pointer called Blaze through the luxuriant gardens.

She threw his ball, patted and hugged the dog from time to time and talked to it.

"Fetch! Good boy."

Miriam was happy in her life. She was a dedicated nurse, run off her feet in the local emergency clinic and had a steady and loving relationship with her partner, Josh.

Blaze ran into the distance near a tree, disappeared from sight, and Miriam was horrified to hear a pain-filled series of yelps from her beloved dog.

"What the heck?"

She suddenly spotted three young people obviously still boozed up from the night before. There were two young men and a young woman, obviously all up to no good. They appeared to be letting off fireworks and were all drinking from large bottles of beer. Miriam saw one young man throw an empty bottle at Blaze. It hit her beloved pet on the head, and he yelped in pain. y

Then the woman lit a bundle of firecrackers and threw them at the dog.

"Hey! Stop it!" screamed out Miriam.

"Shut up, you mangy dog. Stop that," spat out one yob.

The slaggy woman kicked Blaze. One kick connected. Blaze collapsed, yelping again with pain.

"Leave him alone. Can't you see he's injured?" yelled Miriam.

"Get stuffed, lady!" snarled the other yob.

He pulled a Roman candle firework out of his pocket, lit the fuse and as it started to fizz and belch red-hot pockets of fire out the end, he pointed it at Blaze. The dog squealed with terror. The fireballs hit his belly, badly burning his skin and pelt. He did not stop yelping this time. Tears rolled down Miriam's cheeks.

The other man started kicking Blaze in the head as the poor dog rolled semi-conscious on the ground.

"Shut the fuck up!"

"Stop it. Don't! Please!"

But the young man didn't stop. Blaze looked as if he was about to expire.

Miriam looked round desperately to find help.

Nobody was in sight. She suddenly spied a rose garden with a dozen rose plants all secured by metal stakes.

She grabbed one stake and wrenched it from the ground, like King Arthur extracting Excalibur's sword from deep in the stone in the Bosnian lake. Holding it at arm's length she ran towards Gavin and with all her strength rammed it into his stomach area. It appeared to pierce right through and out the other side. Gavin collapsed to the ground.

The other two saw the deplorable sight and took off like frightened rabbits as Miriam pursued them. She then retreated to Blaze and crouched over him. He looked dead. But she then spotted a flicker of life.

The police arrived and several citizens rushed from houses across the road. An ambulance siren could be heard approaching.

An elderly woman came out of her front door,.

"I saw it all. That young man deserved what he got. What he was doing was awful!"

A constable spoke up, "I'll get the dog down to the vet at once. He's breathing. Ma'am. You better come with us."

Miriam was distraught and in tears.

"I was just defending myself and my dog."

The Police put Miriam in a patrol car and sped off.

Mary seemed to have a regular diet of domestic abuse clients. It was legal aid, low-paying work, unless it was farmed efficiently. This meant having all the forms and procedures down to a fine art and time spent very well managed. She estimated she could bring in more than $600,000 per year for a well-run family law practice, with time left to develop other legal work.

Mary loved the hands-on opportunity to try and bring about immediate and positive changes in relationships. This morning, she was interviewing a plumber and his wife, each charged with common assault on each other. The couple were holding hands! Selma Parton was aged 38, plump and rather common-looking. Her husband Trevor Parton looked a little older. He sported tattooed "boob dots" on his cheeks, signifying that he had been to Borstal when he was much younger.

He had clearly suffered a bad burn on his face.

"What on earth happened?" Mary asked Selma. "The police summary of allegations says that you poured a very hot cup of coffee over his head. As you can see, he's pretty badly burned."

"Well, he was needling me and just before I did that, he hurled a cheese sandwich at me. We both ended up wrestling on the ground throwing punches. Very few landed."

Trevor spoke up, "The neighbours called the cops. Each of us is charged with assault."

"Have the police considered diversion?"

"We've done it before. The cops said not this time."

"What do you want me to do?"

"We want someone to speak for us in Court and see if you can get us off, or perhaps be left without a conviction."

Mary thought carefully and took some notes.

"If we start this, we must do a really good job. The Court will not just be interested in hearing the word "Sorry." We should spend some money on a counsellor to get a good report to bring to the Judge. I will need some statements from a couple of close family members."

"What will it all cost?

"Legal Aid?"

"Probably not. We have some savings from a modest inheritance."

"OK then. $7500 for me plus GST. Probably $1000 for the Counsellor's report. And my plan is to go all out for a discharge without conviction. But if we get it, you won't get another chance."

"OK. Let's go for it"

"All right then. I'll choose the counsellor and he or she will ring you within a day or two. But get me your detailed four or five-page statement by tomorrow, setting out the background to your relationship. I'll explain all the facts to the counsellor. We will get together again once next week and a couple of days before the court date and have another detailed talk."

Mary ushered Trevor and Selma out to the lift.

In Melinda's office, the galloping goblin was in the middle of interviewing a young woman, Maria Pender. Melinda's hair was pink today. Maria had just been laid off by her employer. She was 19 and had sought the job in the small local 4-Square store as a chance to get experience in retail.

"I didn't want to work in the shop all my life, but this was a good chance to get some experience and I was going to save like mad for a couple of years."

"Were you told how long the job might last?"

"Jack, the manager, told me the job would be long-term.

"But then only yesterday he gave me a short letter saying that my employment would finish one week on Friday. He said something about a 90-day period."

"Did you have the written employment agreement?"

"Yes. Here it is."

Melinda scrolled through it.

"Yes. Here it is. It's the standard clause which allows an employer not to renew any employment arrangement within the first 90 days. In other words, it's a termination for no reason whatsoever. But it's lawful."

"But my work was perfect. I think he just wanted to employ his niece in my position. That's what happened."

"That's very unfair. But he has the right to terminate within the first 90 days if it's a small business. Under 19 employees."

Maria then added something which Melinda pounced upon.

"Do you know the boss also tried to hit on me? A few days before I was terminated, he pushed me up against a wall in the chiller next to the stacked-up lamb and beef and said, "How would you like a bit of meat in you." I pushed him away and called him a "dirty old man", but he managed to draw his hand over my crotch. I just about spewed."

"Holy Hell! That's a wholly different matter! You've just turned a potentially straightforward lawful termination into a serious unjustified constructive dismissal. You'll be entitled to a minimum of three months' net wages, probably most of my fee paid, plus possibly as much as $25,000, maybe more, for general compensation. And that would surely help you?"

"I had no idea. I decided it was part of growing up."

"Do we have any witness to the indecent assault?"

"Yes. A good friend and a fellow workmate came in just as he was touching me up. She saw him trying to put his hands down my pants and she heard me protesting. She'll be a good witness."

"OK then. Here's what we do. I'll start with the letter seeking six months loss of wages and $45,000 general compensation plus costs. I'll give them three days to respond. If the matter doesn't settle, then we will go to the Employment Authority or the Human Rights Commission and probably refuse to attend mediation along the way. Mediation is usual but I say not for a case like this."

"I'll leave it to you."

"I might just say to his lawyer, "One grope. No hope. Two gropes. Your client's a dope." Short and snappy. You must share pain this with someone. Do you have a good support network?"

"A great mum and auntie and some very good friends."

"Good. You drop in here anytime you want to. I would like to see you every week if possible. I will be on your case every day. Please get the witness to come and see me tomorrow. I'll get a written statement from her."

❧

Back in his office, Richard opened a letter and whooped with delight. It was from the stock firm that purchased Joppy's cattle. He picked up the internal telephone to Melinda.

"Melinda. Can you pop in please?"

Melinda opened the door and came in.

"Yes, Boss."

"We've won for Joppy! Well, they want to cut my costs figure and they don't want to pay interest at 7% interest for two years. But it's still a win/win! Joppy will be over the moon and our firm benefits greatly! We may get over three hundred thousand dollars!"

"Nice one! But we should still pursue the interest. I worked it out at \$36,662.50 per year. That's almost \$75,000 for the two years."

"I like your style. Joppy will make the final decision, but I'll give him a ring and see if they will settle for one year. Wait just a moment."

Richard picked up the telephone and dialled the lawyers for the stock firm.

"Good morning. Mr Parkinson please. Yes. Richard Locksley here. Thanks for your letter. We can still settle but not for your figure. Anyone can sympathise with your client stock firm, but the law is quite clear. You said you don't want to pay interest. But my client will get interest. You have cut my claim for costs down from \$30,000 to \$25,000. But we can settle this. I will voluntarily reduce the costs claimed by the \$5,000 to your figure of \$25,000 but your client must pay one year's interest so that will make total claim of $587,250 but rounded up to $600,000 plus GST on $300,000."

There was obviously a pause at the other end of the phone. "I'm just taking some notes here", said the other lawyer.

"OK. We have a deal. The claim plus $40,000 GST plus one year's interest at 7% rounded up. Please send a signed settlement Agreement today with details of your trust account."

Richard flashed the thumbs up sign to Melinda.

"Yes. Thank you. Thank you for settling this matter with no acrimony. Bye."

Richard hung up.

"Well done! Can you give me a few minutes assistance on my smacking case?"

"Certainly! Give me five minutes to ring Joppy and then pop back in." We get $300,000 plus GST. Joppy gets $300,000. And he will be a very pleased client.

Melinda left, and Richard picked up the telephone and rang Joppy.

"Joppy! Is that you mate? Ritchie Locksley here. I've done a deal with the stock firm. It's almost 100% of what I asked for but to get the rest it might take a year of Court work and maybe we would not get the full interest. But I can get a year's interest totalling $37,000 which comes rounded up to $600,000 and $40,000 in GST for my bill. I demanded that they round it up to $640,000 We simply split the $600,000 amount equally. By the end of the week, I can deposit $300,000 into your bank account. Happy?"

"Too right! You bloody beauty. I never thought I'd get anything."

"If you ever come across Sparky, before you kneecap him, you still have a claim against him probably for an extra $100,000. But only if he is obviously loaded and owns property.

"I'll keep that in mind, but I might prefer death to money!"

"I'll send you out a formal bill as agreed but it will be a one-liner. It will simply say "My costs for knowing what to do and doing it." OK by you? We still must settle with the car firm for the 4WD. There's another $55,000 there probably, but I have decided you can have all of that. Melinda is tidying that up as we speak. Happy?"

"Jeez! Absolutely. Now. About that helicopter trip? OK for you Friday?"

"That'll be great!"

"OK. Meet me at the Rural Helicopters hanger at the airport at 10.00 am on Friday. Great work again. Thanks so much. I'm rapt!"

"See you Friday."

Richard called Janet in.

"Janet. I've settled the Joppy Watson case. Do a one-liner bill please - "My costs for knowing what to do and doing it" for $300,000 plus GST. I get half the recovery rate plus the full costs agreed. The full figure will be paid into the trust account in a few days. At the same time, send the bill and a formal trust account statement and the balance of the same amount to Joppy. He gets a neat $300,000. Then give me the file and remind me to place it in very tidy order, because it may ultimately be audited."

"Will do. Nice job."

"I must run. I have to represent the chief court reporter before the Residential Tenancies Tribunal. I'll be back in about two hours."

He called out to Melinda as he passed her office.

"Melinda, I'm sorry but your smacking case will have to wait."

No probs. And I'll follow up on the 4WD recovery using your letters as templates."

CHAPTER SIXTEEN

The adjudicator, Helen Helm, sat at the head of the table at the head of the Residential Tenancies Tribunal hearing room. Richard sat beside his client, Jenny Stockton, sat on one side of the table and the two rather rough-looking snowboarders sat on the other side. They were unrepresented. The adjudicator started the proceedings.

"The first exercise is to gather the evidence together. I take it the tenants have read the complaints and you have had advance notice of the estimate of the damage which looks pretty accurate to me?"

"Yeah," the two somewhat crestfallen former tenants replied.

"One thing at a time then. You understood it was a genuine fixed term three-month rental period?"

"We didn't read that."

"But Mrs Stockton has said she specifically explained to you both before you signed the Agreement."

"I guess she did. I can't remember."

"Then you must realise that every time she specifically says something happened and you say, "We can't remember," it's more likely I'm going to accept what she said happened."

"Yeah. Suppose so."

"Now, what about these dogs?"

"We didn't think she would really mind."

"But the Agreement specifically said she would mind."

The tenants shrugged but didn't say anything.

"Well, there is evidence here that you had at least four parties with over 90 people and each party was visited by the police after complaints from neighbours. That activity was specifically prohibited by the Agreement. Damage was caused."

"People just turned up."

Mrs Helm turned to Richard.

"Mr Locksley. I think it's time for you to take over."
Richard, the uber cross-examiner, took over.

"Did the landlord give you several Notices to Remedy" and you did not action any of them?"

"No."

"You said to the police on the night of one of the parties, and the police said so in their report, that both of you told everyone in two named bars in the Mall that the party was on. The police also said that they asked at least 30 people at the party who had invited them, and they all said you two. Now look at me! You're just lying about saying that people just turned up, aren't you!"

There was no reply.

"Well unless you have a sensible answer, I am confident this adjudicator will believe the police over you. Did you tell people at the bars that the party was on?"

"We may have mentioned it."

"Stop prevaricating. Did you or did you not tell the whole bar there was a party at this house?"

"Yeah."

"And what about these other tenants? You allowed them to live there?"

"They didn't do any harm."

"But extra tenants put more stress on rental property. And in this case significant damage was done. The toilet bowl was smashed in three places. Wooden parts of the house were torn apart and thrown on the fire. The carpet is burnt. I particularly refer to the architraves in the back two rooms."

"We're sorry about that."

"Sorry is not enough. You're only sorry because you've been caught. Is there anything you want to say today to suggest that Mrs Stockton is not telling the truth in her complaints?"

"Not really. We just can't afford to pay."

"That remains to be seen."

The Adjudicator took over.

"I've heard enough. Is there anything else that you as the tenants want to say?"

"No."

"I will give a brief oral decision now, which will be typed up, signed and available to the parties by 3 p.m.

She took a moment to check her papers then delivered her decision.

"The tenants have attended today, but effectively place no factual defence before this Tribunal. They simply plead hardship and poverty. Those factors are not defences but, in any event, I reject them as being factually incorrect. They are in employment. They spend their time snowboarding and they both own a motor vehicle. The orders are therefore as follows:

- A warrant shall be issued for immediate possession.
- The tenants will pay all outstanding rent down to and including 30 August.
- The tenants will pay for all the damage as claimed.
- The tenants will pay for $200 per week for the extra tenants each for a period of 10 weeks.
- The tenants shall therefore be liable to pay the landlord the total sum of $41,000.
- In this rare case, costs will be added to the above figure of $4000.

"That is all. Mr Locksley, the Tribunal will be here for another three hours so I will get my brief oral judgment typed up and sealed and available for picking up shortly after the lunch break. Any warrant as you know has to be actioned through the District Court."

"I thank the Tribunal," responded Richard.

The adjudicator rose and left the room. The tenants looked disgruntled, and one thumped the table very hard with a closed fist. They left the room muttering threats.

Richard and Jenny discussed the result. She was most happy.

"Great result."

"Now, I will get the order for the warrant typed up immediately and sealed. The police may not be able to execute this afternoon, but I'll do my best. Did you carry out the research on the two cars owned by the tenants?"

"Omigosh, yes. This is exciting. Here are photographs of the cars which I took secretly yesterday. Here is a search of the securities register showing that they are not encumbered. And the securities office provides estimates of values which they get off TradeMe. Each car is worth about $25,000."

"We'll seize both. All the more reason for speed. The bailiff of the Court usually takes a little longer, but my office will get on to the paperwork straightaway. I'll seek emergency action. I'll give you a ring before the close of play today. Thanks for instructing me."

"Well worth it. I am really pleased. Thank you so much."

❧

Richard walked into Melinda's office.

"Melinda. We won at the Residential Tenancies Tribunal. Easy pickings. As discussed yesterday could you please get the warrant for immediate possession and the warrant to seize and sell the two motor vehicles? Here's the folder. You will see the information our client gleaned from the securities register. Urgency required."

"I'm on to it. I've done these before. I'll bully the police into getting on with the job later in the afternoon if we can get the Court staff off their bums to get the document sealed."

Richard added, "I'd be grateful if you and Mrs Stockton could accompany the police and she can have a quick inspection just in case some spite damage has been carried out at the last minute. If so, she can make the criminal complaint immediately and the police will likely arrest the tenants and that gives us an easier job to seize their cars."

"AOK. I'll keep in close contact with you. Botty Potty. Oops. Sorry 'bout that, corporal."

"Ye Gods! Spare me! Exciting day, kiddo?"

Later on that afternoon, Richard was sitting in his office interviewing four Queenstown prostitutes. Serena, Polly, Sunset and Tessie. They were dressed up like four pretty hens.

"What can I do for you ladies?"

Serena opened up first. "We want to retain this firm, and you particularly, for emergency callout work. Our girls up in Auckland highly recommended you."

"We don't have many serious issues, but we probably need legal advice at least once a week," Sunset added.

"We need Trespass Act Notices served on some unruly clients at least a couple of times a month."

And finally, Tessie, "We also need help with our lease. The landlord's a creep. He wants a free shag for every request we make and is now trying to force us to sign a 20-year lease. We need someone gutsy to fight for us."

"Do you currently have a lawyer?"

"He died a month ago. Anyway, he was plenty hopeless."

"OK. I'm happy to help. Do you have the lease papers there? And a letter from him trying to alter the terms of the lease. And do you have any leverage? For example, do you have the possibility, even a faint one, of relocating?"

"Actually, we do. We don't want to, but I see what you mean by leverage. We just want two plus two plus two like we have always had."

"All right. First things first. Don't get in touch with this dude. Let me do that."

"How much will this cost? The last lawyer charged us $7500 for renegotiating the lease."

"It'll be nothing like that. Under half. I'll tell you what I would like though. Simple information from time to time. Running a successful law practice means keeping tabs on everything that goes on in the town like this. I keep what I call a War Chest of information."

"Like our Uglies' Register. I like your style."

"I don't have to use it very often but it's still very useful to have."

"No problems. You don't mind if we just ring you up with this information?"

"Perfectly OK. But supporting written evidence is even better. Perhaps a photo of the local headmaster tied up in bondage gear? Just joking."

"No problem."

"Re-negotiating your lease. How long is it since you had a rent increase?"

"Only late last year. But he's trying it again. It's currently $1200 per week."

"I'll get back to you tomorrow or the day after if he is not available. But I'll knock his door down if necessary. Nice to meet you all."

Richard accompanied them to the lift. Janet's eyebrows were raised in amusement.

"And that's all they do for a living? Really? All day? Wow!"

"I suppose a blow job's better than no job." Melinda couldn't help herself.

"You'll go straight to hell, young lady! Never say that in the High Court."

"Really? Why not?"

They laughed. Richard came out of his office.

"What have I missed?"

"Just ladies' talk, Mr Locksley."

"Here's the current lease for the girls at the parlour. You wanted a bit of commercial work. Could you bring it up to date please? – 2 plus 2 plus 2. Put our style on it. We want clients to like our work. They spread the word. We'll fill in the amount when I've renegotiated."

His office telephone rang. He popped back into his office. Richard picked it up.

"It's the sergeant on the phone," said Janet. "I'll put him through."

"It's Tane again, Ritchie. Serious matter. We have a Miriam Whiting here and she's asking for you. Her dog was being badly molested by some scumbags in the Gardens this morning and she's going to be charged with assault with intent to do grievous bodily harm. Seems she picked up a garden stake and shoved it into the guts of one of them. He'll live. But only just."

"I'll be straight down."

Richard hung up and grabbed his satchel.

He called out to Melinda, "So sorry. Your smacking case will have to wait again. I have a serious GBH by a dog-loving lady and she's crying in the police station now. Janet. I may be a little longer than an hour. Please juggle the interviews."

Richard ran down to the police station where Sergeant Tane greeted him.

"She's through here in an interviewing room. Bail papers have been drawn up. No problems with her leaving when you're finished."

"Thanks, Tane."

The Sergeant led him to the interviewing room where Miriam sat very disheartened, shivering and with tears rolling down her cheeks.

"Miriam. Here's Mr Locksley. Richard, here's a photocopy of the police file including notes of what she said in the patrol car when we brought her to the station. Also, here's a copy of the video statement taken in this room half an hour ago. I'll bring in two coffees."

"Thanks, Sergeant. Nice to meet you, Miriam. I am here to help you, and you are not alone. I have been briefed on the case and we will still have plenty of time to talk but let's get you home where your best friend Betty is waiting, and I think your good friend Roy is there as well."

Miriam was still distraught but was starting to settle down.

"What can be done? I really injured him."

"Plenty can be done. There are some tricky legal issues, but my argument, based on experience, is that you can use reasonable force to prevent a serious crime being committed. In a nutshell, that's the defence. Now let's walk out now and I will drive you home and we will have a good talk at the weekend. But you must not be worried. There is plenty that can be done."

They walked through the office, bade Sergeant Fleming farewell and walked to Richard's car. He drove Miriam to her house high up on Queenstown Hill, where her two friends came out of the front door as Richard pulled up and parked.

"I'll see you at the weekend." He warned her,

"Don't speak to anyone about the facts, except your true friends here and swear them to silence."

She gave Richard a small wave and a smile before her friends gave her a hug and a kiss and took her inside.

CHAPTER SEVENTEEN

In the office later that afternoon, a staff meeting was underway. All the team were present.

"OK. Office meeting. Reports please," Richard began.

Wiremu took the lead.

"I've taken on nine new drink-driving and other traffic offences this week. Seven require limited licences. All are probably pleas of guilty, but some further research is necessary. There's at least $30,000 because three will be defended snd there are plenty of good contacts."

Melinda piped up. "Squeak. Plop. Oops. Sorry about that. Under control."

Willie patted her affectionately.

"I've got five civil cases from Willie's clients. A summary judgment application for over $100,000 so there's a $10,000 fee there. And a rather neat little application to remove the trees on the boundary with a neighbour. The neighbour planted them after our clients took possession of the property and they are now 30 feet tall and still growing and they block all the sun. We'll get an order getting them down. I quoted $10,000 plus GST and disbursements but they will get some coverage of that if we win. I think we will."

"Good stuff," said Richard.

Melinda continued, "I have also now reviewed all the other firms' commercial and conveyancing clients and they all want to stay with us. I think we might need an experienced legal executive soon."

"Excellent news from me," Mary added. "The link has really been established with the battered woman's support groups here, in Alexandra and in Wanaka and I'm setting up a very good email system and protocols which I think will allow us to respond with paperwork within half a day, provided one of us is on deck."

"I can handle the legal aid applications. I've ordered 500 application forms," said Janet. "I will keep fully up to date with legal aid procedures and rates. Legal aid will only work for us financially if we really farm it. I don't mean rort it. But we must be thoroughly organised because of the miserable cap on set amounts for set work."

"But we must develop the most concentrated systems to power through it without wasting time," Richard added a note of caution.

"You have to be really firm with the clients and tell them that a grant for only 8 hours does not mean that we can work two weeks on their file unpaid."

Mary then reported on the relationship property cases.

"I have now also put together a portfolio of over 40 relationship property cases. They come from all over the place. 16 in Wanaka alone. That means really good fees. I've arranged to write a series of articles about relationship property division in the local rags."

"Terrific. Let's keep the profile up. I might take up golf."

Melinda, looking her most impish, piped up again, "Golf is Flog spelt backwards, y'know. We see you have been consorting with prostitutes. We want you working. What have you got?"

"Willie has crammed my diary pretty full, and I seem to be picking up at least ten new clients a day by telephone. As far as I can see, there will not be one Court Day free for the next 12 months, just on clients we have in the office since we started. Is this practice sustainable? Definitely.

Now pay rates. Janet. Your salary increases by 20% as from next week. Willie and Melinda. I raised your salaries a bit when we arrived here. You are obviously on track each to bring on $450,000 annually. Of course, 50% of that is eaten up on overheads which is my headache. Anything above that gross amount and you get 20%. Is that an incentive?"

"Sure thing, Boss and Mrs Boss" said Melinda.

"But there's one other thing I want to discuss. Much of our work requires quick fire advice and action almost on the spot. I want to build up a perfect set of precedents for both forms and procedure. They must be accessible to all through our wall screens and computers. Case law. Documents. "How to" information. The lot. So each of you come up with, say, 10, within the next week and we will look at it. Willie, can you please work out the computer protocols on criminal matters."

"Mary, could you concentrate on domestic disputes please? Melinda, I will leave business and commercial to you, and I'll do High Court criminal and civil. Let me take one simple example. If I am briefed do an urgent limited licence application, I want to be able to find that on an alphabetical index and up will come the following ..."

Richard counted on his fingers...

    ✓ "The relevant part of the Act it is under.
    ✓ Relevant caselaw.
    ✓ Other numbered files of previous clients.
    ✓ Precedents for forms.
    ✓ A list of steps to take.
    ✓ All the law and practice.h

"This will help us enormously to service clients immediately."

"Will do," they all responded.

"And we all must be responsible for updating it regularly. Add case law. Add links to srticles. Add precedents."

The next morning Andrew and Judith Malcolm were being interviewed by Mary on a domestic/criminal matter. The couple were charged with the oddly worded offence of 'making an offensive document.' They had taken nude photos of their own children.

"Show me the photographs. These are your children aged six, ten and twelve? They are all nude and posing?"

"Yes," Judith Malcolm replied.

"And you took the photographs, Mr Malcolm?"

"Yes. My camera's not digital and I used old film and took it down to the Kodak store for developing. I understand what happened is that the manager of the shop developed the photographs and then contacted the police. We're now charged with making an offensive document. I'm not quite sure of the law, but the police officer told us we could go to prison."

"I'm going to get my husband in because I think he is probably the most experienced to handle this matter.

Just give me a minute and I will see if he's free."

In reception, Richard had just walked in from Court and Mary called to him, "Richard. Can you give me a few minutes with Mr and Mrs Malcolm, please?"

"Sure."

He followed Mary into her office.

"Mr and Mrs Malcolm, this is my husband, Richard. Richard, they have three lovely children and while out walking on a sunny day recently Mr Malcolm, in his wife's presence, took these photographs. They were developed at a local Kodak store and the manager referred them to the police. The police have now charged both with making offensive documents."

"Has anyone else seen these photographs?"

"No. In any event, they were simply going into the family photograph album."

"I don't think you have committed an offence. I'll research it a bit more but at this stage it cries out for a plea of not guilty."

"We've done that. Three weeks ago, the duty solicitor entered a not guilty plea on our behalf and the case is set for the end of next week. Can you help?"

"Certainly. Come back on Monday at 4 pm and we will have completed our research by then. A fully defended case will take a fair bit of work. It won't be more than $15,000, but it could be all of that."

"That's OK by us. We thought it would be about that."

"Fine. We'll see you on Monday. Mary, could you see these good people to the lift and then come back with Melinda please."

Once the clients had left, Mary and Melinda returned.

"Yes, Boss."

"Our clients took nude photographs of their children for their own personal use and inclusion in the family photograph album. No more. They are static, statue-like poses. I don't think an offence has been committed. Check the Act please and all the cases. In law, what is obscene? What is indecent?"

Melinda gave a cheeky grin, "Off the top of my head, Boss - Anything that gives the Judge an erection? Is that enough?"

Richard smiled painfully.

"I don't really think that's quite enough research. It may be a start. But a little more research please."

"Will do straight away."

"My God. You're going to be the death of Janet one of these days, my girl. And probably me."

"Rightio. 9 o'clock in the morning."

He walked away shaking his head and muttering,

"Anything that gives the Judge an erection? Anything that gives the Judge an erection? Ye Gods, that girl's a worry."

In Richard's office, Mr Brinsley had come back to see him.

"Bernie. So soon again. What can I do?"

"It's bloody embarrassing. I am a hypocrite. I ask most humbly if you will represent me."

"I don't pass judgement on clients. Certainly I will. What on earth has happened?"

"I'm up before the Law Society on a charge of conduct unbecoming. Luckily, it's only the Southland District Law Society based in Invercargill. It's a bit of a test case."

"I think I'm a bit of an expert in conduct unbecoming myself. But let's see what I can do. What's happened?"

"I suppose not to put too fine a point on it, I've been a bit of a shagger. My wife died 2 years ago, and I've settled down for 12 months but then I seem to be able to "put it around" more than I ever thought I could."

"You're a dark horse. The suspense is killing me. All consensual?"

"Without any doubt. But I went to a stag night do in an Invercargill Hotel.

Three strippers were hired for the night, and they turned out to be prostitutes as well."

"You're obviously building up to a crescendo. What did you do?"

"At some stage we were all a bit drunk, this girl did a couple of naughty things to me on the table in front of everyone and I ended up giving her one in front of everyone. It involved a rocking horse. But a barman told the Law Society, but not by way of a formal complaint. I promise you. I had never acted like that before. I was in the wrong place at the wrong time."

Richards showed his annoyance at the Law Society.

"So those sleaze bags themselves at the Law Society have become all pious again. Rightio. Happy to help. Looks like I'll have to open my War Chest again. You've seen what that can do."

"Christ yes! Don't tell me you've got more!"

"I'll need a second box soon. What paperwork have you got so far?"

"Here is all the material. It is set down for three weeks away. The charge simply reads, "Conduct unbecoming in relation to inappropriate sexual relations. I mean, when Woody Allen was asked if he thought sex was dirty his quick reply was, 'only when it's done right'."

Bernie laughed. The ice was broken between the two.

Richard read the law Society documents.

"Crikey. What the hell does that mean?"

"An accompanying statement of facts stated that I was involved in 'unacceptable sexual relations outside the sanctity of a normal relationship between a man and a woman.'

"That's appalling. Have I your permission to take the gloves right off? It's time to play dirty. We can run the orthodox defence that what you did does not actually fall into the category of conduct unbecoming. I think that's quite a strong defence in itself. But let's try and knock it for a six before we even get to a hearing."

"Go for it. What do you think you can do?"

"A little bullying-blackmail, hypocrisy-hollering and shame-stirring first. You can call it the Harper Valley PTA defence. I've used it before."

"I hope it works this time," said Bernie looking very pale around the gills.

"Keep me up with any further developments. But leave it in my hands for a few days. Get on with your life and your practice and I will make this go away."

Richard shook Bernie's hand and showed him into the reception area.

❧

Two days later, The Queenstown District Court was open for business again. Melinda was about to defend Hetty Jones in relation to the smacking case and the charge of assault. Judge Bradshaw was presiding.

"Now. The next case. A prosecution for common assault. Is Hetty Jones here?"

"Yes Sir. I appear."

Hetty walked to the dock and remained standing.

"You may be seated in the dock."

Sergeant Murray for the prosecution stood up.

"I appear for the police, Your Honour. One witness to call. Just the social worker."

The social worker's evidence began. Moira Tamati was 35 years old with a rather hard face. It went with the stress of the job. Overworked. Undervalued. Underpaid.

Her evidence unfolded.

"... I obviously arrived at a very stressful time and went through the front door unannounced. I saw the defendant pushing and then pulling her four-year-old son into his bedroom. I regarded her force as excessive. I ascertained that shortly before this the defendant had smacked the child. The lad was kicking and screaming. I immediately took him into welfare custody. This complaint is based on the force the mother used and the fact of smacking."

"Just answer any questions please."

Melinda stood up. In the serious setting, Melinda was almost as good as Richard. She did not dance on the tables here. She just needed to keep her Tourettes under control. She started her line of questioning.

"Is it correct that you simply uplifted the boy and took him into your custody and left the house?"

"Yes. I didn't want an unpleasant scene to interrupt."

"Now let us get this clear. You did not ask my client for any explanation at the time?"

"No. I didn't feel I had the time. She did run up to me telling me something about a cat and that the child had sworn at her?"

"And when you took the wee lad away, he was kicking, screaming and crying out for his mother?"

"Yes. It was most unfortunate."

"But you had to lay your own hands on him and pull him by the wrists and the waist?"

"Yes."

"The force you used was almost identical force you saw my client apply to her son."

"Probably. But I have the lawful authority to physically place the child in my custody. She does not."

"Now I want you to be very fair and accurate when you answer this question and I remind you that you are under oath. The red marks you observed on the lad's wrists at the doctors could have been because of your force just as much as a result of my client's force?"

"Do I have to answer that?"

"I think you do, if it is part of the case against Mrs Jones that the redness was caused by her," replied the Judge.

"I'm unsure about that matter," Moira replied.

"I will call evidence in this case. I will call my client as a witness. She will say that her four-year-old son had just stabbed the family cat with a pair of scissors and was about to do so again. And that he was then acting very dangerously towards her with the scissors. Do you have any evidence to suggest that such events did not happen?"

"No, I do not."

"And if her evidence is that she was taking him to a timeout session in his bedroom, do you have any evidence to suggest that this was not the case?"

"I accept that was the case."

"And do you accept that the childcare literature in this country, and in your own Ministry for Vulnerable Children toolkit, recommends that the use of the "timeout" break is an acceptable and worthwhile procedure as a disciplinary tool for parents."

"Yes, I do."

"Finally, do you confirm on this day you were visiting my client simply to ask her to report on any potential child abuse that she may have seen in respect of an unrelated family two doors down the road?"

"That is correct."

"At the same time, could you confirm that your department has neither received nor actioned any complaint against my client relating to her two children – ever!"

"I do."

Melinda sat down.

"Yes, Miss McKenzie," said the Judge asking for details of her defence.

"My client has instructed me she wants to give evidence in this case. For my part, I submit that I have a strong foundation to argue that the charge should be dismissed now, but my client does not wish to be seen to be beating this allegation on some technicality. I wish to call her to give her evidence as to what happened and that I will refer you particularly to section 59 of our Crimes Act 1961. Perhaps I can leave those legal submissions till the end with your leave?"

"Certainly.

"Mrs Jones, could you transfer over to the witness box please."

Hetty crossed the Court to the other side and stood in the witness box. The court clerk put a Bible in her hand.

"Do you swear that the evidence you are about to give shall be the truth, the whole truth and nothing but the truth?"

"I do."

"Mrs Jones. Will you please tell this Court in your own words what happened in the cat incident and describe your actions, down to the time that the social worker took wee Paul away."

"I think it was the most upsetting day of my life. Paulie seemed to be full of hyperactivity that day like I'd never seen before. I understand there had been some bullying towards him at day-care, but I thought that it all been sorted out. After day-care, he started teasing our cat. He grabbed a pair of scissors and first tried to cut Fluffy's tail off."

"What then happened?"

"I yelled at him more out of fright. I was not abusive, but I told him to stop it. But he then actually stabbed the cat and a spurt of blood trickled from her wee paw. I told him, "Right! It's timeout until teatime. That was only an hour away. He looked me in the eye and said, "Get fucked, Mummy." I had never heard him say that before and he said it in an odd way which made me think he was mimicking something he had heard someone else say. He then swung the scissors at me in an aggressive manner."

"So what did you do?"

"I put both my hands firmly on his shoulders and started to push him gently towards his room. He twisted and kicked, and I had to grab his hands because I suddenly realised he still held the scissors. I was only about a couple of metres from his bedroom, and I managed to take the scissors and pull him into the bedroom. I do not think I used excessive force."

"What happened then?"

"The social worker barged in, yelling at me and grabbed Paul very hard and dragged him the other way out the door. It was a horrible incident. She said loudly -

"I'm laying a complaint with the police about you assaulting your son and I'm taking your son with me."

She put my son in her car, so I got into my car and followed her."

"Where did she go?"

"She went to the Medical Centre first and I followed her in and then the police arrived. Luckily, the doctor allowed me to come into the examination room with the social worker and the police waited outside. After the examination, the doctor, who luckily was also my own doctor, and the police and the social worker all had a conversation without me present. Then they came and told me I could take Paul home. I was very relieved."

"What happened next?"

"I heard nothing more from anyone. Not even a visit from the Department. Then three weeks later, quite out of the blue, a cop came to my home and served me with the summons for this assault case. Then I saw you."

"Thank you. Please answer any questions." The prosecutor Sergeant stood up.

"In view of the concessions made by the social worker I do not wish to call any other evidence. This case will become a matter of legal submissions."

"What are your submissions, Miss McKenzie. I can anticipate what you may say. I think I am probably with you."

"The law is all in section 59. I wish to read it aloud."

The Judge flicked open his laptop. "Just give me a minute to flash it up on my computer. Right. Yes, here it is."

Melinda continued her submissions.

"Ten years ago, you could smack your child for corrective purposes provided the force was reasonable. That is no longer the case. But there is not an absolute prohibition on the use of force on a child. Section 59 gives four examples when you can use reasonable force."

She counted on her fingers – a technique learned from Richard.

1. "To prevent or minimise harm to the child or another person. That would apply here as the child, however young, was effectively threatening his mother with the scirrors. The evidence on that point is uncotradicted by the prosecution.

2. To prevent conduct that amounts to a criminal offence. Cruelty to an animal is a

criminal offence. So that justification does apply here.

3. To prevent offensive or disruptive behaviour. Much the same thing. It applies here.

4. To perform the normal daily tasks that are incidental to good care and parenting. In light of the clear fact that timeout sanctions are recommended by the Ministry for Vulnerable Children means that this justification also applies."

"So all four apply. In her own evidence, my client has also raised the distinct possibility of self-defence in relation to the child still holding and being aggressive with the scissors. That is a fifth defence.
The force used simply could not be described as unreasonable. It is an act performed by thousands of parents every day in this country."
The Judge appeared to be nodding in agreement.
"But subsection 4 also raises an interesting concept. It affirms that the police have the discretion not to prosecute complaints when the offence is so inconsequential that there is no public interest in proceeding with a prosecution. In a defended case such as this I strongly submit that this Court cannot ignore the discretion given to the police." Melinda continued,
"Where is the public interest served if the result is that no parent can use any force whatsoever to place a child in Time Out?"
The Judge gave another a small nod in support.
"For those reasons, I submit that this prosecution cannot succeed and that my client can prove her defences. Or put more correctly, she has clearly raised sufficient evidence of those defences which the prosecution cannot disprove."

Melinda sat down.

"Thank you, Miss McKenzie. Your submissions are well put and hit the mark. I agree. I agree. I find that the force used was no more than reasonable to prevent further injury to the cat, defend herself and to attempt to place the child in a time out room."

"It's a good argument about the police discretion but I am not certain I can place much weight on that. This Court cannot be used to review the discretion of the police in this case. However, I do recognise that Parliament recognised that some force was justifiable when applied to a child and I do take that expression of intent into account."

"The charge is dismissed. The defendant may leave the dock."

"May it please the Court," said Melinda with the customary small bow.

Outside the Court, Hetty was crying tears of joy, and her Mum was there with young Paul, and they were all re-united.

"Thank you so much," she hugged Melinda.

"Spend the afternoon with your son and your Mum. Here's $50. My shout for a coffee and an icecream and a visit to the $2 shop for the wee fella. All the very best for the future."

Melinda returned to the office. She had shown herself yet again to be a mature and talented lawyer. But it was the hair colour that really stood her apart.

❧

The next morning at Queenstown Airport, high country farmer Joppy Watson and Richard were waiting for their helicopter pilot. He emerged from the hanger and strode towards them. Shem Sunderland was one of the most experienced helicopter pilots in the southern part of New Zealand. He was in his early 50s.

"Rightio, Joppy. The usual annual trip?"

"Yeah. A couple of hours should do it. This here is my lawyer, Ritchie Locksley. He's coming along for the ride. Churn his stomach up a bit if you can."

"Nice to meet you," Shem greeted them.

"OK. All aboard."

The Squirrel helicopter had effectively two seats in the front next to the pilot. Joppy climbed into the middle seat and Richard took his place in the window seat. The engine wound up into life and the turbines gently whined. In a minute, they were up, up and away heading straight down the Kingston Arm of Lake Wakatipu heading for the first of Joppy's farms. It took them only 15 minutes flying time to reach the northern tip of the farm and they spent 30 gut churning minutes flying around the perimeter checking up valleys and in gullies.

"I'm looking for land movement and slips in the main. You never know when you should move stock."

They flew over almost all the farm, occasionally touching down to inspect a musterer's hut. Outside one of the huts, Joppy broke out a couple of bottles of beer although the pilot did not have a drop.

"Beautiful bit of country, eh boy?"

"Absolutely staggering. How many sheep on this run?"

"20,000 plus. They keep having lambs."

They both took a swig of beer. Shem shut down the engine.

"I've got another wee job, Ritchie. I'm going to be purchasing quite a large farm up in the Mackenzie Country near Lake Tekapo. It's a beauty piece of land and I think I can get another 20,000 stock on it. I think I'd like that Melinda girl to work on the legals, but with you having a pretty close oversight. I'm just a bloody farmer. You leave the stock to me. I just want the paperwork done cleanly and correctly and I'll pay well."

"There's obviously the conveyancing to do. What else?"

"I've settled on a price. $6,700,000. I'll drop in the papers tomorrow, but I'll need the basic agreement for sale and purchase, agreement for stock and plant purchase and there are some tricky little water rights and mining rights which are being transferred as well. Plus 15,000 head of stock."

"Do you need a mortgage?"

"Nah! Always pay cash. Although this time the price is $6.7 million. I'll have to break an investment."

"May I ask, is there a Mrs Joppy?"

"Yeah. And four little Joppys. You don't see them much."

"Have you got a will and a couple of family trusts?"

"Nah! I'd better have a basketful of them too."

"Right you are. I'll get some drafts drawn up. Can you come in tomorrow? You'll need an hour or so with me and then probably a couple of hours with Melinda. Look, I'll give Melinda a ring now and book you in for, say, 10.00 in the morning?"

"Fine by me. I like your style."

Richard stood on a small plateau on the Eyre Mountain range near Kingston with the whole world at his feet and spread out before him.

He held a bottle of beer in one hand and a cell phone in the other ringing Melinda. Joppy and Shem stood by the helicopter. Joppy came closer to Richard while Richard spoke.

"All OK. 10.00 in the morning. She'll turn off the phone, shut the door and take a truckload of information from you. You make sure you draw up a timetable for all of this. Possession dates. The names and contact details of all relevant people. All you need to do is make sure your investment can be released a couple of days before settlement date. Sometimes these jobs run like clockwork. Sometimes we encounter a lot of crap. Vendors can be tricky sods."

"Been there, done that. The bastards say, "Oh, did I not mention GST?" and "Oh, the forestry block is not included. Bastards!"

"We'll sort it all out. Right. Let's get going."

"On the way back we'll touchdown for you at the top of the Remarkables. Amazing views."

"This place is just like it was about 125 years ago. About 1895 and after." The image stuck in Richard's mind.

From Kingston, Shem piloted the helicopter down the lake then steadily up the razorback of the Remarkables Mountain Range and brought it to a hover on the toppermost landing area overlooking the whole lake and Queenstown airport 4000 feet below.

Suddenly, the chopper lurched and shook and started to spin to the right. It coughed and spluttered and clanked. Some black smoke poured out of the engine area.

"Look out! I'll have to put on some more power. Ritchie! You unbuckle quickly and get ready to jump out. Follow him if you can, Joppy. Mayday! Mayday! Queenstown Control. Mechanical failure on top of the Remarkables. Discharging two passengers. Send help and a medic!"

Queenstown tower - "Roger that!"

Richard jumped, followed quickly by Joppy. Richard's left leg landed heavily on a rock, and he felt and heard his knee and ankle twist badly.

"Friggin' heck! That hurt."

Richard blacked out. Joppy was safe and the helicopter hovered and shook for 10 seconds then made a bumpy landing, belching black smoke. But Shem seemed to have it under control and quickly shut down the engine.

☙

A few hours later Richard was in Frankton Hospital, luckily situated at the bottom of the Remarkables. Mary's Mum had been in the same Hospital. It was 6.00 pm. Richard woke up feeling more than a little groggy. Mary was holding his hand.

"Oh, thank God. How on earth are you?"

"Fine. Just groggy. But my knee hurts like hell."

"You've badly bent it. The doctor was worried about concussion, but some tests show that there was nothing to worry about. The medic up the mountain punched you full of morphine and that's why you've been sleeping."

At that stage, the children came in with Grandma.

"Dad! You're OK! We were really worried."

"How are you, Dad?"

"Bloody sore. But the doctor may give me some more very special medicine. You look like Madonna, Grandma."

Grandma was in fine character. "Well, you look like shit!"

Dr Sam Meldrum came in.

"Ah! Back from the 19th Century, I see. You were prattling on about 1895. Here, I'll give you another shot of morphine. But it will put you back to sleep. The concussion tests are very good. We'll keep you in overnight, but you can be discharged in the morning if everything is still good."

The morphine obviously kicked in. Mary and the children said goodbye and Grandma gave Richard a dainty wave.

As they left, Richard slipped into a very comfortable medium. The room started to spin slowly at first, then faster and faster and he saw the numbers of the decades whirl around - 2018, 1998, 1970, 1940, 1920, 1900, 1897, and stopped at 1895 – 125 years earlier. He fell into a deep and comfortable sleep. But he had obviously been hallucinating.

CHAPTER EIGHTEEN

The year was 1895 in the Queenstown Magistrate's Court. A Court sat here at regular intervals. Mr Frederick Joseph Burgess was the Stipendiary Magistrate and the Mining Warden. Richard was interviewing clients outside. Horses and drays clip-clopped up and down the street. A Cobb & Co wagon gingerly rolled down the lower part of Stanley Street. Clients, generally rather lowlife-looking labourers, milled around the door.

The General Merchants and the market verandas smelled of cheese, figs, dates, oranges, raspberries, tea and other produce. Open fire braziers provided warm places to stand and gossip or sell pigs and eat chestnuts roasted over manuka fires. Smoke curled into the air. A gypsy-looking couple were playing a violin and an accordion.

Richard read the court list nailed on to the interior door of the Court Room. It set out the criminal and civil cases for the day.

MAGISTRATES COURT SITTING
Thursday, 29 August 1895

Criminal Cases
Police v. Joshua James Black
Police v. Jeremiah Jenkins
Police v. David Henry Templeton
Police v. Thomasina Lucy Dorset
Police v. Samuel Saul Dobson
Police v. Wan Hung Lee
Police v. Luke Momfort de Villiers
Police v. Abigail Prudence Jardine
Police v. Bessie Nellie Brinsley
Police v. Montague Belfast Winterbottom

Civil Cases
Constantine Illingworth v. Ben Tucker
William Dreyfuss v. Central Groceries Ltd
Jim O'Donovan v. Uriah Clemenger

The Magistrate entered the Court Room. Everyone stood and then sat down when the Magistrate took his seat. He was a stern-looking, bewhiskered man in his 60's. He removed a short, black top hat as he started the business of the day.

"Mr Registrar, call the first case."

"Call **Joshua James Black**."

Richard arose and addressed the Court. He was every inch the Counsel of 125 years back in the future.

"I appear as Mr Black's Counsel, Your Honour. He pleads guilty to a charge of acting with intent to commit a breach of the peace."

"The facts, if you please, Sergeant."

The Sergeant stood up. He was a ginger haired man with a long drooping ginger moustache,

"On the 21st of last month the defendant made arrangements for a prize fight. He sold tickets and arranged illegal gambling. The police heard about this event and took steps to arrest the defendant before the fight commenced. He has no previous convictions."

"Your plea Mr Locksley, if you please."

"My client is age 48. He has never been in trouble before. His 21-year-old nephew asked him to arrange the fight which was going to be held during the weekend of the nephew's 21st birthday celebrations. The only people to be present were family, friends and special invitees. This was not an event to be open to the general public. But he has contravened the Act of Parliament and he has asked me to apologise to this Court and say that it will never see him again for offending of any kind. I ask you to give full credit for those instructions to me. He does have the ability to pay a fine."

"Mr Black. I am going to take you on trust that you have learned your lesson but prize fights like these generally get out of control and many people, not just the two protagonists, get hurt. That is why there is a law against public pugilism. If you come before any Magistrate for offending like this in the future, you will go to jail. In this case I am prepared to fine you. You will pay the sum of 5 pounds and ordered to pay Court costs of 1 pound. Stand down."

"Call **Thomasina Lucy Dorset**."
A prostitutes' Madam flaunted herself into the dock looking like an ageing brood pheasant, feather hat and all. She cluck, cluck, clucked her way into the dock. The Magistrate appeared to take an instant dislike of her.
"Show some decorum if you please. You are charged with running a common bawdy house. How do you plead?"
"Guilty, Your Honour."
"I appear as her counsel, Your Honour."
"Thank you, Mr Locksley. Facts please Sergeant."
"The defendant has two previous convictions. She continues to run a common bawdy house on the second floor of a building in Marine Parade. She takes a commission from eight common prostitutes who are often seen soliciting clients in their underwear at the upper story windows. She has been fined on previous occasions but admitted to one constable that the fines are minimal compared with a profit she makes from these poor souls."
"Oh, does she indeed? I don't know what can be said, Mr Locksley. Your client is at some peril."
Richard summonsed up the most earnest plea.
"She has suffered a tough and unlucky life. Her first husband was killed before her very eyes when he fell into a threshing machine, working on Remarkables Station. Her second husband beat her to within an inch of her life and then left in the middle of the night with her life savings. She was left to care for two children under the

age of five. Not one of the prostitutes has made any complaint. Not one member of the public has made a complaint despite her staff sexually servicing at least 100 male clients a week and four female clients. Yet it is only the organiser who is charged. God has not given this woman a chance. I ask you to do so."

"Nice speech, Mr Locksley. But it does not warm this old, cold heart. You say that nobody has complained. Well, I complain. Parliament complains. The police complain. It's the third time she has been before the score for this disgusting trade. Her disreputable bawdy house is barely 50 yards from the local Presbyterian Kirk. She should have time to think of that church's principles and the law-abiding local members of that church while she is in prison."

Thomasina interjected from the dock.

"Three members of that church committee are my clients along with seven of the regular congregation. And the last visiting Magistrate sitting here paid me for a bit of a cuddle, and a wee bit more. Know what I mean?"

"Hush your mouth. You are sentenced to 6 months prison with hard labour!"

Richard protested, "Oh, Your Honour. That is too harsh! I asked that you temper it with a little more mercy."

"Not one more word! Otherwise, you will join her. Call the next case."

"Call **David Henry Templeton**. How do you plead to a charge of drunkenness in a public place?"

"As God is my Judge, I am not guilty."

"He's not. I am. You are!"

"Drunk in Beach Street last evening, Sir. Spent the night in police cell. Middle of winter. 17 prior convictions."

"Convicted and sentenced to 14 days in prison. Next case."

"Call **Montague Belfast Winterbottom.** How do you plead to the one charge of aiding soldiers to desert?"

"Guilty.

I appear your Honour."

"Facts, Sergeant."

"The defendant is a farm worker from Gibbston. On diverse occasions during May of this year he encouraged two privates in the New Zealand Army to desert their posts. They did so desert, and the defendant helped them hide at his place of work and he gave false evidence to the police when they were called to investigate. The two soldiers were finally arrested and made statements to the police. In times of war, Your Honour, such crimes would be punishable by death. Nevertheless, the police seek a stern penalty but somewhat less than that."

"What do you have to say on his behalf, Mr Locksley?"

"May it please the Court, serious as these allegations may appear, the defendant focused on the need for labour on his farm and did not consider the military ramifications. But this country is not at war, so the seriousness of a wartime offence is not present. He has instructed me to say that he is most remorseful and realises now that what he did was quite wrong. He has asked me to apologise to the New Zealand Armed Forces, to the police and to this Court. A fine will be a real punishment having regard to his minimal income."

The Judge looked stern.

"Mr Winterbottom. I had considered a sentence of six months imprisonment to make it clear that this offence is serious. But I have been persuaded that your remorse is genuine and that you had not properly thought through your actions in this case. But the fine must be high. You are fined £20 and ordered to pay the costs of prosecution."

The conversion rate to today's dollars meant that the fine then was effectively about $1500.

That evening, it was warm and cozy in Richard and Mary's small cottage near Lake Hayes. Candles lit the small kitchen where they sat.

"I slaughtered one of the sheep today and sold one half to the visiting butcher. What's your work tomorrow?"

"I've got three or four cases in the Arrowtown Court, so I'll be taking Amber. He probably needs a good trot."

"You must wrap up well. It looks like a stormy rain and snow night. I've got five blankets on the bed now and we'll need the fire on all night."

"I wonder what life will be like in this region at least 125 years in the future? Will we have faster ways of travel? Will man ever be able to fly in a machine?"

You may as well think man will fly to the moon!" answered Mary.

"I think the only thing you can rely upon is that people will always need a good lawyer."

"Any cases of interest today, love?"

"Some cases under an array of strange Acts of Parliament."

He counts them off on his hands.

- ✓ Deceased's Wife's Sister Act 1880
- ✓ Chinese Immigrants Act 1881
- ✓ Imbecile Passengers Act 1882
- ✓ Lunatics Act 1882
- ✓ And an Act where there is a section which provides for flogging and whipping but prohibited it on a female, or a boy under the age of 16, and allowed for no more than 25 whacks."

Mary looked up in horror. "I hope someday in the future we will not need Acts of Parliament with these disturbing names. Maybe not?"

"Not for 150 years," said Richard. He did not tell Mary he was experiencing a foot in both centuries.

&

The next morning at 9.00 am. Richard saddled up Amber in the cottage corral. Mary was sitting on the covered front porch. Richard swung up into the saddle. He could barely be seen because of his thick oil skins. The rain tumbled down.

"I'll see you before supper. We need some flour and tea."

"I should have my work all finished and back by 4.00 pm. I'll see you then, my precious."

Richard cantered away and jumped the fence at the end of the paddock. He cantered around the side of Lake Hayes and up on to the Dalefield Plateau heading towards Arrowtown. He then dropped down the centre of the Main Street and hitched Amber to the rail outside the Arrowtown Magistrates Court and went into the building with his bag of briefs.

Magistrate Herbert Montgomery was already presiding. He was a thin, weedy-looking man aged in his mid fifties with an inquiring face and a rather long pointed nose and his hair parted in the middle. Richard joined three other lawyers in the well of the Court and listened to the Magistrate finish a rather long sentencing of a butcher charged with performing an indecency in front of a young girl.

"You are a lowlife who committed a beastly act towards a gentle maiden. She was only 14 at the time and you are 34. You are a dastardly villain and you do not deserve to remain in our community for a long time. But fortunately for you, the maximum penalty available to me is only one year's imprisonment. You are hereby sentenced to 9 months imprisonment and within the first 10 days you will suffer 20 lashes, 10 on the first occasion and 10 on the second. Stand down."

"Mercy, Your Honour. I plead for mercy."

"I said stand down!"

Two uniformed constables wrestled Montgomery from the dock.

"Call **William Waters**. How do you plead to a charge of riding furiously in Stafford Street?"

"Guilty."

"I appear for the defendant, Your Honour"

"Thank you, Mr Locksley. Proceed Sergeant."

"On Saturday evening last, there were a number of women and children assembled beside the Provincial Boarding House when Mr Waters rode a horse furiously up Stafford Street and then returned to the hotel. He rode at a head-long pace endangering members of the public."

Richard did his best.

"The defendant thought that the horse had been fully broken in but realised only that morning that it had not. The horse became very jittery, and Mr Waters rode it strong and hard in order to quiet it down. He was not intending to cause any mayhem or disorder. He apologises for his bad judgement. He has not previously been before any Court and is aged 32. He is currently employed as a labourer."

The Magistrate was very stern in his tone.

"Mr Waters. If you had used a modicum of common sense, you ought to have realised that you should have taken this horse beyond the town limits. Although there was no actual danger, the potential for injury was high.

You must pay a penalty. You are fined 12 pounds and ordered to pay court costs. Next case."

"Call **Ann Josephine Kelsey**. How do you plead to the charge of using obscene and indecent language in a public place?"

"Guilty! But the old cow deserved it!"

"Silence! Not one more sound. Mr Locksley, do you appear?"

"Yes, Your Honour."

The Sergeant stood up again.

"The complainant in this case and a number of witnesses stated that the defendant used a long string of abusive and indecent epithets. The defendant says she only said, "You're a grey-headed old wretch." But the police allege she also used four letter words beginning with F, S and C, not once but several time."

Richard did his best again.

"She has pleaded guilty and saved precious Court time and I ask that she be given credit for that. There was some nasty provocation. The complainant had called my client "a lazy whore." She started it! The police do not dispute that. That was the first epithet cast. Had it not been for that first insult there may have been no offence committed by my client. She has not been before the Court before."

The Magistrate appeared to show some understanding.

"This Court will not tolerate obscene and indecent language in a public place. But this Court also endeavours to be fair and even-handed in assessing cases. While not excusing this defendant for the dreadful language she used, it was in answer to being called "a lazy whore." That insult carries with it an indecent imputation and it ill lies in the mouth of the complainant to come complaining to this Court.

I'm going to take the unusual path of dismissing this charge. But I will remember you Miss Kelsey and you will get no further leniency from me. Stand down."

"Call **Alexander Aristotle Howarth**. You have been charged with stealing from a tent. How say you?"

"Guilty."

"My client, Your Honour," announced Richard.

The sergeant read out the facts

"The complainant in this case found his clothes stolen one evening three weeks ago. He returned from his work at the Lunatic Asylum and discovered that his tent had been entered and that his shirt, two neckerchiefs, a pair of trousers, a billy-cock hat, half of pound of tea and some sugar had been stolen. Three nights later, he came upon the defendant wearing his shirt and trousers and the hat in a hotel bar here in Arrowtown. He tackled the defendant and marched him around to the police station."

Richard started his third plea in mitigation this morning.

"The defendant acted with no advanced planning at all. He had been drinking to excess earlier in the day and when he walked home through the area of tents to the south of this township, he stupidly succumbed to the temptation to steal these items from the tent.

I do not attempt to mitigate his offending out of existence. But there is one important matter which has not been advanced to this Court. The day after being caught he took his entire savings and purchased a new set of clothes and tea and sugar and took them personally to the complainant and apologised."

The Judge appeared most impressed.

Richard continued, "The two men then struck a friendly relationship and spent the rest of the day drinking, only both to be cast into the cells at the police station together for a night. They are still friends. What does Your Worship make of that?"

"A smile comes to my lips, Mr Locksley. I cannot send a man to prison with a smile on my lips. He is not going to get away without a conviction, but I simply convict and discharge. Howarth! Don't do it again! Next time – 20 lashes!"

Richard waited while he listened to an extraordinary and skilled performance by a young fellow barrister, who he discovered had travelled all the way from Dunedin to represent his client. The plea took at least 20 minutes, but it was magnificent. It was the last plea of the morning.

"The Court will adjourn," announced the court clerk.

❧

Before the Second World War, Mr Alf Hanlon was a famous lawyer and King's Counsel practising out of Dunedin and frequently appearing as Counsel in the Southern Lakes Courts in the 1890's through to the early 1940's.

He was born in 1866 and died in 1944. Mr Hanlon was a household name throughout New Zealand after he represented Minnie Dean, the Southland baby farmer, in 1895. She was hanged in August 1895 for her crimes. He was still only 29 at the time.

After the Courtroom in Arrowtown that morning had cleared, this rather tall but callow young lawyer, aged in his late twenties, approached Richard. He was that very Alf Hanlon.

"Good morning, Sir. May I introduce myself. I am Alf Hanlon. I am a lawyer practising in Dunedin."

Richard immediately recognised the name of the advocate, who would become one of the greatest criminal lawyers in New Zealand during the following 50 years until his death in 1944.

"Nice to meet you. What a wonderful plea," Richard engaged him in a very friendly manner.

Mr Hanlon returned the admiration. "I must say I was most impressed at the way you handled the Magistrate. Such short pleas are so effective."

"I suppose, just 20 years of experience. You get to realise that too much just starts to sound pompous."

"I have not seen you around before. Are you new to the district?" asked Mr Hanlon.

"Have you got time for some coffee or tea? I have got a story which will rock you!"

"Rock you? What sort of expression is that?

"A modern saying, my good man. Shall we take a stroll down Ballantyne Street and see if we can find a coffee establishment."

They both entered a local building and sat down at a table. A waitress came up. Dolly looked like, well, a dolly. She was a de rigueur hospitality assistant, Arrowtown circa 1895.

"What'll it be, Gentlemen?"

"Cappuccino please," requested Richard.

"Wot! Wot on earth is that?"

"Just an Italian greeting. Black coffee please".

"Same, Dolly," said Mr Hanlon.

They settled back and the coffee arrived.

"Look. I want to tell you something. You are going to think I am quite mad ... but I am not. Just hear me out. Don't walk out. It is to your advantage."

"Rock me!?"

"I know it sounds bonkers, but I am from the future. I don't know how I got here. Don't know if I am going back."

"Bonkers?"

"Means mad. In an affectionate sort of way."

"Go on. I am fascinated."

"Well, I am a lawyer in this region over 125 years into the future and some twist of fate has transferred me back here and I am representing clients in the same way and for the same things as I do in the year 2022. It is amazing! Just hear me out."

"I think we may need some more coffee. DOLLY!"

"Well hear this. You are 29. You were born in 1866. You are destined to become one of the greatest criminal barristers in New Zealand and you will live a long and eventful life. You will represent almost 20 murderers very successfully."

"I seem to do mainly licensing cases and debt collection at the moment."

"All that's going to change. In a few weeks you will be briefed to represent a female client charged with murder just out of Invercargill. It will become known as the baby farming murderess. Her name is Minnie Dean. We will probably not meet again but remember me well when you get this brief."

"Absolutely fascinating."

"You will go on to practise law for almost 50 years. You will be appointed a King's Counsel. You will represent the New Zealand Government in a very high-profile case. You will also write a popular memoir called "Random Recollections" and a popular television series will be made about you."

"Television?"

"It's moving pictures and a sound experience beamed into private homes and played on a screen on the wall."

"I am stunned. Screen?"

"I hope to meet you again, but I doubt it. The best of luck for the future."

Richard left and Alf Hanlon could be seen sitting still and shaking his head.

"Who was that Mr Hanlon?" Dolly enquired.

"I don't know if it was an angel or a ghost, but I think I've just witnessed something very amazing. Cappuccino? Rock me? Bonkers? Television? Screen?"

Richard galloped home. As he jumped the hedge at the bottom of the paddock adjoining his cottage his world turned round and round and moved forward through 1896, 1910, 1936, 1965, 1990, 2001, 2021, 2022 – until he gently woke up in the Frankton Hospital. Mary was holding his hand again.

"Where on earth have you been? You have been mumbling as if you were in Court. And who the hell is Thomasina? And what is a bawdy house? And stealing from a tent? What's that all about?" And 20 lashes! For goodness sake. Where have you been?

"I've been in a different world. Wait till I tell you about it all tonight. Wow! What the doctor gave me was pretty damn good."

"And what's the Lunatics Act all about?"

Mary drove him home. He was back in the 21st Century.

～

One week later, but 125 years earlier, in the Savoy Tearooms on the corner of Moray Place Princes Street, Dunedin, just across from his Dunedin office, Alf Hanlon was sitting having a late afternoon tea. Raisin cake, crumpets and black tea. An assistant ran in puffing.

"Mr Hanlon. You've got a fascinating brief. It's all over the newspapers. A woman called Minnie Dean has been arrested in Invercargill and charged with the murder of several buried babies. The press is already calling it the "baby farming" case. Come quickly."

The look on Alf Hanlon's face was one of complete bewilderment. He sat glancing into space, alternatively shaking and then nodding his head. He clearly remembered the conversation with Richard in Arrowtown one week earlier!

At precisely the same time, 125 years later, Richard was working at pace in his office in Queenstown. On the telephone. Shifting books. Reading law texts. Writing on his whiteboard. Janet coming in and out. Willie dropping in files. Melinda taking clients into her room. Mary was interviewing. Clients coming and going. The practice had become very busy in such a short space of time. He was feeling very happy.

He drank a cappuccino; his television screen was live with "We will, we will, Rock You," by Queen pounding out in the background.

"1896," he thought. "Did that really happen?"

CHAPTER NINETEEN

Now back in 2022, Richard appeared on an important case in the Alexandra District Court. District Court Judge Bill Sinclair was presiding. Richard was representing Grandma Bo for assault on two Aucklanders after she observed them deliberately running over ducks crossing the main Lakeside Road in Wanaka.

The public gallery was full of people in support of her. Many had come from Wanaka. The Auckland family sat in the front row of the public gallery. The only space left were two seats on either side where nobody else wanted to sit. People were pointing at them, and mutterings of disgust could be heard.

"Shame."

"Duck killers."

"Not welcome here."

The police had confiscated some signs to the same effect.

Grandma Bo's case was called.

"Marjory Jenkins. How do you plead to the two charges of assault?"

"Guilty."

"I appear."

The prosecuting Sergeant spoke up,

"Your Honour has the police summary of facts before you. On Friday 12 September last ..." The Judge interrupted.

"Before you start Sergeant, why were these remaining charges not diverted? She has no previous."

"Diversion requires the consent of the complainants. They would not give it."

The Judge looked singularly unimpressed.

The sergeant read out the summary right down to the details of the squashed ducks.

"Mr Locksley," said the Judge. "I don't wish to cut you off in full flight, but I am not going to leave this lady with a conviction. Please just give me your salient points."

"Thank you, Sir. Age 78. Still performs hard-working community service. No previous convictions at all.

The cafe asked that the initial charges of damage and disorderly behaviour be withdrawn when they learned of the true facts."

"Yes, I noted that," said the Judge.

"Mrs Jenkins saw with her own eyes the mother duck and three ducklings squashed before her eyes and the father duck limp away with a broken wing quacking in pain. She had tears rolling down her cheeks and she was heartbroken and severely upset. Her anguish was even the more compelling by seeing the driver smirking and the parents both turning to the children and laughing. She feeds these ducks every day."

The Judge was clearly moved. It's not often you get an overt duck lover on the Bench!

"I can accept that her stress would be palpable," His Honour said.

Richard continued. "Perhaps more of interest is that my client obtained the normal discovery package from the police a week ago and found the notes of the officer in charge of the case, which recorded comments made by the parents to the police. Those comments included the following clear indications of lack of remorse by the complainants...

"They were only ducks."

"We were only having some fun."

"A stupid country Judge will see our side."

"Did they indeed? Would the so-called victims please stand up!"

The arrogance drained from their faces as they struggled to their feet.

"Did you make these comments to the investigating police officer?"

"Yes, Your Honour."

"What say you now?"

"We are sorry for the use of the word "stupid.""

"Anything else?"

"Not really. We don't think it's a big deal."

"Wrong answer! Sit down." The Judge addressed Grandma Bo.

"Marjory Jenkins. As a Judge, I cannot condone violence. I am meant to say you did the wrong thing. Citizens cannot take the law into their own hands. But outside of the complainants, there would not be one person in this Court today, myself included, who feel that the act of brutality to the ducks required swift denunciation. The only problem with physical denunciation is that with a citizen less mature than you, and with a less explicit set of circumstances, physical retribution can always spiral out of control.

But I'm not going to leave you with a conviction. You are hereby discharged without conviction.

And I say to the family from Auckland - It's very unlikely that you will be welcomed back in this region. It's not too late for the police to consider a charge of wilful mistreatment of animals under the Animal Welfare Act which carries a penalty of up to 5 years imprisonment. The fact that you have not been charged means that you have been lucky. But it's not too late and just think on that as you return to Auckland. I can tell you that if this "Stupid District Court Judge" had been hearing such a charge on these facts a sentence of six months imprisonment would not be out of order.

Mrs Jenkins leaves this Court without a stain on her character. But your characters are both besmirched."

"Stand down Mrs Jenkins. But please don't do it regularly. I'll take a brief adjournment. 10 minutes."

"Thank you, Your Honour."

The public gallery cleared. A constable, upon the directions of the Sergeant, stood by the Aucklanders and accompanied them out a side door.

"We don't want a lynching here. Better come with me for 15 minutes."

"What a pathetic Judge! We were the ones who were assaulted."

"You just don't get it do you? Get out of town! Please don't come back!"

Outside the courthouse. Marjory Jenkins was surrounded by her supporters and family. A small tear ran down her cheek. Richard walked up to her.

"I'm very happy with being discharged without conviction. But I am not happy that I have had to go through this, and I am not happy for the ducks. Seeing them killed will be with me for the rest of my life. But thank you so much for your support and assistance."

"I completely understand. Marjory, I am not going to charge you one cent. Every now and again there comes a case where I will not do so. I am proud to have represented you."

A little jig was performed by Grandma Bo. "I'll send you a month's worth of homemade muffins."

They all had a hug and returned home.

The next morning, Janet popped her head around Richard's door. "Richard. It's that Bernard Brinsley on the telephone. The creep."

"Right. Put him through ... Bernard. Not another meeting with the Law Society I hope?"

"Not at all. I don't think I could take another one of those."

"Quite."

"I hope you can call me Bernie. I seek your help. In just a few short weeks you have certainly become the leader of the bar in this area, and I salute you for that. I have a murder case I want to brief you upon. I had briefed one of the two lawyers who died not long before you came down. It's a bit beyond me so can I come round?"

"Certainly. Come round now if you can. Coffee or tea?"

"Tea please. Just a little milk. I'll be there in five."

He was there in just three minutes. Queenstown's a bit like that.

Janet showed Mr Brinsley into Richard's office.

"Are you prepared to call me Bernie now?"

"Certainly. All those matters are behind us."

"I'm glad of that. Thank you. I was a jerk."

"Forget it. It's in the distant past."

"I act for the Mahon family. They have a daughter, Sally, who is 25 and she married a right scumbag who has abused her every which way for three years. A couple of months ago she had had enough and, while he was sleeping, she got a carving knife and knelt on top of him and pushed it right through his heart."

"Jeez! A jury won't like that for a start. I heard something about that."

"I have managed suppression of name up to now, but murder is certainly not my field."

"Do we have a battered woman's syndrome here which we can weave into a pre-emptive self-defence case?"

"You're right on to it. Luckily, she had been seeing a senior and gifted clinical psychologist referred by a social worker and we have a formal report which provides compelling evidence on that possibility."

"I only hope it's Dr Marian Stewart. I've used her several times before. She is really credible."

"It is. Her main practice is in Auckland, but she maintains a house and clinic here in Queenstown as well. Probably a tax dodge but very fortunate for us. I've taken the liberty of booking an appointment for you tomorrow at her house up here on Queenstown Hill. Is 1:00 pm OK for you?"

"No problems. Is that the file?"

"Yes. Here's the report and full discovery documents from the police. And here's a DVD of her recorded police statement. Dr Stewart was very savvy. Sally telephoned her first and the doctor got to her almost an hour before the police arrived. Sally gave a perfect exculpatory statement to the police in a video interview, detailing the long-standing abuse and the depth of her despair. It's all pitiful reading."

"So it's unlikely we will need to call Sally to give evidence?"

"That's what I think. Unfortunately, she is a legal aid case, but two Counsel have already been certified, so I'm wondering if you will let me sit in with you. You get the lion's share of the legal aid of course, and you act a senior Counsel."

"Delighted for you to be a Co-Counsel. But I insist that we simply split the legal aid cheque 50/50. I wouldn't have it any other way."

"That's very generous of you. Shall we meet again in a few days?"

"I'll take over the preparation today and you attend to the legal aid requests immediately. The Legal Aid Board is fairly generous on murder trials.

"Certainly. Thanks for the brief."

Richard shook Bernie's hand and escorted him to the lift.

Mary was interviewing a 30-year-old mother, Sara McDonald, about a child access case. The father of the child was being horrible.

"It's a bit complicated. My former husband and I have been separated for two years. We have a wee girl in my day-to-day care called Eve. She is now five and has just started school. He has her every second weekend. But in recent months he runs me down to the wee girl and says that I will burn in hell because I am in a relationship with another man, and we are not yet married."

"Burn in hell!!??"

"You need to know the background. Up until the time we separated I thought we were just a normal married Kiwi couple. We were not particularly religious. But he was seeing another woman behind my back, and he left me for her and started living with her immediately. A few months later they both converted to the Jehovah's Witness religion. They became deeply involved in that religion. It was a big surprise."

"What went wrong?"

"A full year after we broke up, I met a man, and we have a girlfriend/boyfriend relationship although he does stay one weekend a month. Because we are not married my former husband now bashes his Bible and tells this dear little girl I am evil and describes the flames of hell that will consume me when I die. She comes home really upset about her Mummy being burned to death. What can I do about it? I don't want to cut out access, but he simply must not continue saying these things to Eve."

"That's one of the most appalling things I've heard relating to the welfare of children. A Family Court Judge will be totally on your side."

"What do we do?"

"You stop access completely. Tell him why! And tell him that your lawyer is taking him to the Family Court. I want you to write out a detailed statement of all the facts. About four pages. Email it to me. I will draw up an application to the Family Court to redefine access and to get some Court orders set up to stop him in his tracks."

"I'm only on a Benefit. Can I get legal aid?"

"Almost certainly. I'll get Janet our office administrator to go through an application form with you before you leave.

She also passed Family Law with top marks at university. This office is happy to do this for you on legal aid. Do you have a computer?"

"Yes."

"Within a day of you emailing me back a full Statement, I will email you back the Family Court documents and you tell me if you want any changes made. I will then get you in for signing and will get the case underway within 48 hours. We can probably get an emergency hearing within two weeks if he starts pestering you."

"Thank you so much. I feel much better. I didn't really know what could be done about it. After all, he is the father."

"Strictly speaking, he does not have absolute rights because in any decision relating to children, the Care of Children Act says that the interests and welfare of the child is the paramount consideration."

"I thought there was something like that. I'll send you my Statement tomorrow morning."

Mary accompanied her in the reception and introduced her.

"Janet, this is Sara. Could you fill in a legal aid application please and a formal Information Sheet. It's an application to redefine contact by the father with the child, Eve."

"Technically a Parenting Order?" asked Janet.

"Certainly," answered Mary.

"Nice to meet you, Sara. You come and sit round here beside me," Janet gave her a big supportive smile.

"Melinda. This is Sara. We are stopping access by her former husband to young Eve until we get an emergency hearing. Could you do a standard letter to the local Family Court and the Invercargill Family Court telling them that we have been instructed by Sara and are filing an emergency application to suspend contact with her former husband and that therefore no unilateral application by him should be considered without our input. We have done it before."

"On to ir immediately," replied Melinda.

Mary retreated into her office as Richard came out of his.

"I've got to get down to Court. I have two defended fixtures this afternoon, so I probably won't be back until the office closes."

CHAPTER TWENTY

Within 30 minutes the hate speech prosecution where Wiremu interviewed Tom Finlayson was about to be heard. Richard was leading for the defence. Willie sat beside him. Judge Lydia Langham entered the Court.

"Silence for Her Honour, Judge Langham. I call the first fixture on today's list. Thomas John Finlayson."

"I appear, Your Honour. With me is Mr Pihama.

Good morning. Yes Sergeant."

"I call my one witness, Constable Rosewood."

The Constable commenced giving his evidence. He covered some preliminary matters first then described what he had heard that night.

"I was in the audience. I was off duty and obviously not wearing my uniform. Approximately eight comedians performed that evening, and the so-called comedy was rude and offensive humour from the outset. I took great exception to the humour and was disgusted by almost all of it."

"Did you observe and listen to the defendant's contribution?"

"Yes. It was the worst of the lot. I took exception to two particular so-called jokes. The defendant said that Maori didn't feature in the AIDS statistics, and I quote, "because they don't get off their bums enough to catch AIDS." He then ended his monologue by saying, and I again quote, "It's hot in here. I'm sweating like a Jew at a money machine."

"Yes, Mr Locksley," beckons the Judge. "You may cross-examine."

Richard rose to his feet.

"I suggest you have only given a thumbnail sketch of the events of this evening?"

"Probably. But I think I had heard enough."

"I suggest to you that the eight monologues you heard that night were spread over 2 to 3 hours?"

"Yes, I suppose so."

"And there was much loud and long laughter all through the evening, until the very last minute."

"Yes, I accept that."

"And the joke about the Jewish person at the money machine offended three American tourists who may have been of the Jewish faith?"

"Yes."

"And no other member of the crowd supported their protest?"

"That's correct."

"And they advanced up to the stage, each carrying a sign declaring "Stop Offensive Jokes" and they waved the signs around right under the nose of the defendant."

"Yes, they did."

"So it was obvious they had come to the evening prepared for some sort of confrontation without even hearing a word uttered by the comedians?"

"I suppose so. I don't see the point."

"You don't have to. The Judge does."

The Constable looked to the Judge seeking some form of support. He did not get it.

"Now I want you to think very carefully about your answer to this question. At the time the American tourists protested physically and vocally, did even one member of the crowd yell at them, denigrate them in any way, abuse them or make any move to attack them."

"I must accept that they did not."

"So Constable, and I have the charge against my client in front of me, where precisely do you say that his monologue and his words were likely to excite hostility or bring into contempt any person of a particular colour, race or ethnic or national origins of that group of persons? Think carefully before you answer."

"Um. I think by inference you can say that."

"Do I take it from your answer that you saw no evidence of hostility or contempt directed by members of the crowd, EVEN ONE, towards citizens of a particular class?"

"But the Americans were extremely upset."

"But that's not the essence of the offence, Constable."

"I feared that hostility or contempt was likely to break out."

"I have two matters to ask on that answer and I want your comments. Firstly, no hostility or contempt was shown by others towards the American Jewish people."

"No. You are right."

"And secondly, Constable. In the three weeks which have gone by since the comedy evening, you can bring no evidence to this Court that hostility or contempt manifested itself during that time."

"It was very nasty humour."

"It may well have been when analysed. But do you confirm that all of the advertising for this evening warned potential customers that some might find the jokes offensive."

"Yes. I saw the advertising."

"And Mr Finlayson's monologue actually was underpinned by a constant theme relating to free speech. I suggest it had an intellectual quality about it, however offended you may have been."

"I can't remember his full monologue. But I was very offended."

"Thank you, Constable."

"Do you intend to call evidence, Mr Locksley?"

"I do, Your Honour. I intend to call only the defendant. My legal submissions will become obvious from my line of cross examination. May I reserve them until the end of the evidence?"

"You may. Will you please come to the witness box, Mr Finlayson?"

The court clerk swore him in on the Bible.

"Do you swear to tell the truth, the whole truth and nothing but the truth?"

"I do."

"Mr Finlayson, how long did your monologue last? And could you repeat it accurately?"

"No more than four minutes. And yes, I made full notes before I started."

"Your Honour," submitted Richard. "The orthodox way of presenting examination in chief is by me to ask questions and elicit short answers. In this case, it is the very nature and quality of my client's monologue which is under analysis and attack. What better and more accurate way to present that evidence than to have him repeat it and then recall the Constable to say whether it is an accurate repetition?"

"I think I agree, Mr Locksley. I hope I won't regret it. On with the show."

"Mr Finlayson. Please repeat your monologue accurately in accordance with the way you presented it on this comedy night. Please employ the same pauses, timing and accents you used on the evening. Firstly though, are you a final year law student?"

"Yes."

Tom then took out his notes, drew himself to his full height, gave a slight bow and flashed a broad smile. The Court room was immediately transformed into a Comedy Club filled with a rowdy and an appreciative crowd. The Judge looked nervous. Tom employed the appropriate accent whenever dialect cropped up during his monologue. He was very good at it. He started with a grin.

"Rightio! All you bastards out there, listen up!"

The Judge looked up, startled.

"Don't worry Judge, I won't say the N word, or the F word ... or the C word. I didn't on the night."

"I'm most glad to hear that."

Tom continued. He was at his best.

"Freedom of speech in this world is at great peril of being slaughtered on the altar of political correctness. But the law does not require you always to speak in good taste.

Otherwise jokes about the Irish and Scots would be obliterated. Punishable by imprisonment if you uttered one! Let me present to you some examples of offensive humour and then you tell me whether you did or did not crack a small smile or whether my humour incites in you hostility or contempt towards the subjects of my humour. It is not an offence to tell an offensive joke. So let us start."

The Judge and Richard exchanged a sly wink. The Judge held her hand in her hands and looked down at her Bench. The public gallery was transfixed. Richard may have pulled off the coup of his life.

"I'm gonna tell some jokes about Horis, Coconuts, Chinks, Wogs, Poms, Coons, Dagos and Abos. AOK so far? But you tell me whether I have broken the law relating to hate speech. I don't hate these people. I just like jokes."

"Your Honour, the audience laughed non-stop through my monologue. But I continue."

Tom (Abo accent) –

"An Abo is met coming home from the Family Court by his friend. He is carrying half a sheet of corrugated iron. His friend said, "Crikey, Brownie. Did you lose?"

"Nah," was the reply. "I got half the house." That's a joke about the poverty and the humour of a race. Should it be a crime?"

The Judge could be seen sneakily smiling, then she straightened her face.

"Did you hear the one about the Abo at school? The teacher was singing "Old MacDonald Had a Farm."

"OK, Bundy," she asked a small aboriginal pupil. "Can you make a noise like a pig?"

"Sure", he said. "OK you coons. Get out of the car, put your hands on your heads and spread your legs!"

Tom commented with a smile, "I find that funny, not offensive. Should it be a crime?"

Tom's jokes were coming out of his mouth like a machine gun.

"Ya'll know what roadkill is. It's an Abo's first meal.

.... probably his first root too!"

His timing and pausing was impeccable.

Even the prosecuting Sergeant was heard to utter a muffled laugh.

"Now just take care, Mr Finlayson," said the Judge.

But she barely suppressed an outright laugh.

"And do you know why Maori men don't get Aids? Because they don't get off their bums long enough to catch it. That's an awful joke, but I should I go to prison for it? Billy T James would still be doing time if he had not died."

Willie looked at Richard and smiled and whispered.

"Jeez, Boss. A black bastard like me shouldn't be finding this funny."

Tom continued, "Russians. Can a joke offend them? A Russian wouldn't know what a joke was. A Russian judge walks out of his chambers smiling. A colleague approaches him and asks why he is laughing.

"I just heard the funniest joke in the world!"

"Well, go ahead, tell me!" said the other Judge.

"I can't – I just gave someone ten years for it!"

"Well, I like that one," said Judge Langham.

"A baby duck and a baby skunk meet in a park. "You are yellow, and you have a bill and webbed feet. You must be a duck." The duck replies - "You're not quite black and you're not quite white and you smell bad. You must be Mexican." Whew! That's getting a bit rough!"

The crowd at the public gallery were now starting to enjoy this and the Judge looked a bit worried. But she bit her lip.

"Judge, the whole audience at the bar were wild with laughter. But I continue.

I learned something the other day. I learned the Jehovah's Witnesses do not celebrate Halloween. I guess they don't like strangers going up to their door and annoying them."

What's an Irish seven course dinner? A six-pack and a potato.

Chinese? Everything is made in China ... except for girl babies.

Apparently, animals make different sounds according to different languages. For example, in China a dog makes a sizzling noise.

What is white at the top and black at the bottom? Society! Now there's a satirical joke. Satire should NEVER be a criminal act. Don't be racist folk. Racism is a crime. And crime is for black people.

Greeks - What do you call a Greek with 200 girlfriends? A shepherd.

A customs officer is interviewing a traveller from Afghanistan at Heathrow Immigration."

Tom put on an English accent for the customs officer and a thick middle eastern accent for the traveller.

"Name?"

"Abdul Al-Rhasin"

"Sex?"

"10 to 15 times a week".

"No. no. I mean male or female?"

"Yes, male, female ... sometimes camel."

"Holy cow!"

"Cow? Yes, sometimes."

"Oh dear!"

"No, no deer. Deer run too fast. Hard to catch."

The public up the back of the Court laughed out loud.

"Here's one for the Trump supporters. This is gross but because it ties Trump in, I say it becomes a political comment. A white supremacist tells the bar, "In my family tree there are black guys, and if you look closely, you can see where they're hanging from.

And I laughed when I heard Trump say the other day, "I'm not racist. My butler, cook and servants are all black."

And then there are the simple Scottish and Irish jokes, but ask yourself whether you think they are so abusive or insulting enough to bring into contempt those particular people. If you do think so, then I should be locked up.

A Scotsman is wallpapering his front lounge. His friend walks in and says, "Are ye renovating, McTavish?"

"Nay, moving house."

Now that is a joke about the meanness of Scots? It is insulting, but it technically fits into the definition of an offence and our important freedom of speech principle ought not to be bruised and battered this way if the joke is classified as hate speech.

Look, I better go. It's really hot in here. I'm sweating like a Jew at a money machine. Oops, there I go again.

I just want to finish by praising the braveness of my heroes Rowan Atkinson, John Cleese and Ricky Gervais who have all spoken out against the censorship of comedy, even if that comedy is crude. I have woven my comment into a little limerick –

> Atkinson, Cleese and Gervais
> are right on the button when they say –
> "Comedy's broke
> When you're censored by WOKE
> And the speech laws you're told to obey."

Tom finished and looked serious. The public gallery was still laughing until the Judge hit her gavel.

Richard rose to his feet. "I just want to ask Constable Ramsey one thing. Was the monologue you have just heard from the defendant very close to the original you heard in the bar? Nothing more and nothing less?"

"Yes. Identical."

Her Honour was impressed.

"Mr Locksley. What a skilled and innovative defence. You always seem to be able to entertain this Court. But on a serious note, you have advanced your legal defence through the words and evidence of your own client. Your skills have been expertly employed. I am prepared to give the decision in favour of your client right now. I have section 61 of the Human Rights Act 1993 in front of me."
The Judge slowly and deliberatively delivered her decision.

"I have had the benefit of hearing the actual words and their context from the defendant in his evidence. While there would be many who might find many of the jokes offensive, I do not think our criminal law, as set out in the Human Rights Act 1993, has been breached. If they have, then it is a sad day for freedom of speech in this country. If there had been a hint of an attempt to excite hostility or contempt against the races or ethnic origins raised, then naturally I would have been much more concerned. But the time, place and circumstances of this monologue fall far short of a criminal allegation."

"The charge is dismissed. My Chambers, Mr Locksley?"

"As the Court pleases."

Richard knocked gently and entered the Judge Langham's Chambers, where she was pouring two cups of tea.

"Richard, cup of tea? I rarely do this, but I just wanted to call you and tell you what a simple and effective defence you ran. And actually, I almost wet myself with laughter."

"Me too. I know we shouldn't laugh at such matters, but the world will become very dull if political correctness becomes the order of the day."

"You must call me Lydia from now on outside of Court. And isn't it about time that you thought about joining us on the Bench?"

"I like the idea, but I've just set up the new practice here in Queenstown. I understand that sometimes it is the kiss of death to let it be known that one might be interested. After all, one who wants to be a Judge probably is the sort of person who should not be a Judge."

"We all say that on the Bench. It's our wee joke. We weed out the crawlers. But I'll let you into another wee secret. It's not announced yet, so I swear you to strict secrecy. In about two weeks, I'm going to be appointed as the new chief District Court Judge and I would welcome you to the Bench."

"That really honours me. Thank you for raising it. I am most obliged. But I need a few more months here first to settle in my staff. But I raise one idea. This area is serviced by Invercargill Judges and Alexandra by Dunedin judges and both those cities are under pressure. I think there is now room for a Queenstown-based Judge to handle Alexandra, Queenstown and Gore with perhaps visiting satellite courts in Wanaka and Te Anau."

"I'll certainly keep that in mind. I know the attorney general has similar ideas."

"Take care. And until then, keep my Court entertained."

"Thank you, Your Honour."

CHAPTER TWENTY-ONEb

Barely a day passed, and Richard was back in Court after a heavy load of interviews. His client Miriam Whiting was waiting for her case to begin. She was charged with assault with intent to commit grievous bodily harm on lowlife Gavin Porteous for his physical abuse of her dog in the Queenstown Gardens. She had pleaded not guilty. Judge Andrew Jamieson from Invercargill entered the Courtroom.

"Silence for His Honour the Judge. Call Miriam Joan Whiting."

"I appear," announced Richard. "This case is set down for two hours. The salient facts are admitted."

"Thank you, Mr Locksley. Yes Sergeant."

"The prosecution and the defence have agreed that the victim and his two friends were physically setting upon the defendant's dog with the use of fireworks, kicking and throwing bottles at it. The police also accept that the dog was almost killed and still has a residual blindness in one eye.

The defence accepts that the defendant picked up an iron rose bush stake and rammed it into the stomach area of 22-year-old Gavin Porteous who was the main abuser of the dog."

"I call Gavin Peter Porteous." The prosecutor beckoned. Mr Porteous moved into the witness box and was sworn on the Bible. He related his subjective and patently unreliable evidence to the Court. But he finished with the most damning part.

"I then saw her pull the iron bar from the ground and she pushed it brutally into my stomach area. I passed out and I woke up in hospital. Luckily, it did not strike any vital organs, although I was in hospital for 10 days. I have made a slow recovery, but I have scarring on my stomach and some pain."

"Just answer any questions please," said the sergeant. Richard stood up and looked the witness right in the eye.

"Do you accept you were seriously injuring my client's dog?"

"It was only a joke."

"Do you think the dog was enjoying your joke?"

"I suppose not."

"Would you like to revise that answer and say definitely that the dog was showing signs of serious distress?"

"Yes."

"Well, let's get the evidence crystal clear. You threw approximately eight lighted and exploding firecrackers at the dog?"

"Yes."

"And most of them exploded in a flash on or very near the creature?"

"Yes."

"And you threw a lighted Roman candle – that's the one with the six fireballs spewing from its end – at the dog?"

"Yes."

"And that action actually set the fur of the animal alight, and fire and smoke curled up."

"I suppose so."

"Yes or no!" Richard raised his voice.

"Yes."

"And you and your friends kicked at the dog at least a dozen times with eight of those kicks connecting and breaking three ribs?"

Mr Porteous hung his head and remained silent.

"Answer my question!"

"Yes. You don't have to go on about it."

"I do, and I will! You and your friends, particularly you, threw bottles and cans at this poor dog! True or false!"

"Yes."

"And those missiles hit the dog on each occasion because you were so close?"

"Yes."

"And throughout your attack, my client was crying and screaming at you to stop? Over and over again?"

"Yes."

"Did the police show you the vet's report? Did you read it? It's before the Court."

"Yes."

"It is six pages long! Listen to what I say carefully and tell me if you accept the following findings by the vet."

- Three broken ribs.
- 12 bruises.
- 7 square inches of burns.
- Significant damage to the left eye.
- Medium concussion.
- Three gashes requiring 23 stitches.

"Do you accept that you caused those injuries?"

"Yes."

"And all this time, my client was pleading with you to stop with tears rolling down her cheeks."

"Yes."

"Finally, Mr Porteous. Can you tell us what you would have done if you were in her situation?"

"Is that relevant, Mr Locksley?"

"Not as to guilt or innocence per se, Your Honour, but as the defence relates to an assessment of reasonable force his answer may be relevant."

"I will allow the question."

"Mr Porteous?"

"I think I would have done the same thing."

"Thank you, Mr Porteous."

"That only leaves the playing of the video of the interview with the defendant, Your Honour."

A constable pushed the play button on the Court video facilities and Miriam could be seen answering questions from a detective in the formal setting at the police station an hour after the incident. She was crying, obviously upset and hyperventilating. The interview contained most of what Mr Porteous had just told the Court.

"… I only wanted to protect my beloved dog."

"I could smell flesh burning and saw his fur on fire."

"He was yelping and crying continuously."

"… It was obvious he was in great pain."

"I quickly thought of what else I could do. Nobody was near."

"I just wanted to stop this dreadful cruelty happening."

"I pleaded and cried for them to stop, but they would not. They were actually laughing."

Richard felt his own emotions rising in his throat but, most importantly, he thought he saw a tear run down the right cheek of the Judge. The Court was deathly silent.

The video recording ended with Miriam breaking down in loud sobs.

"That is the evidence for the prosecution."

"I have only legal submissions to make, Your Honour."

"Yes, Mr Locksley."

"Her act was violent. I accept that. Her act caused serious injuries. I accept that. But the defence involves several points of law.

Section 48 of our Crimes Act 1961 allows a citizen to use reasonable force to protect themselves or others. But a dog or a chattel is not covered by that section. So we disregard that it although it raises the consideration of reasonable force.

Section 52 relates to chattels or what are termed "movable things." Reasonable force can again be used to protect those "things" provided there is no actual strike and no bodily injury. So that section must be disregarded.

But then there is a little-used section which initially appears to refer to the prevention of suicide. But let me read it.

41 Prevention of suicide or certain offences.

Every person is justified in using such force as may be reasonably necessary in order to prevent the commission of suicide, <u>or the commission of an offence which would be likely to cause immediate and serious injury to the person or property of anyone,</u> or in order to prevent any act being done which he or she believes, on reasonable grounds, would, if committed, amount to suicide or to any such offence.

"Let me find it here on my laptop. Yes, I see it."

"The section specifically states, "or other offences".

"I submit that this is what we have here. My client's dog was her property. Immediate and serious injury was, not just imminent, but occurring. There simply remains for a decision to be made as to whether her one action of one strike was reasonable in the circumstances to prevent the "immediate and serious injury" to her dog."

"I had overlooked that section. I think you may be right," said the Judge.

Richard continued, "But I go much further. I have referred only to statute law. Our Crimes Act lays down specific crimes but reserves all defences at common law to be still valid. I refer to section 20 (1). This section rarely is used because our Act tends to cover all defences. But if you look at English common law, clearly shown from the up-to-date website of the Crown Prosecution Service in the United Kingdom, reasonable force can be used for the <u>prevention of any crime</u>."

Richard underlined his words with some force.

"And if you go back to our Crimes Act, a crime is defined as any offence punishable by imprisonment. If you then go to our Animal Welfare Act 1999, then you will see that cruelty to any animal can be the subject of imprisonment up to 5 years."

"I see," said the Judge.

Richard continued, "So I say that the law is on Miriam Whiting's side and that it would be an inappropriate response to the horrific circumstances of this case to say that her force was unreasonable.

Accordingly, I submit that she is entitled to the benefit of that defence and this charge must be dismissed."

The Judge paused for a full two minutes, rustled some papers and checked his laptop. She then delivered her decision.

"Mr Locksley's defence succeeds. I have given anxious consideration to the degree of force used and the fact that an iron stake was rammed into the stomach with such force that it penetrated out his back. Luckily, no permanent damage or death resulted. But her actions cannot be condemned by the suggestion that "this was just a dog. This was a living thing as precious to her as a baby would be to its mother. And Miss Whiting did not strike twice.

She did not elevate her violence to a repeated beating or striking of a body while it was already down. She took immediate action to prevent a crime continuing. Not every animal protection case will justify force at this level. But the vile and cruel behaviour visited upon this dog by these three young adults was so disgraceful and at such a level that I find as a fact that Miss Whiting's actions were justified. Perhaps more technically correct, I cannot find that the proescutions can exclude her actions as. The charges are dismissed. You may step down."

"May it please the Court."

Mr Locksley, could you please come to my Chambers for five minutes?"

Richard asked Miriam to wait and he proceeded into the Judge's chambers.

"Goodness me. I'm not in trouble, am I?"

"Certainly not. I didn't welcome you back down South before. I just wanted to do so on behalf of myself and my fellow Judges in Invercargill. We need some experience around here and that was a very neat defence. I want to congratulate you."

"Thank you, Your Honour. You honour me."

"Call me Andrew in the right circumstances. Now, I adore gossip. Tell me. Everyone is remaining tight lipped. What on earth did you do to Judge Christie. He was a dreadful old fart. What happened?"

"Well, my lips are sealed ... but ..."

❧

The next day it was Wiremu's turn again in the Queenstown Court. He was defending a possession of cannabis case against Simon Tonkin, a rather arrogant second-year law student. The constable in charge of the case had just started his evidence. Judge Jamieson was presiding. Constable Curtis began his evidence before the Court.

"Three Saturdays ago, on October 1, I was patrolling in an unmarked police car through the Central Business District of Queenstown. I noticed two youths, one of whom was the defendant, who I recognise in Court today sitting in the dock.

"My attention was aroused when I saw them approach another male who I knew from previous experience to be a dealer in cannabis. When they saw the police car, the defendant and his friend started running. I caught up with them and asked them what they had been doing. They told me that they were intending to buy some cannabis from this man, but they were not able to do so.

They consented to a search when I said I could smell cannabis on their breath and clothes. I have had 13 years' experience in the police drug squads in Auckland and Christchurch and have been trained to detect the smell of cannabis.

When I searched the defendant, I found a small brown paper bag with clearly identifiable traces of cannabis in it and the subsequent analysis proved it to be cannabis. I produce the relevant certificate to that effect. I arrested and charged the defendant with possession of cannabis."

"Yes, Mr Pihama," said the Judge, inviting Wiremu to begin his cross examination. Willie jumped to his feet.

"Constable, the police file discloses that the professional you engaged to analyse the substance found in the bag could not obtain enough for a positive test in the first instance. He states on the certificate that he had to use a razor blade to scrape residue from the bag in order to get enough of the second test. Those are words he used?"

"Yes."

"Those are my only questions, Your Honour. That is all of the evidence now before the Court. I do not intend to call evidence for the defence. I have legal submissions to make."

"Certainly Mr Pihama."

"My client is charged with possession. *Not* use. The evidence for the prosecution alone establishes that the cannabis was only a trace. It was evidence of past possession but, even then, not necessarily past possession by the defendant. But the main defence is supported by many cases. I refer to the case of *Worsell* in particular. What we have here is merely evidence of past possession.

And, Sir, the following advice is on every Community Advice website in the country –

> "For you to be convicted, the drug has to be found in a useable quantity, not just a measurable quantity. So you can't be convicted of possession if, for example, the police find only some small traces or particles of cannabis along with some cigarette papers in a tin. However, the police only have to specifically prove it was a usable amount if you raise this issue in your defence."

The Judge expressed his preliminary view.

"I totally agree. Sergeant. Why was the defendant not charged with using cannabis? I may have drawn a reasonable inference that his possessing a bag with traces of cannabis and the smell of cannabis enough for a using charge."

"I don't know the reason, Your Honour. I missed it myself. The sharp eyes of defence counsel spotted it and capitalised on it."

"Well Mr Pihama made it clear that the evidence was closed, and I do not feel like exercising my discretion to allow you at this late stage to amend the charge. Mr Tonkin. You are a lucky young man. I will make no further comment. The charge is dismissed. You are free to go."

Simon Tonkin gave a large sigh of relief and bent with a slight bow to the Bench and accompanied Willie out of the Court.

"Congratulations. I've been close to that situation myself when I was at university. But we were both taking extraordinary and stupid risks. You want to be a lawyer. You simply can't break the law however wrong you think the law might be. If you want to do that, then become a politician. But not a lawyer. And what has it cost you? $7500 to me and your travel costs from Dunedin."

"Well stuff everyone! It's a stupid law."

"Many people think you need to be arrogant to be a lawyer. You've obviously got plenty of that. But just mark my words. Take care mate."

"Thank you. I probably needed you to say that to me."

CHAPTER TWENTY-TWO

When Richard arrived at his office, by arrangement with Janet, two members of the Southland District Law Society were present. Malcolm Stoddart looked an earnest young man in his early 30's but was obviously full of his own moral importance. Jim Hendry was about 55 and seemed a lot wiser and more experienced. But Richard immediately perceived a large element of nervousness in their demeanour. He had already noted that they had driven 120 miles to see him rather than the other way round.

"Good afternoon. Thank you for coming."

Richard buzzed through to Janet.

"Janet. If Bernie is here, please show him in. And Melinda as well."

Janet showed Bernie and Melinda in. Melinda's hair was magenta today.

"Gentlemen, Melinda is my young Associate. She has been admitted to the bar for almost four years. She has been assisting me on this matter.

Bernie does not know precisely what I am about to say but he did give me clear instructions to represent him to the best of my ability."

Mr Stoddart then spoke up, "We are here because I thought it best that we have a full and frank discussion about the "conduct unbecoming" allegations against Bernie Brinsley."

"OK", replied Richard hesitantly.

"Yes. We hoped we could do some form of softening deal."

"What sort of deal?" asked Richard.

"Here is a written summary of the allegation. We thought a quick admission by Bernie and a slap on the wrist and an agreement to pay $5000 costs to the Law Society for the work in formulating and bringing the complaint."

Richard raised his voice, "Did you think my request for a meeting was along those lines? How sadly mistaken!"

"We are just acting out of principle."

"The last time I heard someone say that I knew he was about to do something extremely mean! And I was right!"

"OK. We have the authority to settle this, but we say at the very outside that there must be some penalty. And the complaint must be made public."

Richard spoke sternly, raising his voice. The tiger was about to let itself out of its cage.

"There will NO penalty! This matter will not proceed past this meeting. There will be no publicity. After you have heard what I have to say we will adjourn for 20 minutes, and you will come back and announce that this matter will not go any further. The only concession I will make on Bernie's behalf is that I won't demand that the Society pays my fees of $10,000."

Bernie looks a little startled, but not as startled as the other two men.

The younger Mr Stoddart responded.

"Because of your attitude, I don't think we've got much more to say."

Richard was at his finest. He rose to the occasion.

"You might not. But I have. You want attitude? Well, here it is! You will have to excuse some crude terms employed by me. I refer to the incident alleged. No member of the public was forced to watch this display. It was in private. It was consensual."

Stoddart spoke, "It was conduct unbecoming for a member of our profession."

Richard countered, "But applying that standard must not be carried out arbitrarily or inconsistently."

"How do you apply that test?" asked Mr Hendry.

"I'm glad you asked that question," said Richard. "Let me give you some help in understanding the kind of evidence I am going to produce and release to the public."

Bernie had been down this track before. His heart fell then. It rose as Richard continued,

"My overall defence is that this was not the stuff of "conduct unbecoming". In support of this defence, I will raise an alarming parade of hypocrisy within the Law Society amounting to a breach of natural justice."

The two rather pompous Law Society members looked startled –

"What do you mean?"

Richard stood up,

"I mean an indiscriminate and inconsistent approach to immorality in the profession, amounting to conduct unbecoming for many, many members of the profession and Judges."

"I assume you have examples?"

"I have indeed. Your allegations must be of sterner stuff."

"Your current local President, who initiated this very complaint, has an ex-nuptial child and pays the minimal amount of child support while living with his family and children. Normally I would turn a blind eye to that. But you start firing bullets at my client and you better start providing protective vests."

"I didn't know that," blurted out Mr Hendry, looking more than a bit nervous.

"I did," said the younger Mr Stoddart.

"Why didn't you tell me? Particularly when you drag me up here to fight the cause for the Society! Wue're just going to look silly!"

"Oh. I can assure you, it gets even better," added Richard.

"A member of your current Society and two young male clerks caused havoc within the last month in the local brothel here in Queenstown." I have interviewed the prostitutes concerned and the police and here are the statements and the names. They are my clients. The allegation was one of indecent assault where the three men inserted a beer bottle into the anus of one of the prostitutes while they all laughed. There is CCTV footage. It was only her request that the men did not face formal criminal charges and the matter ended with a Police warning. I have the file from the Police. I have the footage. Have a goosey gander! I will produce it."

Richard handed them three pages of a Police Report. He continued. They paled.

"But there was no suppression of name agreement, and I will have no hesitation in outing these men."

"But that's blackmail!"

"Don't push me, Sonny. It's not. This is a meeting for me to put forward my defences and the obvious consequences of those defences. This disgusting stuff will see the light of day when I pursue these defences."

"Shut up Stoddart. He's right," said Mr Hendry.

Richard was not finished yet.

"I will also raise the case of High Court Justice Leslie Parmenter. To everyone's knowledge in Auckland he has been shagging a 30-year-old associate lawyer in a large Christchurch firm that regularly appears before him. He is 58. No lesser person than The Chief Justice flew up from Wellington to put a stop to it. The Law Society knew about it. The abuse of power and privilege to say nothing of the obvious potential conflict was palpable. Yet the Society has done nothing about that."

"When did you get all this stuff?" asked Mr Hendry.

"I have a War Chest. I listen. I don't forget. People send it to me. I will not hesitate to use it when hypocrisy offends me. Prostitutes, taxi drivers, criminals and barbers are better sources of information than the New Zealand security services."

"Have you got much more?"

"Heaps. There's that Family Court Judge who liked the look of a female witness in a relationship property case and passed a note to his court clerk to hand to her at the break. She complained to the Court manager. The note read, "You're a good-looking woman. Would you like to have dinner with me tonight? Wink, wink". For God's sake, the Chief Judge stood him down for a week and gave him a telling off ... But no more! And you guys persecute my client!"

And another Family Court Judge who deliberately touched the breasts of a female practitioner at a Law Society dinner. The Society placed some pressure on the female not to take the matter to the police, then assisted the Judge to another post up North. No disciplinary action! Nothing. Not even an informal expression of concern. You bunch of hypocrites!"

"How do you know all this?"

"Simple. I acted at the time for the female practitioner. You don't do your homework very well, do you?"

By this time both Mr Hendry and Mr Stoddart were looking sick.

"I have not finished yet. I have an Employment Court Judge enticing a stripper out of a cake at a Law Society sanctioned function.

And the Waikato Law Society member aged 42 living with a 16-year-old girl just out of Welfare care. Quite strong evidence that he was having a sexual relationship with her before she turned 16. The Society did nothing! So don't talk to me about principle."

Richard started winding up. He was uncharacteristically running short of breath. So much to say.

"No fewer than four other District Court Judges have been seen in brothels up and down the country all of whom I am prepared to name, and another lawyer only warned about "inappropriate behaviour" in writing to a 14-year-old girl. Oh, and a list as long as your arm of lawyers in sexually inappropriate situations."

Melinda burst in supportively.

"And, if I may be permitted, all the objects were females. The culture stinks. And what did the Society do against any lawyer in the large Auckland firm debacle a few years back? Nothing!"

Richard raised his voice yet again.

"And it is Bernie who is singled out. What you need to consider is the uproar this will cause when the profession realises that investigations of moral sexual conduct may now become commonplace. And that you two started it!"

Mr Hendry responded. "Please give us 20 minutes," he stammered.

"OK. Let's all go and have a breath of fresh air. But there is no wriggle room here. You go down to the water. Collect your thoughts. We'll meet back here in, say, 20 minutes. Look. Sexual immorality should not really be a basis for any "conduct unbecoming" allegation. Criminal conduct, yes."

Bernie and Richard remained while Hendry and Stoddart left.

Bernie asked Richard, "Where do you get this stuff?"

Richard smiled. "It just seems to stick to me like horseshit to a picnic blanket. Sometimes I get anonymous tip offs."

"Blimey! You're pretty impressive."

"And people just don't like hypocrisy. Just since you briefed me, I have had several such tip offs. And, of course, I brought my War Chest with me from Auckland. You've had a dose of that yourself."

"I have indeed. What do you think they'll do?"

"They will cave. They'll be back in 15 minutes."

His phone rang. He answered it.

"Thanks. Send them in. Sooner than I thought."

The two men knocked and entered Richard's office.

"Gentlemen," greeted Richard.

"The Society will not proceed with this charge. We wish to warn . . ." but Richard immediately butted in.

"There will be no warning by the Society. There will be no notes on the Society's file of alleged impropriety. I will have some choice words to say to Mr Brinsley, but they will be the words of his Counsel and not the Society."

"Understood. Confidentiality?" queried Mr Hendry.

"Yes. Both ways. I will draw one up and Bernie and I will sign it and you come back in half an hour and, subject to approval, you can sign and take away a copy. It will be conditional upon complete confidentiality between us. If there is a report left in the Society's file, then that will be treated as a breach of the confidentiality agreement. This matter must be buried. Understood?"

"You have our word."

"Excellent. This matter is finished after you have signed the Agreement."

Melinda showed the two gentlemen to the door and left the advocate and his client alone.

Bernie looked highly relieved and said to Richard,

"Now – the lecture?"

"Yes. SILLY BUGGER! Lecture finished. Let's go and have a beer. Then I'm off to see the psychologist tomorrow morning for the murder."

"Richard. Thanks so much for handling this Law Society matter. The fee? I will pay anything."

"Think no more of it. No fee. I was bluffing them."

CHAPTER TWENTY-THREE

At 8.30 am Richard rang the doorbell of the home of the psychologist engaged in the murder case. Dr Marian Stewart greeted Richard. She was a very professional looking person of Richard's age and exuded total competence in her subject.

"Good morning. Richard Locksley. Good to see you again."

"Yes. Thanks for seeing me at such short notice."

"Come on in. We have a lot to talk about."

They moved through the house to Marian's study.

"I understand the trial is set down for Wednesday week in Invercargill. I think you probably know my professional qualifications and experience. I think I can help in the defence of battered woman syndrome."

"That's great," Richard replied. "I'd like to call it the defence of self-defence, based on the psychological condition of the accused at the time the killing took place. A jury won't like it being classified as a freestanding defence in its own right."

Marian agreed. "I need to keep reminding myself of that. I have some useful information. I interviewed her on at least five occasions, both before and after the killing. I had been counselling her about her severe depression in the marriage."

"I've read the report. It is most compelling."

"I also took the precaution of getting her to jot down notes as events occurred. Here are the notes. They are very basic and clearly in her own handwriting with bad spelling and syntax but, to me, it lays down the foundation for the defence."

Richard read it and rubbed his forehead.

"Whew! Pretty powerful stuff! But I don't have to sell this defence to a lecture room full of clinical psychologists. I have to sell it to 12 ordinary Southlanders, and I have a dead body here with a deadly-looking knife sticking out of his heart, rammed there while the poor bastard lay sleeping."

"That's the image we must dispel. He wasn't the innocent victim here."

"A jury will need to be convinced that her mind had got to the stage where it would not allow her to process or rationalise avenues of retreat."

"I think I can do that. I will argue that this pre-emptive strike by Marie was justified under our existing principles of self-defence. Your job is to convince the jury that your medical diagnosis helps my submission."

"Absolutely."

"Rightio. We'll have a long talk a few days before the trial. It is almost certain that I will not call her to give evidence, because her video interview with the police immediately after the killing is exceptionally helpful. That's all I need. But one thing both you and I must keep in mind. The jury not only has to like me and feel sorry for her, but they have to like both you and me. Any hint of a slick lawyer and a clever dick psychologist will be seized upon by an unsympathetic jury."

"I quite understand. OK. I'll see you again in about a week."

Two days later, Richard and his client, Invercargill Mayor Tim Shadbolt, were waiting to start Tim's defamation case. They had elected for it to be heard as a Judge alone hearing, deciding not to blow it up into a full jury trial.

A Wellington Judge, Judge Cynthia Townsend, had come down especially for this hearing. The three regular Queenstown Judges resided in Invercargill, so they could hardly have heard his case. Richard spoke to Tim.

"I know Judge Cynthia Townsend fairly well and she's a splendid lawyer and very fair."

"Couldn't you at least have found one who attended your wedding and owes you money?" laughed Tim.

"I tried. Oops, here she comes."

The Judge came into the Courtroom. The case began.

"May it please the Court, Mr Shadbolt pursues this claim in defamation against the National Spotlight weekly tabloid. His statement of claim says it all. I leave it to him to give his own evidence on the matter. I call him now as my only witness."

Mr Shadbolt walked to the witness box. He started into his evidence after the oath was administered by the court clerk.

"As Mayor of Waitemata City, I had access to the valuable gold mayoral chains. They were lost. I had nothing to do with the loss.

"How long ago?" asked Richard.

"This all took place over twenty odd years ago. All of a sudden, without interviewing me at all, the National Spotlight ran a front-page headline and an article on page 5 which I say did three things. The article effectively accused me of stealing the chains. By clear inference that also accused me of lying about them being lost."

"Anything alse which concerned you?"

"I take great offence also because it accused me of not caring at all for the environment when I was Mayor of Waitemata City. I claim they were all defamatory statements. I produce a copy of the tabloid."

Richard addressed the Judge.

"It's as simple as that, Your Honour. The words speak for themselves. The Plaintiff can now be cross-examined."

Rosemary Brownlie stood up to cross-examine on behalf of the tabloid. She was a fierce-looking advocate and went on the attack from the start.

"Where does the article say you actually stole the chains, Mr Shadbolt?"

"It doesn't say so directly. But I say the overwhelming inference in the allegation of "knowing where the chains are" carries with it the sting that I am a thief."

"And where does it say you are a liar?"

"It reports me as saying I do not know where the chains are. But then in the headline it says "Come off it Tim. You know where the chains are." I say that from those two short sentences the clear inference is that the newspaper is saying that I am a liar. I go further. I say it is a direct allegation and not an inferential one."

She looked a little non-plussed. She thought it was going to be easier than this. Tim was as bright as a button. Incisive and credible.

"Well let's turn to your complaint about the newspaper saying that you did not care for the environment. That's a true statement, isn't it?"

"Absolutely not! I could speak for hours about the practical measures it took over six years to put in place showing the strongest of environmental standards promoted by me. I have here a 37-page list of the successful motions I put to the Council directly concerning the environment. This list contains 117 specific motions. All were instigated by me and guided through the relevant committees. You have already had that list."

"It's a petty complaint."

"No it is not! If you don't care for the environment, perhaps it is of no moment. But I suggest my record on environmental issues is impeccable. I value my reputation!"

"Ah, yes. Your reputation. Let us turn to that."

The Judge leant down and butted in.

"Ms Brownlie. Are you still pursuing this defence of existing bad character?"

"Yes, we are."

"So let me get this right. You are going to rely on convictions of the plaintiff dating from civil rights protests almost 40 years ago when he is currently the longest serving Mayor of a local authority in this country."

"Yes, Your Honour."

"Your client takes the view that this defence allows anyone, for life, to say anything they want of Mr Shadbolt without civil recrimination?"

"Yes Sir."

"Extraordinary. I suppose you'd better proceed then."

"Mr Shadbolt. Do you have 18 previous convictions for criminal offences?"

"Yes. But can I say that not one of them is under the Crimes Act 1961. They all related to protests 45 years ago. There is not one conviction for dishonesty, violence or drug offending. What is the most serious conviction you are alleging?"

"You don't ask the questions here!"

"Well, I can!" interrupted the Judge. "What is the most serious conviction you are alleging?"

"I suppose it's disorderly behaviour."

"Oh, for goodness sake. Proceed," ordered the Judge, with just the hint of a sneer and shrug of her shoulders.

Ms Brownlie continued to push this line of questioning.

"You have a conviction for disorderly behaviour in June 1981."

"Yes. This was at the height of the Springbok tour protests. Over a megaphone I urged the crowd to cry down the President of the New Zealand Rugby Union. He complained. The police arrested me. The Judge convicted and discharged me."

"In 1971, you were convicted and fined $100 for obstructing police."

"Yes. Me and about 500 others were protesting the presence of the vice president of the United States of America, Spiro Agnew, who was staying at the Hotel Intercontinental. We were still involved in the Vietnam War. I refused to be moved from the front of the crowd. I pleaded guilty immediately and again was convicted and discharged."

"Again, in 1981 you have a conviction for obstructing the footpath."

"Yes. I was on a soapbox on the corner of Wellesley Street and Queen Street. The Springbok tour protests again."

"And 1970. There is a conviction here for wilful damage."

"I can't remember. Oh yes. Was that spray painting a beer billboard with the slogan "No Racist Tour"?"

"Yes. And there's another disorderly behaviour here ..."

"Are you really going to take me through another 14 of these, Ms Brownlie? Look at the list. Pick your worst one. Show it to me."

"Well there is one of here for criminal damage and he told you he had nothing under the Crimes Act."

"What's that all about? Oh? Was that about taking down and destroying the signs saying - "Scumbag Shadbolt Shags Sheep"? The police withdrew that charge. Do you have a record of the conviction? If so, it's wrong."

"Do you have such evidence, Ms Brownlie?"

She ruffled through her notes and folders.

"No, it seems not, Your Honour."

"Stop right there. No more. These are not stains of dishonour! Many would call them badges of honour! Even if there are 18 of them, they fall woefully short of the suggested defence that Mr Shadbolt is of such bad character, but he cannot be defamed any further."

Rosemary Brownlie looked crestfallen. Those convictions were the crux of her defence. It now lay in tatters.

"That is the evidence in defence. I submit that the evidence is not strong enough to support the complaints made by Mr Shadbolt. It is a factual matter now solely in the province of this Court."

Richard presented his legal submissions.

"The oft quoted test is what would the average man sitting at home with his newspaper in one hand and a cup of tea in the other think about the meaning of the article. It is not a test to be answered by a highly trained wordsmith or a professor of semantics at the University. I submit that common sense answers the issue.

"Agreed," said the Judge.

"On the question of damages, this newspaper did not even see fit to interview Mr Shadbolt before publishing the scurrilous article. I submit that is an aggravating factor. I asked that damages be significant. My client is frank enough to instruct me to say that he is not asking for many hundreds and hundreds of thousands of dollars. This is not a million dollar claim otherwise it would be in the High Court. But I submit that a correct level of damages should start at a minimum $250,000 plus costs."

The Judge made a few preliminary comments before adjourning. "I intend to retire for 30 minutes to read over the paperwork and my notes. I shall give a brief oral decision today and then a fuller written judgment within two weeks."

"All rise."

The Judge left the Court room and Richard and Tim also went outside for a breath of fresh air.

"I didn't think it would be so short."

"There are few facts in contention. I think the newspaper was unwise to defend it in its entirety. The Defamation Act 1992 says that an early apology must be considered in assessing damages. If they apologised early on and we were only arguing the level of damages they might well have been able to minimise them down to a very low level. But I think the Judge didn't like the fact that they did not interview you and was seeking to make a monetary gain out of the salacious front-page headline. We shall see."

30 minutes passed. They returned to the Courtroom. The Judge re-entered and sat down.

"I shall deliver a brief oral judgment now. I shall release a fuller written decision in about a week. I find the article about the plaintiff to be actionable and defamatory on all grounds. I find the defence that the plaintiff did not have a sufficient good character not to have weight at all. Even a person who has been convicted of murder 30 years previously cannot be defamed with impunity by a false allegation that he is a rapist in the present time. But Mr Shadbolt's convictions do not place them within a country mile of a claim that he has a bad character.

I find that the evidence falls short of establishing that the plaintiff stole the Mayoral chains. I do not think an inference can be drawn to that extent. But the article directly accuses him of being a thief and a liar and that would be upsetting to any person, let alone a person who has served in local politics with distinction from for so many years.

I also find that the allegation that he did not care about the environment to be utterly ill founded and understandably the plaintiff has alleged that is a ground for a defamation action as well. So I find for the plaintiff on these two latter allegations and regard them both as being serious. I also find the fact that the defendant newspaper did not take the trouble to interview the defendant to be an aggravating factor.

What should be the level of damages? Mr Shadbolt himself is a strong and resilient character, but that does not mean he should have to put up with this sort of stinging front-page attack. My findings in this case completely exonerate him and that will go some distance in assuaging the sting of this publication.

He is entitled to an award of compensation. There is no scientific exercise, but I think a sum of $200,000 is not excessive, having regard to some recent awards which have been upheld by our Court of Appeal. I am influenced to some extent by the fact that this was a nationwide tabloid newspaper and that the words complained about were set out in large type on the front page and therefore also advertised on street frontages for all to see regardless of whether they purchased the publication. That fact alone must add to the award of damages.

I therefore find for the plaintiff and order the defendant pay to him the sum of $200,000. I reserve costs. Mr Locksley is to file a memorandum as to costs within five working days. This is a simple matter. I shall give the defendant five working days to respond, and I will then make a decision on costs."

"This Court shall rise."

The Judge left the courtroom after a short bow to Counsel.

Tim let out a whoop and a holler. Richard quietened him down.

"It's not even 3 pm. Over in a day. Bloody amazing."

"Congratulations. You were a great witness. I secretly thought you might have been one of the worst but, frankly, you were magnificent. Cool, calm, collected and the underdog at all times. Congratulations."

"I think you handled that so professionally and I am really grateful. As you told me, stick to the basics. I could see the whole case change when she started cross-examining me about those convictions."

"Well, I can tell you now. The court clerk told me that the Judge back in her university days had been involved in protests involving occupying the university registry and refusing to move. There's a picture of her in the Auckland student newspaper with long oily hair and grunge clothing. Apparently, the police gave her a formal warning, kicked her up the arse and now here we are."

"What a great story. It proves there is a God in heaven and she's on our side."

"We'll get about $50,000 in costs, just dividing up the lot gets us each about $125,000. Happy?

"Too right. Beers. My shout."

"Pearler."

❧

At the Irish Bar around the corner from the office, Richard, Sir Tim, Mary, Willie, Melinda and Janet were standing around a leaner table. That bar was about half full. It was only early in the evening and already disorderly behaviour and mayhem was starting to unfold outside. Mary started the conversation.

"Look at all that mayhem. This is one of the most beautiful spots in the world and yet we have scumbags and low lifes almost completely ruining it at night."

Richards added his comment.

"Well in other places I would be talking poor upbringing, lack of jobs and lack of education. But here, there is an overabundance of overseas young visitors who simply want to party party party. The possibility of any arrest and Court penalty is half a world away from where their parents and family live.

Willie spoke his mind.

"I don't like to say it but maybe we need a little more Singaporean police tactics. I simply mean that more foot patrols and police presence might do the trick backed up with zero tolerance by the courts. Our police are well-trained enough not to overstep the mark."

Then Sir Tim, "I think you're right. This is not the behaviour of the alienated young person. As you say, it is a party party attitude fuelled by gallons and gallons of grog. Of course, having people like you getting them off all the time doesn't really help."

The "oldies" started to trickle off and Melinda and Willie ambled off to a nightclub. Holding hands??

"See you all Monday."

It was Saturday morning again. The family climbed out of the Gondola high on the top of Bob's Peak and moved quickly to the observation deck looking out over all of Queenstown and the lake. The scene spread to the East towards Southland, to the South towards Glenorchy and North to the Remarkables. The kids were gobsmacked.

"Look at the view, Dad. It's just like being in a plane."

"I can see right over to the other side."

"I haven't been up here for almost 10 years. It's amazing."

"I think I'll go look for some new clients."

"Don't you dare! You stay right there. Weekends are for the family."

The family spent the rest of the weekend together with no clients or phone calls. Mary had turned the cell phones off.

CHAPTER TWENTY-FOUR

It was midnight in the Mall in Queenstown on a typical Thursday evening. The place was packed with partygoers under the age of 30. Most appeared to be drunk and disorderly. There were fights. The police were there in numbers. A window was kicked in. An overhead sign was damaged by revellers who simply laughed and walked away.

"Go the All Blacks!"
"Who are you looking at?"
"What the shit?"
"Get this in the head for a start!"

One lout pushed the swaying second yob and, without any further warning, punched him very hard in the head. The punched man fell to the ground. The assailant kicked him in the face.

Two police officers quickly arrived and placed him in handcuffs and dragged him up to the police paddy wagon at the top of the Mall.

A policewoman tended to the man on the ground. His face was bloodied, and blood was oozing from one ear.

Another group of young drunken men and woman surrounded the policeman taking the assailant away.

They pushed and shoved and screamed obscenities.

Three more policemen arrived with batons drawn.

This mayhem continued. Arrest after arrest after arrest.

"Leave me alone. I just wanna have fun," screeched one layabout.

"Just calm down. You're going to sleep it off for the night."

Richard and Mary sat in a nearby restaurant. They stepped out into this mayhem and quickly attempted to take a shortcut back to the car down a side alley. Two drunken men lurched past them, and one bumped heavily into Richard.

"You clumsy prick!" The lout barely could get his words out.

He pushed Richard up against a wall and moved to strike him with a closed fist. Mary bravely tried to intervene. She was almost knocked to the ground. Slowly morphing out of the shadows as if weeping from the surrounding brick walls appeared four tough figures. They were not wearing their gang patches but were instantly recognisable as Richard's Mongrel Mob clients. Two of them quickly moved up, side-by-side, to protect Mary, the third corralled the second drunken lout against a wall and the fourth, the biggest, stood nose to nose with the thug threatening Richard. It was Hemi. Built like a brick outside dunny and steaming as much on a cold night.

"Now now then. There's a good mate," he smiled right into the lout's face."

He then gave the man a massive clout across the face with the back of his hand. The poor fellow collapsed to the ground.

"You a foreigner? Where from?" demanded Hemi, bending over the lump on the pavement.

"Aussie."

"Thought so. When are you leaving?"

"This weekend," he cried, spitting blood.

"No you're not! Here's what you'll do. If we catch you in the next three nights in the middle of this town after 7.00 pm, you'll be taken to the airport in an ambulance. Got it?"

"Yes sir".

"Less of the sir. It's HEMI. Goodbye from New Zealand."

The lout got up and ran.

Richard showed his admiration. He was a bit of a Mongrel himself on occasions.

"Jeez, mate. Thanks. I wish Judges could impose that sort of summary punishment."

Mary gave Hemi a hug.

"Do you guys need a lift home?"

"Nah. Crikey. Night's a pup. Worse, and better in some ways, than Auckland Central. And it's not even 8.00 pm. See you Bro."

The big boys shuffled off.

Richard and Mary got home quickly. It was a bit rough out there some nights. The scourge of the most beautiful township on earth.

"Apart from that disorder though, I'm really beginning to like this town," said Mary.

"I know. It's real Southern man-type stuff."

"What's on tomorrow?"

"I've got that All Black case and then on to preparing the murder. That'll take three days next week."

"I am pretty full in the Family Court. Any regrets shifting down here?"

"Not at all. It's been three months now and I find it wonderful. The kids seem settled and quite frankly I'm much happier than I was in Auckland."

"I feel the same. Such a change in lifestyle. And the kids love it."

Five people including one young woman sat in the waiting room. Two looked ashamed. Two had bruises and dried blood on their faces. Three remained as arrogant as they did the night before. Richard came out of his office.

Richard cheekily thought to himself that they all had fallen out of the "stupid tree" and hit every branch on the way down.

"I understand you all know each other. Shall I interview you altogether to save time?"

"No problems. They say you're the best."

"That's why I charge the most. But I'm good. Come on in. Have you got your police bail papers ready? We'll try and sort all this out."

He ushered them into his office and signaled to Wiremu to come in as well.

"All sit around this table. This is Willie. He's a first-class lawyer. Rightio. First up. Is there any conflict of interest here?"

"Wot?"

"Does anyone blame the other or have any objection to me representing each one of you?"

"No. I think we're all OK."

"Well, let's look at your papers."

"Noel. Assault with intent to injure. They say you picked up a full rubbish bin and deliberately hurled it at a police officer. Guilty or not guilty?"

"Guilty, I suppose. Can I plead insanity?"

They all laughed.

"Get your act together everyone. Unless I can work magic, you will probably each get 12 to 18 months in prison. But I at least need to work out whether the police can prove the charges against each one of you."

That quietened them down.

"Trevor, it says here you used threatening language and obstructed a police officer. No – the charge is threatening to kill. That carries a maximum of seven years in prison. That's serious stuff."

"I suppose I did!"

"It says here you have five previous convictions for assault. Two for assault with intent to injure."

"Yes, but the last one was over six months ago."

"The Judge will say, "the last one was ONLY six months ago." Everyone must get real right now. You are all facing serious charges. Simon, what about you?"

"Pissing in a public place."

"Peanuts. Only a fine. What else?" Sammy spoke up.

"Looks like it's attempted arson. I lit a newspaper and threw it into the front door of a bar. It was just a bit of a laugh. I wasn't intending to burn the place down."

"Says here that 142 people were in the bar at the time. Nobody was laughing. Unless I can get the police to consider dropping the charge to intentional damage, or pull some sort of miracle, you could get three years in prison."

Simon's face dropped and he started to get real.

"Garth. What about you?"

"It says here assault on a female. But she dissed me."

"How?"

"She said she didn't like No 1 haircuts."

"What were you doing at the time?"

"I was trying to pash her."

"How long had you known her?"

"About 10 seconds."

"So you bashed her? For goodness sake, man!"

"Yeah. But only once."

"But your bash broke her nose?"

"But she deserved it, didn't she?"

"Well, NO! The Judge won't see it that way. You could well get a year. Jenny. What about you?"

"I got done for disorderly behaviour, intentional damage, biting the policewoman and peeing in the gutter."

"What positive things can I say about you and about these allegations?"

Richard handed out a three-page questionnaire to each client.

"You're all due in Court the day after tomorrow. I have much work to do to put the best spin on these events. Here's some questionnaires. Please fill them in with as much detail as possible. Full names, contact details, employment history, education history and family background. The last half of the form is where you fill in neatly anything you believe is relevant to the allegations against you and to your own background. It's essential that you do this intelligently. Put some real thought into it. Fill them in and give them to me in the waiting room before you go. If it takes an hour, then spend that time.

Make sure I can contact you on your telephone number this evening between 8 pm and 10 pm."

"OK," they all said.

"Fees. I need $2500 plus GST from each of you, except the piddler, paid into these offices by 11.00 am tomorrow morning. Does everyone understand? Oh, and if you can get a written reference from a boss, that would be helpful as well."

"Yeah. Sure."

"Don't come on Thursday looking hungover or dressed as bogans. Clean and tidy and dressed neatly. I'll have a separate word with each of you before you come up before the Judge. I do all the talking."

The clients stood up and shuffled out looking a lot more crestfallen and a lot less arrogant than when they went into Richard's office. But at least four of them managed a muffled "Thank you" before they left. Richard turned to Willie.

"Willie, make up standard files please. I'll take them home tonight and do some polish with each client tonight by telephone."

"Don't forget you've got the defended case with the All Black at 11.45 am. I think you've got a good defence. Here's the case law."

"Great stuff! What have you got on today?"

"I have three formal proof civil cases largely about debt collection, but all the amounts are over $100,000 so fees will be good."

"Don't hesitate to ask for help."

"Work seems to be pouring in. Melinda has a slew of drink-driving cases but has also picked up a couple of new commercial clients for work, which seems quite lucrative. Mary has also been busy interviewing on family matters. A number have come from the law practices we took over and scheduled Family Court disputes are starting to pop up all over the place including three in

Dunedin. We'll try and get them scheduled for the same day. You may have to lend a hand there."

"Good. For this first couple of months at least could I delegate to you the role of reporting to me each day as to how the incoming work is settling down? I think we may need to set a half-hour management meeting, probably every second morning first thing."

"Will do."

"What do you think that Tom Finlayson would be like as an intern for us? The hate speech guy. He seemed to have a good edge to him. He's in his last year at Law School, isn't he?"

"I think he would be a good pick. Let's talk to Melinda and Mary."

At the same time, Mary was at the Police Station discussing the local plumber and his wife's domestic assault charges with the Police Diversions officer, Sergeant Lesley Paine.

"I act for both Selma and Trevor. Neither one is better than the other."

Lesley replied, "They've both caused us more than a bit of trouble over the years."

"I know that. But I think they finally realise that the relationship is up against the wall unless they get some professional help. I've spent the last week organising help for them through the local Community Relationship Services Council. They are also having highly professional psychological counselling with Tony Rapson, who you will know well. They had three sessions already."

"I don't feel I can make any promises of diversion at this early stage."

"Fair enough. I accept that we can't make positive value judgements right now. What I seek is that you will consent to a two-month adjournment. Then I'll see you in two months with both of them and present two full reports to you from the Council and from Tony Rapson. If those reports persuade you that tangible positive supervision is in place, I will then ask you to consider diversion."

"We know Tony Rapson well. He provides psychological assessments for the force, so we trust his judgement."

"So you'll agree?"

"Yes. But no promises about diversion. That'll depend on the reports."

"OK. Thanks. I'll arrange for a registrar's adjournment to, say, 8 November. Because it's a domestic case and because there's at least a possibility of a diversion will you accept an interim suppression order?"

"No problems. I've got an adjournment consent sheet here. I can fill it here now and sign it. You take it down to the Court. I'll mark the police file 8 November and we'll have another talk a couple of days out from that date."

She filled in the document, they both signed it and Lesley photocopied the document and handed the original to Mary.

A few minutes later, Mary walked into the Court office, filed the paper with the clerk. On the way out she peeked through the No 1 Courtroom door and saw her husband Richard about to start the case of the All Black charged with disorderly behaviour. A visiting Judge, Judge Veronica Waldron was presiding. She was a rather prim and proper Judge and looked in her late 60s with white hair. She had been a Judge for 14 years and was widely respected. Mary entered the court room and sat up the back.

"Call Jono Lewis Mattson."

Jono walked from the rear of the Court up into the witness box.

"I appear. The plea of not guilty is confirmed. The case should take no longer than 20 minutes."

"One witness, Your Honour. I call Constable Drew Hunter."

Constable Hunter got into the witness box. The clerk stood beside him.

"Please place your hand on the Bible. Do you swear that the evidence you are about to give touching the matter now before this Court shall be the truth, the whole truth and nothing but the truth?"

"I do. On Saturday evening, 16 August, at about 5:30 pm I was on patrol on the beach front across the road from the old Eichardt's Hotel premises. I observed the defendant, who I identify here in Court today, as part of the crowd which was generally boisterous and noisy. I observed him strip down to his underwear and dive into the lake. He shrieked with the cold and then started swimming towards the jetty in the general area of the underwater fish observation facility.

I called for him to exit the water. He did not do so. I called a second time, and he did not do so. The third time I raised my voice loudly and ordered him to get out of the water. He did so immediately. I arrested him for disorderly behaviour."

Richard rose to cross-examine.

"Constable. He apologised and told you he had not heard you at the start?"

"I accept that."

"And I take it you do not suggest he was telling you a lie on that matter?"

"I accept that."

"He got out of the water straight away?"

"Yes, he did."

"There was no behaviour from the rest of the crowd which concerned the police?"

"No."

"There were about a dozen ducks on the top of the water? Would you agree that they appeared unperturbed?"

"Yes."

"And the attitude of the fish was unknown?"

The Judge butted in politely – "Uh Oh. I can see where this is going?"

"The fish, Constable?" Richard repeated his enquiry.

"I couldn't see. No discontent has been reported to me. He smiled. Something was dawning on him."

Richard sat down.

"That is the evidence for the police, Your Honour."

"Kinney's case, Mr Locksley?"

"Exactly."

"Then you know I was the junior Counsel in that case when I was a youngster at the Bar? My maiden name is on the Law Report."

"No I did not. It's the law students' favourite case delivered by Sir Owen Woodhouse in *Kinney v Police*. He had to decide whether a young man who waded up to his knees in an ornamental duck pond at a "daylight festival of amplified pop music" in Napier's Botanical Gardens had been guilty of disorderly behaviour. I still like reading out his quote from page 925 of that year's volume of reported cases."

Richard read from a volume of New Zealand Law Reports.

"Normally the pond is occupied only by goldfish and a few wild ducks, but on this occasion, they were joined for a few brief moments by the appellant.

The ducks seemed unperturbed – they remained on the surface of the water with scarcely an increase in their rate of stroke. The attitude of the goldfish is unknown."

Judge, the learned Court of Appeal Judge dismissed the case of disorderly behaviour."

Her Honour commented.

"And you have rather neatly woven his comments into your cross-examination by establishing that the ducks seemed unperturbed, and the attitude of the fish was unknown. Clever move."

"I submit that the prosecution case falls well short of proof beyond reasonable doubt that an offence has been committed. I asked that the charge be dismissed."

"Sergeant, not to put too fine a point on it, I think the police may have goofed in this case. And where is the evidence of a likelihood that violence or offensiveness was to break out? That is an integral part of the charge."

"I think I have to agree, Your Honour. There were 27 arrests that night."

"I apologise. I was not meaning to be critical of the police. You have a hard-enough job in this village without being berated by a visiting Judge. But a disorderly behaviour charge requires a little more than hijinks or exuberant behaviour. There also must be some evidence of the surrounding public believing on reasonable grounds that some sort of violence or serious disorder could break out. Those facts do not exist in this case."

"I must concede that, Your Honour."

"Case dismissed. Mr Mattson, I advise that you confine your energy to the sporting field where you have excelled."

"I thank the Court."

He jubilantly left the Court, to be met by a loud haka immediately outside in the foyer of Court which was still sitting.

"Now Sergeant. That might be disorderly behaviour."

"A minute of your time, Ma'am?"

The Sergeant strode to the foyer and a booming voice can be heard.

"SILENCE! Or I'll arrest the lot of you!"

Immediate silence reigned. He returned.

The Judge laughed. "Call the next case. And I think you should apply to be the next Coach, Sergeant. Your discipline would help."

Richard and Mary strolled back to the office, chatting.

"I wanted to wait for Willie, but he's got a rather interesting theft case. His client had a nasty dispute with the supermarket's employer, and they were obviously looking for a bit of dirt on her.

"What's the charge," asked Mary.

"After she finished work one night, she was walking past the rubbish skip out the back of the supermarket and saw a half-dozen pack of beer with four of the bottles broken. She took the other two and drank them."

"But surely they were abandoned goods? How can you steal them?"

"Well Willie is turning into a damn fine lawyer. He will argue that you can't steal abandoned goods."

Willie was already back in the Courtroom. He was defending the former supermarket employee, Janice Shrimpton. Judge Waldron was hearing this case as well. Willie started to cross examine the main prosecution witness.

"Mr Judkins. You are the owner of the complainant supermarket?"

"Yes."

"And three days before this beer was taken from the rubbish skip my client had a confrontation with you about unpaid overtime."

"Yes."

"And you threatened to fire her if she raised the matter again?

"She was being a real pest."

"That's not what I asked!"

"Yes. Perhaps I went a bit too far."

"Well do you accept today that you had no grounds to fire her on that day?"

"I had no grounds."

"On the day in question you knew that my client finished work after stacking shelves at midnight? And you knew my client was the last one on the premises with the other employee leaving at 11:00 pm."

"Yes."

"The police file discloses that the very next morning you asked your floor manager to secure for you the CCTV security footage for outside the building in the vicinity of the rubbish skip?"

"Yes."

"The disclosure by your floor manager also shows that you asked him to look out any footage of my client."

"Yes."

"And you saw on the video Miss Shrimpton look into this rubbish skip, which incidentally is owned and placed there by the local Lakes Recycling Centre, and take out the damaged six-pack and retrieve two unbroken bottles of beer? Do you accept those propositions by me?"

"Yes."

"Let's be absolutely clear on the next point. The supermarket had no further interest in the discarded six-pack. In fact, you knew that the skip was emptied each morning at 6 am?"

"But she had no right to take it."

"It's for this Court to decide whether she committed a crime. Finally, the police told you that she had no previous criminal convictions of any kind?"

"Yes. I accept that."

Wiremu sat down having finished his cross-examination.

"That is the case for the prosecution, Your Honour."

"Yes, Mr Pihama."

"Your Honour, I do not intend to call evidence. The evidence is now closed. A new matter has arisen from the evidence which justifies the submission that there is no case to answer. But even if that submission is not successful, I submit that proof of the criminal intent of theft beyond reasonable doubt simply does not exist in this case."

"All right. I'll hear you will now on both matters."

"Firstly, I ask you to read the charging document in this case. It obviously accuses my client of theft, but it specifies that the two bottles of beer at the time were the property of Lakes Supermarket."

"Yes."

"But we now know from the evidence that the supermarket had abandoned it into a rubbish skip owned by the local Recycling Centre. It is too late to amend the charging document when this matter has been on foot for over two months. The prosecution framed the charge and assumed the onus of proof and I have closed the evidence part of this hearing."

"I accept that."

"But I also submit that all of the facts together do not establish the charge beyond reasonable doubt. Where is the unlawful nature of her actions? It is not here! Was there sufficient legal ownership in the two intact bottles of beer for it to attract a criminal conviction? I submit that the answer is "No."

Finally, I invoke the rarely used doctrine of de minimis non curat lex. The law does not concern itself with trivial matters. This principle is still alive but has largely been superseded by the system of diversion. In this case, diversion was not possible because Mr Jenkins took strong exception to it, which is very regrettable. His refusal to cooperate placed my client in quite an unfair position, compared with others who have been charged with more serious crimes yet still receive diversion."

"I accept that comment," said the Judge.

Willie continued in his legal and factual submissions.

"But I submit that the principle of de minimis non curat lex is not dead and should be invoked in this case. I ask that the charge be dismissed."

Willie sat down. He rested his case. It was the Judge's turn.

"Thank you for those submissions. They were short and to the point. I am reminded of a good piece of advice that the senior retiring Judge of our Court of Appeal, Sir

Duncan McMullin, said in his farewell address. He said the Court was concerned about receiving up to 100 pages of written submissions, culled from every possible article on the Internet, when all the Court really wanted was for Counsel to say – "I have three short submissions to make" – and then to summarise those submissions. You have done precisely that. Congratulations."

"I am obliged for that comment, Ma'am."

"I agree with your submissions. I am not prepared to amend the charge. Although it does allege theft, which is the main issue, it specifies ownership, and the evidence does not support that ownership. Secondly, I could not be satisfied on the evidence that the required criminal intention was present. Thirdly, although I have never applied the principle of de minimis non curat lex, I think it could very well apply in this case, particularly when it may have been dealt with by way of diversion.

The charge is dismissed."

"May it please the Court."

Janice flashed a broad smile, nodded courteously to the Judge and walked out of the Court doors, into the foyer and out into the sunshine.

"Thank you so much. What can I say? My Dad gave me his credit card and I'll come down straightaway and pay it. You said $4500, did you?"

"That's fine. Here, I have my portable internet Eftpos machine here. No time like the present. I'm sorry you had to go through the experience. All the best for the future. I'd better fly. I have some more appearances to complete. Just ring me if there's anything else you want me in the future. Happy to help."

Wiremu got a clap of admiration when he returned to the office.

CHAPTER TWENTY-FIVE

The next day was bright and sunny and the week was still not finished. At 10.00 am Mary was representing husband and wife, Andrew and Judith Malcolm charged with making objectionable publications, involving photographs of their three children naked. In the rather foreboding surroundings of the criminal Court, Mary stuck out like a single yellow rose in a rock quarry. She was a very striking advocate.

Detective Constable Clare Ramsay was giving evidence. Judge Lydia Langham presided.

"On Wednesday 27 October, I was called to the premises of Kodak Photographic Ltd in Bellingham Street, Arrowtown. The proprietor had called the police because he was concerned that the defendants had asked him to develop 22 photographs of young girls under the age of 12. I produce the photographs. The girls were all naked and I subsequently ascertained that the photographs had been taken in the disused cemetery at Mace Town. No public complaints were received, but I deemed the photographs to be offensive and I duly arrested Mr and Mrs Malcolm. I understand the defence accepts all of these facts but denies that the photographs were objectionable."

Mary stood up to cross examine.

"Detective. Mr and Mrs Malcolm fully cooperated with the police?"

"Yes."

"Neither had any previous convictions, nor have come to the attention of the police in any way whatsoever?"

"I confirm that."

"And will you confirm that this family including the children have been members of two Naturists clubs in the Auckland area, as well as a private club in the Central Otago region."

"Yes. They showed me two large photograph albums of their whole family naked on many occasions at these Clubs and in what appeared to be secluded parts of a country setting."

"That is the end of my simple cross examination, Your Honour. I don't intend to call evidence. But I do have legal submissions to make."

"Thank you. I'll hear you now."

"Obviously, these photographs have not been classified as being objectionable by any tribunal. You as the Judge must now decide whether they are legally objectionable, but you have clear statutory directions."

"Yes, it's a mouthful of a statute, but it's called the Films, Videos and Publications Classification Act 1993.

"Yes. It's an offence to "make" an offensive publication. I refer to section 123(1(a). I accept that the taking of the photographs itself constitutes "making." It's interesting that it is arguable that the innocent Kodak Shop is also guilty because of the strict liability imposition in subsection (3). And I make nothing of that."

"Interesting. I see what you mean," replied the Judge."

"But the main issue is determining whether these photographs are objectionable under the Act."

"And section 3 directs the facts to be considered? I have the Act on my laptop now."

"Absolutely. And not one of the criteria are present in this case. I invite you to follow through with me as I summarise the definitions."

The Judge fiddled with her laptop.

"Yes, here it is."

"To find my clients guilty, you must find as proven beyond reasonable doubt any or all the following definitions:

That the photographs were likely to be injurious to the public good. Of course not! They were not, and were not

284

going to be, in the public arena. And the prosecution must end there."

"I see your point," said the Judge.

"But there are then other tests. Are the photographs sexual in nature? That cannot be the case. They are simple poses mostly with the children standing."

"I agree."

"Do they exploit the children for sexual purposes? Obviously not."

"Do they depict violence, coercion or a dead body, for goodness sake! Of course not!"

"Are they degrading or dehumanising? No."

"Do they involve torture, extreme violence or extreme cruelty? Not one jot! Those are the statutory tests!"

"I see the basis of your submissions."

"Well not one of those facts is present! Your Honour, in presenting this case I had considered calling as a witness a member of my staff to present at least 20 publications purchased from local bookstores and dairies.

"I know the stuff. They are generally referred to as Men's Magazines."

"Yes, Judge. Worrying names like "Stiff", "Throb" and I found one entitled "Big Juicy Jugs 3.""

"MEN!!" exclaimed the Judge with a twinkle in her eye.

"Exactly my thoughts," enjoined Mary.

She then continued.

"They were all submitted for classification to the Indecent Publications Tribunal as objectionable but were all passed as not objectionable. I am going to rely on your own knowledge of the world about such magazines. Although photographs contained in those magazines do not contain the more extreme pictures of dead people, acts of torture, extreme violence or acts upon children, it can well be argued that many of them degrade and dehumanise or demean the females in those photographs. But they are not classified as objectionable by our national assessment body."

Mary wound herself up.

"Not one of these photographs come anywhere near the tests in the Act. That is my case. I ask that these charges be dismissed, and, in this case, I submit there are strong grounds for full suppression of names. I just know that the national press will pick up on this case and make a mountain out of a molehill and the reporting will be salacious and demeaning. For the sake of the children, I ask for the suppression."

Mary sat down.

"I can make a decision now. Mrs Locksley is correct. I have the photographs in my left hand and section 3 in my right hand. While having a collection of naked photographs of one's family might be regarded as unorthodox, the photographs in this case do not come near the intention of section 3 to classify these photographs as objectionable. That is my judgement. I do not think I need say any more. The evidence was short. The submissions were carefully presented and to the point. My decision need not be longer.

The charges are dismissed. There will be orders for suppression of name or any facts leading to the identification of this family."

The Judge looked at the defendants.

"You are free to go. Thank you, Mrs Locksley. This case was impressively argued. I shall retire."

The Judge left the Bench. Mary walked with her clients out into the foyer.

"That was the right decision. I am happy for you. But I'm so sorry, I have to run because we have a case about to start in the Family Court. I'm happy to have a de-brief and a coffee with you if you drop in this afternoon about 3.00 pm."

"OK. We'll see you then. Thank you so much."

"You and the Judge of the only two people who have not made us feel dirty."

❧

Mary climbed a flight of stairs and entered the Family Court just as the Judge came into the Courtroom. She was now about to represent her client, Sara McDonald, in relation to the Jehovah Witness case, where her former husband had been telling their five-year-old daughter that her mother would burn in hell for her adulterous behaviour. Family Court Judge Judith Trenworth was presiding. She was a young appointment to the Bench aged 39 and had three pre-teen children herself. The Judge was usually based in Invercargill. Mr Andrew Beaumont appeared for Mr McDonald. He Honour stared the proceedings.

"This is an interim, urgent application, so it is set down for only 30 minutes. Counsel, please summarise your respective cases to me first. First of all, Counsel for the applicant. Mr Beaumont. You start." He began his argument.

"Mr McDonald makes this interim and urgent application for a direction as to immediate re-instatement of contact with his five-year-old daughter. The couple separated just over two years ago. He has remarried. Up until recently he had been enjoying contact almost every second weekend with young Eve. Mrs McDonald has now stopped access. My client wants that contact reinstated. It's as simple as that."

"Your turn, Mrs Locksley."

Mary pointed at Mr McDonald. She spoke passionately -

"It's not as simple as that! *He* (she pointed to the father) tells Eve several times during each access period that her mother will burn in hell, because she is not married and occasionally shares a bed with another man. It's the height of hypocrisy, because he and his wife lived together for a year before they got married. He has now just embraced a "fire and brimstone" religion!"

"Is this correct Mr Beaumont? Surely . . ."

Mr McDonald himself butted in –

"It is not right! It is contrary to God's law! Non-believers live in Satan's world!"

Mr Beaumont tried to call his client into order but could not do so.

"Be quiet Mr McDonald!" snapped Her Honour.

Mr McDonald would not stop -

"The Bible commands us to shun sexual immorality. This also includes other unclean acts between unmarried people, such as fondling the genitals of another person and oral ..."

"Now stop right there or I'll have you removed!"

The Judge pushed a button under her desk and within 10 seconds the door burst open and a burly bailiff and a uniformed policeman entered on the double.

"Ah. Gentlemen. Could you remain here until we finish this case please. The emotions are running high."

"Counsel. What more do I need? Isn't the evidence before me already in the most graphic of ways. And I see it's laid out in the affidavits as well."

"But I ask that some trust be placed in my client to recognise that the welfare of Eve is the paramount consideration."

"How can I possibly do that after hearing that outburst? No. I've heard enough. I'll appoint a lawyer to represent Eve and I also order a psychologist report on the potential effect upon Eve of the very strong religious views of Mr McDonald and his new wife. Maybe those reports will be helpful to Mr McDonald. But in the meantime, until I am satisfied that Eve will not be confronted with such harsh outbursts by her father, he will not have any contact with her! He will have to convince me that his and his wife's views will not be visited upon this child. Burn in hell? Really Mr McDonald!"

"I see you are a servant of Satan as well." Mr McDonald exploded.

"NO! That's enough! Take him away. He's clearly in contempt. Mr Beaumont, I will deal with him at 3.30 pm.

You will no doubt advise on how he can purge his contempt by that time. Application adjourned at this stage. I will retire."

Mr McDonald was led away by the bailiff and the constable. The Judge left the Courtroom and Andrew Beaumont and Mary looked at each other.

"Never a dull moment, eh?" Mr Beaumont smiled.

"I'm just an ordinary conveyancing solicitor for the Kingdom Hall. Is it always like this at Court?"

"They don't call it the Agony Court for nothing. My client's a good woman. Tell him to tidy up his act and we will return to unsupervised access quicker than he thinks. But he better start apologising to Her Honour before 3.30 pm."

"Thanks."

When Mary returned to the office, almost everyone was interviewing, and the waiting room was full.

"Busier than Auckland," was all that Richard could whisper to her when he came out to meet another new client.

"Talk at tea-time, love."

On the same day that afternoon. Richard climbed the steps to the Kit Kat Klub to discuss the premise's lease with his four sex worker clients. The premises were small and neat and tidy. Four sparsely decorated individual rooms were situated off a central corridor. A small lounge and bar faced Richard as he entered the premises. He was lucky that there appeared to be no clients present. The whole parlour smelled of cheap perfume, incense and lubricating oil.

"No problem. We've put together a few juicy bits of gossip for you to store away."

"Hi, Richard. How did she get on with the landlord?"

"He's a bit of a wimp. He gave the game away in the first minute by saying he really wanted you to stay."

"And do we stay?"

"Yes. And on good terms. I hope you agree. You get three two-year terms with the rent staying the same for the next two years. OK by all of you?"

"Fanbloodytastic! How did you do that?"

"I offered five tie-up sessions with the four of you and three dozen blowjobs. He wanted 100, so I had to beat him down. That'll cost you!"

"Really?"

"He's joking, stupid! Are you?"

"Of course I am! He was a bit of a push over. He now actually wants me to do some unrelated work for him. So it's win-win. My office will complete the new lease and you can come in and sign it with Melinda tomorrow at, say, noon. $2000 plus GST OK by you?"

"Sure. We make that in an hour on a Sunday afternoon!"

"Here are some bits and pieces for your Warbox."

"This out-of-town solicitor visits us every time he comes over for a client in this Court. He likes kinky stuff. Bondage. Golden showers. The lot."

"And this Doctor gives out prescription drugs for free without an examination."

She passed Richard another note.

"This teacher is having full sex with this 16-year-old student."

"This chemist sells prescription drugs without a prescription."

"This 72-year-old pensioner continually asked us to procure him a 12-year-old girl. We have just trespassed him from the Salon."

"Is that enough to go on? We will bring some more and every time we see you. You look after us and we'll look after you."

"Gratefully received. I shall keep them quite confidential. In my profession, we always need an edge.

Richard hurried back through the Mall to his offices.

CHAPTER TWENTY-SIX

The High Court was sitting in Invercargill. Richard, his Second Counsel, Bernard Brinsley, and 25-year-old Sally Mahon and her parents entered the building for the start of her trial for murdering her husband while he was sleeping.

In the foyer of the Court. Richard surrendered Sally to the Court escort.

"They technically take you into custody and you will be downstairs in the cell until your trial starts, but that's only 30 minutes away. Keep your chin up."

"I'm scared," she said, weeping.

"Everything will work out. You'll be brought up the stairs into the large High Court where we will all be present. The charge will be put to you by the court clerk, who will ask you how you plead. All you must say is "Not Guilty." From then on, it's up to us."

"OK."

The trial started with a brief opening by the trial Judge, Justice Brian Hardie-Boys.

Jury selection took an hour, as individual citizens from the summoned members of the public had their names called from a ballot box and advanced towards the front of the Court. They were either challenged or "stood aside" by the Crown until 12 selected members entered the jury box. Richard and the Crown challenged only three each. No reason had to be given. The Crown may have some inside knowledge about a particular juror and Richard usually made a gut judgement about whether he could relate positively to a potential juror.

It's not a science," he told Bernie. "It's an art. Bullshit probably."

The Crown Counsel and then Richard delivered their own short opening statements to the jury.

It was a sombre and dignified atmosphere, as is usual in the High Court, far from the pressure-cooked pace of the busy District Court in Queenstown and Alexandra.

Large display boards of bloodstained clothing and photographs stood on five trestles around the courtroom.

The public gallery was packed. The press bench had at least a dozen reporters sitting like pigeons, and all were scribbling notes.

The officer in charge, Detective James Warrington began his evidence.

"On arrival at the scene I examined the body. A large carving knife was still protruding from the chest. It had passed through the body and the tip had just exited from the upper part of the back. All exhibits and the clothing of the deceased were sent for analysis."

The detective related in rather boring detail a description of each room of the house.

Richard began cross-examining the detective.

"You recorded a comprehensive video interview given by the accused and we will see that soon?"

"Yes."

"And you will also have examined the deceased's body and clothing together with Doctor Holden."

"Yes."

"On the neck and upper body of the deceased you observed at least four lesions commonly known as love bites?"

"Yes."

"And you and the doctor found lipstick on the penis of the deceased, which was subsequently analysed to be fresh, and it was found the not to match one old lipstick tube found in the house."

"Yes. I accept that the lipstick did not belong to the accused."

"And you and the doctor noted down at the time that you smelled the strong odour of a woman's sex on the deceased body."

"Yes."

"And there was urine and vomit in the bed which has been analysed as that of the deceased and the police accept that this was deposited there by the deceased at least 30 minutes before his death."

"Yes."

"You were present when the doctor examined my client's body?"

"Yes."

"And on her body, you found multiple bruising and cuts which were explained by my client in the video interview as being inflicted by the deceased?"

"I agree."

"And you know from the doctor's opinion at the scene, and from the subsequent analysis, that those injuries could be accurately dated. I mean, some had occurred that day and some were over a month old."

"Correct."

"Some needed stitches?"

"Yes."

"You can then confirm her description of those injuries and when they were inflicted upon her with the dating exercise carried out by the doctor and subsequent analyst."

"That is correct."

"Let us be crystal clear. Every single description given by the accused matched the dating exercise of those bruises and cuts carried out by the analyst and the doctor."

"Yes."

"And do you confirm that you have no evidence which might suggest that those injuries were inflicted by anyone other than the deceased?"

"No. I accept that he was a violent man frequently."

"Thank you, detective."

The Crown Solicitor then assisted another Detective to set up the video interview so it could be displayed on television monitors on the Judge's desk, four in the jury box, two at

Counsel's tables and one larger screen on the wall of the court. He addressed the jury.

"Ladies and gentlemen of the jury. You can now view the full interview conducted by the Invercargill police shortly after the tragic events of the evening in question."

The detective stood by a large television monitor which was playing the recorded interview by the police with Sally. Sally looked simply wretched in the video. She could be seen reciting her feelings of despair on that evening.

"Everything was just a blur. I felt as if I was outside my own body. I was as scared as I have ever been in my life. I believed he was going to kill me when he sobered up and woke up. I tried to leave. But that made matters worse. I knew that he would track me down and cut me up. He had threatened as much. I barely remember doing that to him. What I do remember is an enormous sense of relief when I knew he was out of my life.

Looking back now I am really concerned about what I did, but I was in the grip of total fear at the time. He had seriously beaten me before and threatened my life and my baby's life.

What was I to do? What was I to do?"

Sally broke down at that stage of the video and sobbed and sobbed. It took only a few seconds for the jury members to realise that the image on the screen before them was mirrored in real life on the face and the body of the Sally they saw sitting in the dock before them. Some had remarked that she was the saddest-looking soul they had ever seen.

The video continued playing.

"He assaulted me almost every evening. Sometimes they were sharp taps on the head. Sometimes they were full blows with his fist. He would frequently slap the baby hard when she cried."

"The thing that really scared me was the told me he would kill me on at least ten occasions during the previous two months. On two occasions, he said that if I left, he would track the baby and me down and would kill the baby in front of me before pushing me over a cliff.

I was absolutely petrified of him."

Crown Counsel rose to cross examine Sally.

"Why didn't you simply turn your back and leave the sorry situation?"

By this stage Sally was crying throughout her evidence.

"I was so scared of him. He was capable of really belting me. The fact that he said so often that he would track me down and kill me scared me dreadfully. I thought I wouldn't even be successful getting to the police station without being killed.

I didn't know what to do."

"But you didn't even try!" snapped the Crown Solicitor. It was obvious the Jury found this a cruel and unnecessary question.

"The turning point. We're almost there," whispered Richard to Bernie. Sally kept giving her story on the video. It was all coming out.

"My priority was to protect bubby. I was in a dizzy way. That's the best way I can describe it."

"It's going well," thought Richard to himself.

"On this particular evening I was having short blackouts from fear. I would be very quietly sitting in the toilet, and I would blackout and the next thing I knew I was in the kitchen.

I wasn't really thinking, but what I do know is that throughout that evening I feared for my life. I definitely thought he was going to kill me if he woke up in a bad mood. He always woke up in a bad mood. He is much bigger and heavier than me. He is a sick man and I believe he would kill bubby in front of me and then kill me."

Sally broke down in long sobs as the video finished and the Court remained silent.

"That completes the evidence for the Crown."

Richard stood up solemnly.

"Yes, Mr Locksley," said the Judge. "Will you be calling evidence?""

"I intend to call one witness, Your Honour. Dr Marian Stewart, both a registered general practitioner with a degree, a doctorate and a considerable number of years' experience in clinical psychology. I waive my right to a short opening before this jury. I shall have the ability to address it in full shortly. I call Marian Jane Stewart."

Dr Stewart walked up to the witness box.

"Do you swear that the evidence you are about to give touching the matter before this Court shall be the truth, the whole truth and nothing but the truth?"

"I do. I have professional qualifications in medicine and psychology. I have practised in these fields for 21 years. I lecture in psychological medicine at the medical school in Auckland. I hold a PhD in clinical psychology. I have written over 35 articles published in medical journals around the world. I am the author of a textbook entitled "Serious Psychological Ailments." I have also just completed a book entitled "Forensic Psychology", which has been praised by the International Society of Forensic Psychologists."

The Judge acknowledged her qualifications.

"Thank you, Dr Stewart. You are eminently qualified to give evidence as an expert witness. I am aware of your high reputation in this field."

"Thank you, Sir. At least two months before the killing of this case, Sally Mahon was referred to me urgently by a social worker who believed she was suffering from battered woman's syndrome. I do not like using that term myself. But there is a clear and documented line of medical authority which recognises that some people, including men and not necessarily restricted to woman, can become so psychologically impaired that they genuinely feel that they are in a life and death situation and need to take immediate action against the would-be assailant. In most cases, the fear is quite justified. In a small number of cases the fear can be entirely genuine, but ill-founded in fact."

"Did Sally fall into this second category?"

"No. In the eight interviews I had with her I ascertained from those conversations and from the clear evidence of bruising and injuries on her body that her fear was well-founded. I therefore very carefully applied my findings to the global literature which has contributed to the advancing knowledge on this syndrome."

"Can you do your best to explain this to the jury in simple terms?"

"As I understand it, the law allows a person to use reasonable force to protect themselves or another. In this case, the baby is the other person. The law also recognises that on some occasions a pre-emptive strike is justified."

"It is my considered professional opinion that Sally suffered from a recognisable and clinical psychological condition in which she believed on reasonable grounds that the only means of protecting herself and her baby child was by killing her husband."

"Does the International medical literature support this theory?"

"Without a shadow of a doubt. The condition explains the way abused people may not seek assistance from others, fight their abuser or leave the abusive situation. Sufferers will likely have low self-esteem and are often led to believe that the abuse is their fault. The overwhelming conclusion from the case studies is that in serious cases of abuse the victim suffers from a psychological condition, where their minds are controlled by the deep-seated sense of direct danger and abuse in their lives and, in this case, the life of her own child."

"Thank you, Dr Stewart," the Judge said. "Mr Crown Prosecutor. Do you wish to cross-examine?"

He stood up.

"Dr Stewart. Surely these abused people can simply leave?"

"Not in the extreme cases. And this is an extreme case. Sally was in such an advanced and terrible psychological state that it affected her control of her own body and mind. I do not believe she had the capacity to rationalise properly, and any consideration of retreat was simply overridden by her fear for her own life and that of her baby."

"But that's an absurd proposition!"

"You don't have to answer that! Mr Clinton," The Judge intervened.

"Are you intending to seek and call professional rebuttal evidence in response to Dr Stewart?"

"No, Your Honour."

"I will not permit you to present your own personal views against the professional evidence of an expert witness. You knew that this evidence was coming. It was incumbent upon the Crown to prepare contrary professional evidence."

"Well, that is my cross-examination then."

"That is the evidence for the defence, Your Honour."

"Thank you, Mr Locksley. Ladies and gentlemen of the jury, it will shortly be time to hear Counsel for the Crown and then Counsel for the defence sum up their respective cases. I remind you that you must keep a completely open mind until you have heard them and then my own summing up. I call upon you first Mr Clinton."

The Crown Solicitor started his address, which was not very well-prepared and rambled on some of the key points. He spent only 20 minutes and wound himself up only at the end of his address.

"Members of the jury. For goodness sake! Apply your common sense. She had the power and the right to retreat. No, she had the duty to retreat!"

The Judge could be seem making notes with a grim look on his face.

"She could have walked right out the door and obtained a restraining order, police protection and then, if necessary, change her identity and live somewhere else. You can't just kill someone because you're scared of them."

The members of the public in the gallery were listening intently.

"You cannot plunge a knife into a man while he is sleeping. You cannot!"

Richard and Bernard Brinsley looked ready to spring to their feet but restrained themselves. Richard would have the last say.

"You must reject this psychological mumbo-jumbo and find her guilty of this charge of murder."

Sally sat in the dock flanked by two burly prison officers. The jury noted large tears trickling down her cheeks and dropping out of sight on to the floor behind the front of the dock. The Crown Solicitor finished his address to the jury.

"Mr Locksley. I now ask you to address the jury on behalf of the defence."

Richard whispered to Bernie Brinsley.

"It's do or die time."

"You're up to it. Give them hell!

Richard stood up to present his defence address theatrically, tugged on his gown and rose to his full height. He fixed his eye on each of the jurors and held his right hand outstretched with his fingers slightly curved as if to embrace the jury, and only the jury. It was a friendly and inclusive gesture and without uttering a word he had grasped their full attention. It was a grasp which would not diminish for the rest of his speech.

It was a split jury of six men and six women. The foreperson was a male. He was a six-foot two burly Southland farmer, which did not bode well, but Richard was quick to note a quick wink from him as he rose to his feet.

Richard started his address, building up to a crescendo as he developed the defence argument. He made the defence sound credible and the only interpretation which fitted the evidence.

"I am not asking you to make new law. I am demanding that you apply the current law. The current law allows her to use reasonable force to protect herself or her baby if, in the circumstances as she perceives them to be, it is necessary for that protection. Let me repeat those all-important words –

"in the circumstances that she perceives them to be."

He was deliberate in emphasising that part of the law.

"That is a subjective test. It is what was in her mind. What was in her mind was the dreadful fear of a deathly beating or likely death itself and serious harm if not death to her child. And that is simply applying the law of this country as it stands today against the facts of this case.

Please assist this poor young woman and her child into a new life and acquit her. That is your duty."

Justice Hardie Boys then summed up right down the middle. He laid out the facts which had been adduced by the prosecution and by the defence. He made it clear that it was for the jury to decide questions of fact, but that anything that he as the Judge said about the law had to be followed.

He took the jury carefully through the law in relation to self-defence.

"You can really start and end with our definition of self-defence. I believe that says it all. Evidence of her psychological state can clearly be considered as part of the factual decision that you must make relating to the plea of self-defence. So-called "battered woman's syndrome" is not a defence in its own right but, and it is a big "but", the opinions expressed by such an experienced expert as Dr Stewart are highly relevant to your determination as to whether the accused believed, on reasonable grounds, that she was acting in self-defence.

Although it is entirely a matter for you, I think you will be greatly assisted in your deliberations by Dr Stewart's evidence."

All members of the jury were listening intently, and the entire court room was silent, but for the erudite directions by His Honour.

"Dr Stewart has told you that in her opinion, battered women become so demoralised and degraded by the fact that they cannot predict or control the violence that they sink into a state of psychological paralysis. They become unable to take any action at all to improve or alter the situation short of killing the abuser.

She has told you on oath that the accused fits fairly and squarely into this category. That is the factual matrix that you must determine.

I have directed you on the issues of law and you must follow those directions. But issues of fact are for you, and you alone, to determine. Please retire and consider your verdict."

The jury filed out of the Courtroom accompanied by two police officers. Richard and Bernie left the courtroom and moved along the corridor to sit in the law library.

"I think you got to them. I think they are on our side. I could tell that from the body language."

"I think you're right. That big sod who was the foreman scared me until I stood up and he shot me a wink. That's pretty rare. I'd love to be a fly on the wall in the jury room."

The jury room was hot and a little sweaty. Voices were raised.

"No problem. Let the poor soul off!"

"I'm not so sure at this early stage. Let's talk about it. But I certainly have sympathy with her."

"He certainly had it coming! I just can't make a decision that sends her to prison for a minimum of 10 or 12 years."

"I took full notes of what the Judge said on the law. I was listening to him carefully to see whether he said what the Crown Solicitor said. But he did not! He effectively told us that Mr Locksley was correct."

"I feel the same way. A verdict of "not guilty" does not mean we are saying to other wives that they can easily kill her husbands while they are asleep."

"Put it this way. I wouldn't let her off it was just the sex with other women and drinking. But it is the regular violence, coupled with the threats of injuring her and the baby and even killing them which really gets me."

"Then there's the psychologist expert who was very certain about the psychological grip of fear that Sally was under at the time. It all ties up for me."

All jurors were talking and gesticulating, and the foreman distributed and collected voting papers.

Back in the main Courtroom, the Judge was gone, but the police officers and detectives and members of the press were still present. Richard and Bernie went back in.

"Great address, Mr Locksley. I was really impressed," a pleasant detective commented to Richard.

"Thank you. Call me Ritchie. Everybody does."

"You came down from Auckland, didn't you, and you're now practising in Queenstown? You defended one of my cases on the North Shore about three years ago. Terry Spithill. The little bastard picked up his son's budgie which was lying stunned at the bottom of its cage, bit its head off and threw it in the fire simply to punish the son."

"Oh yes. I remember."

"We charged him with aggravated cruelty to an animal."

"I remember it well. You were unable to prove that the budgie was not dead already when its head was bitten off. Hence, no proof of cruelty. But I hated that case. I think he was one of the nastiest clients I have ever had."

"Well, you might like to know he got a few whacks when we took him back to the station. We had a couple of other minor charges on him, and we said we would waive them if he took his punishment from us and not tell anyone."

Richard smiled, "I didn't know that at the time. Good on you, mate."

The door opened and in walked the court clerk.

"I'm off to get the Judge. The jury has reached a verdict."

The public started filing back in. The press resumed their benches. The well of the Court emptied except for the lawyers and everyone waited for the Judge. The door opened and the court clerk came in first followed a few seconds later by the Judge from behind a curtain at a higher level.

"Silence for His Honour, the Queen's Judge!"

The Judge and Counsel bowed.

"Place Sally Mahon in the dock."

Sally trudged up the steep steps into the dock. She looked tired and haggard. Aged beyond her years. Her face was stained with tears. The jury filed in. The atmosphere was electric. They sat down. All twelve.

"Members of the jury. Have you reached a verdict?"

"We have."

"On the count of murder, do you find the accused guilty or not guilty?"

There was a long pause which seemed an age, but in reality, was only three seconds.

"NOT GUILTY!"

There were large gasps and drawing in of breath and some spirited clapping for a few seconds, but the Judge raised his hand, and the Court immediately quietened down.

"Sally Mahon. This jury has found you not guilty. You are hereby discharged and are free to go. I wish you the best for the rest of your life."

Bernard grasped Richard's hand.

"Richard. Thank you so much. Your performance was most impressive. I hope we can collaborate again in the future. I will tidy up all of the legal aid matters. I think the final grant was almost $140,000 with all the medical costs. So there will be a cheque in it for at least $100,000 for you. I will not split it equally. Maybe next time."
"Thanks for that. Much appreciated. Let's go and check on Sally. I think Dr Stewart is going to run her home. We better then hit the road."

CHAPTER TWENTY-SEVEN

All the staff were present when Richard walked in. Melinda's hair was green.

"Congratulations!" they all cried out and clapped.

"Thanks everyone. We wrapped it up in two days. It's now glorious Friday."

"I told him he must take the day off!" Mary kissed Richard.

"Maybe. A long lunch perhaps? Everyone?"

"Yeh! Big tum! Big bum! Whoops." You can guess that's Melinda talking.

"I've just got to deliver something to the Court which I want to do myself. It's a note to the Chief District Court Judge. I will be back in 10 minutes. Janet, please book the best lunch place in town. Re-schedule appointments. We can all take a couple each after 4.00."

"No. We won't," said Janet sternly. "The whole afternoon is cancelled!"

Richard did not argue. Sometimes you did not argue with Janet.

As he walked up to the Court House a suited businessman tapped Richard on the shoulder.

"Excuse me, but are you Richard Locksley?"

"Yes."

"Name's Pete Watson. I'm Joppy's brother. He told me I could grab you here."

"Sure. How can I help?"

"I've got caught speeding again. The cop flagged me down. I was doing just under 100 but it was an 80k zone. Trouble is that I have four previous within the last 2 years."

"So that means you must get an automatic three-month disqualification period for excess demrit points?"

"Yes. And I've already had a limited licence in the last 5 years so I'm not eligible for another one."

"So what do you want me to do?"

"I've got a proposition for you. I wrote in and said I was going to defend the charge and I required a hearing. It took them several months to send out a notice of hearing and it's this morning before two Justices of the Peace. About three weeks ago I asked for a copy of the certificate of compliance for the speed camera and I have not received that yet. I suppose they'll get it today."

"Jeez Mate! What's your proposition? I've just finished a murder trial yesterday in Invercargill and I was going to take the day off."

"Well, look. Being able to drive is absolutely essential to my business and I need to see my kids every second weekend and they live 200 miles away. I have estimated that a full-time chauffeur for 3 months would cost me $30,000 because I have early morning and late-night meetings. I know it's not much to go on, but I would like you to test the evidence and, if there is no loophole there, then I want to try and get a discharge without conviction, so I don't get the three-month disqualification."

"It will cost you. And no guarantees."

"Joppy has fully prepped me. He's told me to offer you $3500 cash up front and to bring another $3000 to give to you if you save me from being disqualified. I know it is highly likely that I will be disqualified but $6500 would be well worth it to me if we win."

"OK. You're on."

"Here's the first $3500. The court staff told me my case should be called at 11.00 am."

"Give me your documents. Be outside the court room door just before 11.00. I'll work on it in the small room beside the Court."

Richard immediately started working at high pace in the small office next to the court room. Word by word, he read the court documents given to him by Pete, frequently consulting the internet on his iPhone and making notes.

He used the Court office to have some documents printed off. Finally, he emerged from the small room and accompanied Pete into the Court room.

Two Justices of the Peace were just entering. They bowed and sat down.

"Call the case of Peter James Watson."

"I appear, your Worships."

The prosecuting Police Sergeant looked a bit forlorn.

"My constable witness does not appear to be here. I have just telephoned the police station. Luckily, he is on duty. He did not realise this case was on today. He's grabbed the file and will be here very shortly."

"That bodes well," muttered Richard softly.

The Court waited, silent for a few minutes. The rear door swung open and red-faced sweating constable rushed in.

"I am sorry Your Worships."

"Proceed Sergeant."

"Constable, please go to the witness box."

"Do you swear to tell the truth, the whole truth and nothing but the truth?"

"I do."

He read from a file in front of them.

"On the second day of February last, I stopped a vehicle in the back road travelling towards Arrowtown. It was travelling at just over 99 km/h. I spoke to the driver and told him he was speeding. I issued the standard infringement notice. A defended hearing was requested and here we are today."

Richard rose. "Please show me your notes."

He quickly read the notes.

"There is a letter here requesting the certificate of compliance for your speed detection device. Where is the certificate?"

"It should be on file."

"It isn't."

"I'm sorry."

"Please produce these Notes to the Court as Exhibit 1."

"That is my only cross-examination Your Worships."

"Your defence, Mr Locksley. Is there one here?"

Richard rose to his feet again. He was every inch the advocate that had been before his murder jury yesterday. He presented as impressive and persuasive. He fixed his eyes on the Justices and asserted his legal acumen.

"I do not intend to call evidence. The prosecution case is closed and cannot be re-opened."

"Accepted."

"I have six watertight defences. Many things have gone awry on this prosecution file. Please note as a foundation fact that this alleged speeding took place on February 2 of this year. It is now November 14."

"Firstly, when the Constable gave his evidence, you will have noticed that he read entirely from notes. I did not object at the start, because I wanted this Court to note that the evidence came, not from memory, as it should, but from notes. He did not even tell this Court that they were *his* notes. Look. There are two distinctly different kinds of handwriting in these notes!" That is enough to raise real concerns with the reliability of this prosecution.

Secondly, the use of notes means "notes taken contemporaneously" of the event. Courts over the years have allowed for notes to be used to refresh memories if they are made by a police officer when he or she returns to the station. But rarely beyond that timeframe. So I ask you both to note the words "contemporaneously" and "used to refresh memories." Now look at the notes I got this Constable to produce. They were dated February 10. Eight days later! Accordingly, the evidence given by the Constable simply must be excluded based on my first two points without anything else. The charge must be dismissed on this submission alone.

Thirdly, there was no identification of my client as the driver. None whatsoever. One might sympathise with the constable witness not realising that the case was on today, but sympathy is not relevant. The charge must be dismissed on that ground alone. How do you link the constable's evidence with this man sitting here?

Fourthly, this speed alleged was 99 km/h. There was no evidence to establish that the location of the driving was governed by an 80 km/per hour speed limit. Up to 100 km/h is permitted in New Zealand except for special zones. There is no evidence that this was a special zone. The constable obviously and simply forgot that vital part of the prosecution case. The charge must be dismissed on that ground alone.

Fifthly, please look at the notes. There is a request from my client that the compliance certificate verifying the accuracy of the speed detector was required to be produced. It has not been produced. Such production is required under the Act when requested. So not only was the Act breached, but this Court has no evidence of the accuracy of the alleged speed detected. The charge must be dismissed on that ground alone as well.

Sixthly, and this is the complete death knell to this prosecution, the notice of hearing is out of time. It is before you. It is dated 22 October. The police file indicates that it had been misplaced for over four months. Section 21(8)(d) requires the notice of hearing to be filed within 6 months. It was not. Sub section (ii) states the notice of hearing is treated as that charging document and therefore the Criminal Procedure Act 2011 applies.

The charge must be dismissed on that ground alone.

To use a layperson's term – Chuck this case out!

I hand up copies of the legislation."

Richard stepped up to the court clerk and handed him photocopies.

"There are therefore six unanswerable points as to why this charge must be dismissed. They are simply unanswerable."

Richard sat down, the prosecuting officer smiled and extended a pleasant but silent clap and a wink to Richard. The Justices drew their chairs closer and huddled quietly together. They then separated.

"Bullseye on each one, Mr Locksley. Very expertly prepared and executed. Mr Watson, the charge against you is dismissed. We will adjourn."

Richard and Pete walked out of the Court and into fresh air. Outside the Court house. Richard felt more elated than after the murder acquittal in Invercargill the day before.

"Holy shit! What happened there! You got me off! Not just on one ground but on six of the sods. Joppy said you were good. Here's the other $3000."

"Thanks. Happy to help. Where is Joppy? Is he in town today?

"He is. I was going to have lunch with him."

"Well, then join us. Tell him the whole office is coming, including Melinda, and we'll be at that big fancy restaurant at the Steamer Wharf in one hour. We expect it to be a three or four hour lunch. After all, it's Friday. We'll have some fun."

"Is Janet coming too?"

"Yes. Do you know her?"

"Been out a couple of times."

"She's a dark horse," replied Richard.

"Great idea. And I'll tell you something more! Joppy and I will pay for the whole lunch as a bonus. No arguments."

"Sounds great to me. See you there in an hour."

Richard rang the office.

"Hi Janet. I got caught up with Joppy's brother in the traffic Court. Jeez. A million miles away from the High Court yesterday. I just made $6500 cash, got him off a speeding charge and he is shouting all of us to lunch today. I told him it would be expensive. I've invited both Joppy and his brother, Pete. I don't think Melinda will mind.

"I don't think so," said Janet. "I think her eyes are on Willie."

"Tell me about it"

"My lips are all sealed."

"Truly?"

"But we're all booked. I'll ring and add a couple. Melinda's hair is orange today."

"I'll go down there now. Get Melinda to put on some women's clothing for a change. Our guests don't come for an hour, so close up shop and bring everyone down now, so we have some office time first. Oh. Perhaps we better postpone most clients later in the afternoon until Monday."

"Sometimes, in these sorts of things, I'm the boss. I've already done the cancellations. Got all afternoon free."

"Good on you, mate. You're a legend."

❧

They all gathered at the Steamer Wharf Restaurant. Fancy pants setting, quality food and expensive drinks. Richard and all the office were there before Joppy and Pete arrived.

Melinda had done herself up and looked like a sexy courtesan from the late 19th century. She was dressed as a French actress in a burlesque theatre.

"Men like me like this, because when . . ."

"Too much detail! Far too much detail! Take that dress off!"

Melinda disappeared for five minutes and came back dressed AS A PENGUIN! She continued to crack jokes and flapped her flippers together. One was conveniently cut to allow her tiny hand to slip out and hold an ever-full flute of champagne.

"I might ask you for a dance later. Boss. Do we congratulate you on the murder result yet, or the speeding case result?"

Wiremu cracked, "Watch it, Boss. She's in her "Galloping Goblin" mood."

Richard told Mary about the speeding case he had just concluded.

"Technically speaking, my hourly rate for the murder was $580 an hour, but my hourly rate for the speeding charge worked out at about $15,000 per hour."

"Absolutely wonderful. Now, love, I demand a quiet week. You must take a rest".

"I will. Good week everyone?"

"Getting better every week. We need the new young lawyer soon. You can also take a lease on two extra rooms and some storage for a song."

"What about young Tom Finlayson? I get the feeling he might be one of us."

"We all agree. Willie and Melinda can make the first approach." Richard replied.

"Do it!"

"What about the extended premises?"

"Yes. I think we will probably get a little bigger and a modest Board room would be nice."

"I'll slip away now," said Janet. "It will take me 15 minutes tops."

"Willie and Melinda. You put your heads together and come up with a few ideas of people you know for head-hunting. They have to like Family Court work but tell them that there will be a bit of everything. We'll talk on Monday."

"More champagne anyone?"

Much hilarity continued.

The double restaurant doors opened and Joppy and Pete walked in clutching six bottles of the finest BYO champagne. Smiles and whoops rang out.

"Everyone. This is Pete, Joppy's brother. Great guy. Just don't drive with him."

"And don't fraternise with Richard. He hangs out with criminals and prostitutes. Been with about 20 this week alone," screeched Melinda.

Janet returned. "All signed up. Three more rooms."

"Now. Where's me drink?" asked Pete.

"Coming up, my love. A Fluffy Duck?" Wow. Janet said this?

Willie confronted Melinda for a dance.

"Later on, much later, sweetie. I'll dress up like ..."

"TOO MUCH DETAIL!" everybody shouted.

Melinda was just getting warmed up.

"Look out!" shouted Willie. "She's in her gibbering goblin mood now! She'll dance on the table and burst into song!"

"Not a song," spouted Melinda, with a hiccup, "A limerick!"

She actually got up on a table.

"Oh no," exclaimed Mary. "There's no stopping the goblin." Melinda addressed the gathering –

"There was a young lady from Tottenham,
Who once had good manners but 'ad forgotten 'em,
At tea at the Vicar's,
She ripped off her knickers,
Because, she exclaimed, she felt 'ot in 'em."

"And I will now repeat it in mime!!"

"NOOOOO!" yelled Richard, "I'll get the handcuffs."

"Ooooooo! Let Willie put them on me!!"

"There once was a lady who walked like a duck
    She said she'd invented a ..."
"Drag her down!" commanded Richard. "Melinda, tone it
down!" But he was smiling.
You couldn't stop Melinda once her fuse was lit.
But Wiremu exercised the steadying influence. He raised
both his open hands towards Melinda, then curled down his
outside three fingers and gently raised both forefingers.
    "Whoa girl. Easy. Down you get. Careful."
She almost fell and he caught her. He pulled her gently
close to him .... and gently kissed her.
Janet and Mary will swear they saw Melinda swoon.
It was a very long afternoon, finishing after midnight.

Two days later, tragedy struck. Richard came home and
found Mary in a flood of tears.
    "Mum's died!" she wailed. "I know she was old and frail,
but she loved life."
    "What happened?" enquired Richard gently, holding her
closely.
    "I don't know if this is sad or a blessing, but she died in
her sleep. She had an ulcer which didn't seem to cause
her any pain or stress, but it burst and leaked while she
was asleep, and she lost blood pressure and just faded
away."
The children walked in. Mary flashed a warning shake of
her head to Richard, indicating that she had not told them
yet.
    "Come and sit down, kids."
They both sat down and held a child each. The news was
broken carefully, but as often happens with children, they
moved to comfort their parents. They knew how to say the
right caring things about Grandma's frailty.
Mary loved them so much.

They spent the evening together, remembering all the good things about Grandma and the fact that she was almost 90.

The next morning the telephone rang, and a tear-stained Mary answered it while Richard was taking a shower. She spoke for 20 minutes before joining Richard, who by that stage was cooking breakfast in the kitchen. The children had walked down to the local playground. Mary turned to Richard.

"Have you ever had days where your range of emotions have been so at variance that you think you are losing your ability to think rationally?"

"Goodness me," said Richard. "What now?"

"That was Mum's solicitor. He's just told me about the will. I know we were going to get the house because I am the only child. But that's all I thought. I knew there were a few Bonus Bonds. Well, "a few Bonus Bonds" is a little bit of an understatement."

"How much?" queried Richard.

"There's $1,270,000 in Bonds and a further $174,000 in savings, as well as a share portfolio of a value of about a further $750,000. He says it will be a over two million dollars when it is all tidied up in a couple of weeks. And it's all ours."

"What the . . ."

Mary butted in, "Apparently, Mum did not know the full extent of the Bonds or the shares. What do you think of that?"

Well, it's not the time for high fives or jigs," said Richard. "But what a lifestyle and security that will give us and the kids until the day we all die. That's incredible!"

"For the near future, let's tell no one at all." They both agreed.

At that moment the children came in and all Richard and Mary could do was alternately smile at each other and lightly cry together.

It was a bitter/sweet moment that very few people experience in their lifetimes.

※

The next Saturday morning, Richard, Mary, and the children family walked through the beautiful Queenstown Gardens with their lively new Springer Spaniel puppy, Charlie.

"Saturday morning again!"

"And no clients."

"Bliss!"

"We'll talk about a Judgeship at home tonight."

"Sounds a possibility", said Mary. "But perhaps a bit soon?"

Later that day, the family all travelled up to Coronet Peak where the snow had melted, and the air was warm and refreshing. The chair lifts were still operating for the summer tourists and the family was gently shuttled up to the top of the peak. The views of the Southern Alps to the South and North were staggering beautiful to behold.

The kids were then treated to over an hour on the luge slide, which operated from the top to the bottom of the chairlift. They could not do that in Auckland.

Richard and Mary simply loved their whoops of delight.

They all knew that Grandma, her ready laugh and gentle personality, would be in their hearts forever.

Her home, Queenstown, was now their hometown.

THE END   *But there's more to come.*